I can do so little
for you [that?]
I worship [you so?]
that it seems almost
desecration to touch you;
and yet when I
am with you I can
hardly let you a
moment out of
my arms. My purest
queen, no man was
worthy of your
love; but I shall
try very hard to
deserve it, at least
in part.

Goodbye, my own
heart's darling

Your loving

If a Poem
Could Live
and Breathe

Also by Mary Calvi

Dear George, Dear Mary:
A Novel of George Washington's First Love

If a Poem Could Live and Breathe

A Novel of Teddy Roosevelt's First Love

Mary Calvi

ST. MARTIN'S PRESS
New York

To my father
for always believing in me

First published in the United States by St. Martin's Press, an imprint of St. Martin's Publishing Group

IF A POEM COULD LIVE AND BREATHE. Copyright © 2023 by Mary Calvi. All rights reserved. Printed in the United States of America. For information, address St. Martin's Publishing Group, 120 Broadway, New York, NY 10271.

www.stmartins.com

End paper content and art: Longworth, Alice Roosevelt, 1884–1980. Family papers, 1878–1918. MS Am 1541.9 (64–111). Theodore Roosevelt Collection, Houghton Library, Harvard University, Cambridge, Mass.(87) Theodore Roosevelt, Letter to Alice Hathaway (Lee) Roosevelt; Oyster Bay, 17 Oct 1880; bird: Roosevelt, Theodore, 1858–1919. Juvenilia and childhood correspondence, 1867–1922. MS Am 1541 (288–290). Theodore Roosevelt Collection, Houghton Library, Harvard University, Cambridge, Mass. (288) 16 autograph sketches of animals, etc.

Frontispiece: (pg. xi): Roosevelt, Alice Hathaway (Lee) seated with Theodore Roosevelt, Rose Saltonstall standing: portrait. Boston, Mass., 188–. Cabinet card. Alice Roosevelt Longworth family papers, MS Am 1541.9, (122–169). Houghton Library.

Designed by Donna Sinisgalli Noetzel

The Library of Congress Cataloging-in-Publication Data is available upon request.

ISBN 978-1-250-27783-1 (hardcover)
ISBN 978-1-250-27784-8 (ebook)

Our books may be purchased in bulk for promotional, educational, or business use. Please contact your local bookseller or the Macmillan Corporate and Premium Sales Department at 1-800-221-7945, extension 5442, or by email at MacmillanSpecialMarkets@macmillan.com.

First Edition: 2023

10 9 8 7 6 5 4 3 2 1

Contents

Part III

Part IV

Note to the Reader

I had thought the letters you'll read in this book did not exist, at least not in their entirety. I remembered what one biographer wrote, that "all trace of any letters that passed between them [Theodore Roosevelt and Alice Lee] has vanished." But here I was examining their writings to each other, albeit carefully; after all, they date back to the 1800s.

As I transcribed the letters between a young Theodore Roosevelt and his first love, Alice Hathaway Lee, I was moved by their painful beauty, and realized everyone deserved to hear her voice, to hear his. Their story, I wanted to craft based on these letters, as well as the diary entries, witness accounts, newspaper articles, publications, and other sources related to Theodore Roosevelt, Alice Hathaway Lee, and those who influenced their world and bore witness to a turning point in our nation's history. The novel would present readers with both written and spoken words from preserved documents, and also illustrate the changes underway in a defining era—the Gilded Age.

After reading through the last of the letters, I decided it might be a good idea to take a photograph with them while seated at one of a number of long wooden tables inside Houghton Library at Harvard University where they are stored. As I did, I was taken aback by what was hanging on the wall behind me: a portrait of President Roosevelt.

Maybe he wanted them to be seen.

When does the light shine, when the dark
refuses the dawn?

When does the heart open, when the mind
declines the invitation?

When will love be seen, when all turn away
from its truth?

In the year 1878, no matter history's rebuff,

the forgotten lived with such passion that life
changed forever.

Part I

---◆◇◆---

I have never done anything to deserve such good fortune.

—THEODORE ROOSEVELT

Chapter One

Here Roams Theodore

COWBOY LAND, NORTH DAKOTA

WINTER 1884

THE PRESENT

The cold broods so mercilessly, the once-golden prairie ices into a bed of frosted steel. Still and silent, the lands idle, until a whoosh sounds, drawing me to the window. A cluster of scrub pines sways outside my cabin. Leaning against the pane, I feel the freeze on my cheek as I close my eyes and listen. Glassy branches touch one another, chiming like the chords of an Aeolian harp—ethereal notes sinking, rising, floating. The melody evokes memories of the first day I saw Alice Hathaway Lee, when she moved with such elegance the word itself could not have known the depth of its own meaning.

The breeze calms, the music quiets. I remain motionless. Where has she gone?

I pause to think of what to do. Shall I wait for another gust? There is a spot in the gorges where winds tunnel through. For certain, the pines will shake there. It is not so far, or I can stay here alone in this simple ranch-house built with unhewn cottonwood logs and smelling of moss. There is not much time as night draws near; I can see only a sliver of dying daylight on the horizon.

I step back from the window and look over at my one treasure amid these primitive things, the picture of us framed in gold that sits on the desk built by my hands.

Getting to the deep narrow passage may prove dangerous. In these brutal midwinter months, the air currents can pick up quickly and thunder through the naked canyons, bringing knife-blade cold.

I refuse to go on without her. I'm to the threshold, turning the creaky knob, opening the door to the madness.

Yes, I want more. I need more.

Chapter Two

———◆◆◆———

Pretty Alice Lee

SALTONSTALL ESTATE, CHESTNUT HILL, MASSACHUSETTS

OCTOBER 18, 1878

THE PAST

Born into a class considered elite in any circle, Alice knew to sit as a Boston Brahmin should: politely. Mindful of her manners, she folded her white-gloved hands in her lap atop a billowing indigo tea dress frilled with flounces. The prim belle, nine months shy of an eighteenth birthday, wore her light brown hair in an updo with finger waves styled in tight fashion. She kept an erect posture while seated on the east-facing veranda in a high-spindled, substantially carved rocker, yet the demure presentation ruffled due to the chair's erratic creaking forth, back, stop, back, stop, and forth.

"Nothing more than a questionable experiment," argued her cousin Richard Saltonstall with harsh inflection.

This spurt of utter nonsense vexed her, along with the ones from his classmate Hodges Chate. Both of the fellows were seated in front of her. Alice had read the news article printed in *The Cambridge Tribune,* to which they referred, on the proposal to allow women admission to Harvard College, not on the same campus, but an off-site, women-only annex.

"I fail to understand the reason for such an exercise in foolishness," came from tight-jawed Hodges who had a most unattractive nasal voice.

Craning her neck to the right, Alice tried to distract herself by watching an oddly colored bird land on the branch of a hemlock. If not for the cherry-red head, the feathered darling might be challenging to spot as only black and white feathers covered the rest of it. From its big chisel-like bill emerged a rolling *churr* sound.

"Clearly ludicrous" came, gravelly, from Richard after a noticeable breath.

Becoming increasingly agitated, Alice attempted to maintain a staid disposition, knowing she came from an impeccable pedigree with her Coast aristocrat ancestors hailing from Lincolnshire, home to the likes of Sir Isaac Newton and Alfred, Lord Tennyson.

She focused on the wings stretched wide. Whether the bird was male or female, she could not tell. Maybe an ornithologist could, she imagined. In some genuses, she had heard males sport bolder colors to compete for females' affection, while the females blend into the surroundings to protect their nests. This flying charmer flaunted a perfect combination of the two, a back of black feathers with white ones patched about and the unique, crimson-colored head.

"Absurd!" The balderdash continued from the non-blood who specifically targeted one of the possible female candidates who had excelled in private instruction from Harvard professors. "I say again with certainty, she'll turn into an old maid."

Alice bit her bottom lip to hold back the vocables about to release in a splenetic outburst. Not even the scent of her lavender perfume, usually so calming, could ease her tension. Her chair halted its pen-dulation in the shade. Patience wore thin. Teeth clenched. Eyelids shut tight. A simple, stinging question escaped from her mouth: "Why, gentlemen, do you never speak of an old bachelor?"

The backs of the men straightened as straight as their rigid-back chairs.

Alice verbalized the argument in an affable tone, realizing she may have come across a smidgen too forceful. "You converse about one and not the other."

Each angled toward her. They wore matching navy morning coats and tan trousers, with hair parted in the middle, trim beards, and quizzical looks.

"Old bachelor?" asked Richard.

"Old maid." She used the sweetest inflection she could muster. "Old bachelor."

Her cousin's forehead furrowed. He huffed. She stared directly at him. "Are they not one and the same?"

"An old bachelor chooses to live the single life," insisted Richard.

Alice felt heat rise to her face. "And an old maid does not?"

"An old maid is an old maid!" exclaimed Hodges, chortling after his comment with more than a hint of disputatiousness.

Alice unfolded her hands and took hold of the chair's arms. Her lace-up boots stayed firm on the ground as she rocked.

Hodges scanned her body up and down. "An old bachelor may ask to marry whomever he desires."

"Ancient prejudice!" She blurted this out and was glad of it.

Hodges's eyes on his long, narrow face widened to where the whites showed.

"Ancient prejudice must be dug out root by root." These words could not be stopped from spewing from her mouth.

"I see you are in better health, Alice." This came from Richard with a smirk.

Yes, after two weeks in bed, she was, but that had nothing to do with the fact that their bias was insulting. "Is it not significant enough that women outnumbered men in the last census?" They did not answer her question. She continued, "By 888,000!"

Swift, short footsteps interrupted. Out rushed Richard's sister; Cousin Rose displayed a jolly appearance with a rounded chin, full neck, big brown wandering eyes, and a nervous smile. Her black hair sat in a high bun with finger waves clinging to her head. Rose seated herself in the empty rocker to the left of Alice, landed a hand on Alice's tight grip, and practically sang out, "I know of an old bachelor whom no belle of sane mind would have." Rose brightly asked: "What about that creepy one in the musty shop in town?"

Alice knew exactly of whom she was speaking: a taxidermist whose grim studio had stuffed specimens in the window.

Rose angled into the male row. "Even an old maid would give that spongy geezer the mitten."

The male lot reacted with snickers.

"That man is a drunken ol' loon." Richard took a quick inhale. "However, the truth is the truth, Alice."

"This student, Miss Abigail Leach, is already twenty-three from what I know." Hodges's jaw muscles clenched, thickening his air of persiflage. "This would put her at twenty-seven upon graduation, that is if she is even able to achieve a college"—Hodges held up his fingers, gesturing quotation marks as he delivered the next word—'degree.' The lady will not be able to marry. I repeat, old maid."

"No law mandates an age requirement for nuptials. Besides, why would Miss Leach need to marry?" Alice glared at him. "Education may be her partner."

"Forget about birthing children," replied Hodges abruptly. "Too late for that."

Alice seethed as she leaned into him. "Miss Leach may be more interested in the birth of intellect."

An uneasy sigh emerged from Rose before she spoke, her voice a singsong. "I hear Miss Leach can talk like a book and reads Latin for amusement and such."

"Shakespeare, Spenser, and Sir Philip Sidney, too," came from Alice.

The fellows made no response. The aroma of fresh-baked bread shifted their attention to the porch door where out bolted Alice's little brother. Footsteps at a reckless pace, giggling mischievously with a full mouth, George Cabot carried a teetering silver tray with nearly a dozen hot cross buns piled high. He set the fare on a small table next to Alice as she put herself back in the seat properly.

Her brother neared his face to her and spoke in a muffled high-pitch through bulging cheeks. "I don't want to be one of those old bachelors."

"It will be your choice," she responded quietly.

"But, sister, how will I be sure such a fate does not find me?"

"You have plenty of time to worry about such things."

"I am almost six."

"Very well then, Georgie." She suppressed a laugh. "First, you will have to chew." He gulped. Alice brushed crumbs from his jacket, a miniature version of the one worn by the older lot. "Second, either way, you will need to groom yourself better." Her brother straightened his jacket, seized another bun, and flew like a shot.

Richard stretched over Alice's lap for a bun from the tray. "One of my Harvard mates will be here late this afternoon."

She granted him no reaction.

"Take note. He is an athlete."

She stayed quiet.

He stared at her until she finally offered her attention. "His name is Mister Theodore Roosevelt." A sly grin appeared on his lips. "Alice, this gent possesses trophies of all types. Give him a minute of amusement."

Chapter Three

———◈◆◈———

Slippers Slipped

CAMBRIDGE, MASSACHUSETTS

OCTOBER 18, 1878

With his mouth wide open, Theodore inhaled deeply. He decided, as he studied his reflection in the washroom mirror, that he appeared as an abbreviated edition of a hippopotamus. He held his breath for ten seconds. Life hadn't given him much of a choice other than to perform this daily ritual. That feeling of a belt tightening around the chest, gasps coming on without warning. Those torturous asthma attacks went far back to childhood.

Three, two, one, a long exhale, and Theodore shot a glance at his bare chest, pectoral muscles finally appearing defined. A physical crusade drawn from drudgery is what had been needed to build this body, even for a nineteen-year-old. His father once told him he had the mind but not the body, and without the help of the body, the mind could not go as far as it should. There and then, he made a promise to himself: I'll make my body.

His deep-set blue eyes scrunched in frustration. He had little time before Richard's arrival, yet the deed needed to be done. The snip of the scissors sounded as he trimmed the muttonchops. They had carried enough weight to make his jawline appear an inch bigger on both ends. Staring at himself, he moved on to using a straight-edge razor. He drew it down his right cheek. He would have to repeat this, not once, but three times. He moved to the left side and made several passes. Upon completion and a soapy rinse, his face looked naked, except for a tamed mustache above a generous upper lip. His altered appearance, he figured, would be more fitting for a weekend at the Saltonstalls'.

He still needed to deal with the bane of his grooming ritual: his warlike curl, the nemesis at the right of his side-part, inherited from his father. He recalled how they named it "warlike," for a battle always brewed to keep the waywardness aligned. A wet, stiff rubber comb helped to put his thick, wavy hair in place. Whether the taming would be more than temporary after his five-mile ride to Chestnut Hill was unlikely, but there was no time for a second pass, as Richard would be there shortly.

After splashing himself with a forest-scented cologne, he tightened the white linen towel tied around his waist, exited the second-floor washroom, and headed into the wood-paneled hallway inside Mrs. Richardson's boardinghouse, a two-story, off-campus home on Winthrop Street with a straw-colored exterior, black shutters, and fancy white columns at the entrance. About two blocks from Harvard Street and on the way to the Charles River, good air could be found here. He was glad he listened to his father's wise advice to make his home off campus, being that the college dormitories, especially the ground-floor rooms, came with some unhealthy breathing conditions.

Such a weak, sick child should have never made it this far, he knew. A junior at Harvard College! Besides the sickness, Theodore had not been educated in the formal sense; he never attended a school or even sat in a classroom due to his debilitating ailment. If it had not been for his father, would he have even survived childhood? Those desperate nights when he was a boy, Theodore pictured them clearly:

"Our little boy can't breathe," his mother cried to his father, who'd just returned home.

Heavy steps came louder. Hands lifted young Theodore from his bed and into strong arms. "Breathe, boy. Breathe," a calm, firm voice pleaded. Back and forth they paced, father holding son, in the hall-way's dim corridor.

His little chin felt scratchy wool while taking a rest on the sloping shoulders of a father who had not had a chance to undress out of his formal black suit.

The gas chandeliers went dark. Only moonlight found its way through the lead-outlined window, spotlighting artwork on the wall. Theodore made out the wood carving depicting a big hunter on the side of a mountain eyeing a small antelope across a ridge. A shiver of fear went through Theodore as he looked upon the undersized calf trapped for eternity, threatened by a sizable pursuer thirsting to make the littlest his prey. He hoped to never be that wee creature. Teedie, as his family called him, was small, too.

"Teedie, my son, you must find breath any way you can."

Wheezing came from the boy's throat. Teedie did not like that sound. His father seemed grateful for it.

Teedie tried his hardest to get hisses of air in and out.

NOW A PANG of guilt struck Theodore, knowing that he carried on with his college studies as if nothing had happened. Something did happen. Every kind act and word of encouragement from his father should have been written down. Why hadn't he taken the time to do so? He spoke words aloud to his father, wishing Theodore Senior could hear him. "You gave me breath, gave me lungs, gave me strength—you gave me life."

With urgency, his bare feet slapped along the cool mahogany-planked floor until halting. The door to his residence lay open. Had he forgotten to close it? He was not one to forget things.

Nothing seemed awry in his modest residence, a large study with four sunlit windows, two facing north and two east. He inspected around the fireplace, the settee, the table, and the carved mahogany desk, which appeared untouched. His black leather-bound diary and metal fountain pen were there, just as he had neatly left them.

He looked around at what else filled this space—nothing one might normally find in a student's room, no college banners or memorabilia. Instead, plenty of trophies stood mounted on rectangular pine bases under glass domes: *Erinaceus europaeus, Sciuridae, Crotalus,* and *Vanellus spinosus.* He'd usually have to explain to a layman that those obscure-sounding names in his museum of sorts were binomial nomenclature for hedgehog, squirrel, rattlesnake, and plover. Below the shelf holding a glass-eyed *Bubo scandiacus,* otherwise known as the snowy owl, something was askew. He rushed to his impromptu vivarium, squatting to check the two enclosures where he kept the live animals. In one, snakes slithered over and around each other. In the other sat an eerie emptiness.

Theodore kept his body fixed and turned his head. Eyes scanned the room. Ears listened closely for any heavy shifts in the flooring. He heard nothing. To his feet, he jumped and hurriedly inspected the room. He halted and kept quiet again. Again, nothing. He got on his hands and knees for another look.

A shriek echoed.

Then another.

A third made it clear: Mrs. Richardson was in a complete panic.

Theodore leaped up, raced out the door, and rushed down the stairs toward the ruckus. Staccato yelps echoed from the first floor.

Besides the shrill screams coming from the woman, his nose told him he was getting closer.

Messy-haired and stout, she stood in the hall with her mouth twisted, a broom in one hand, and from the other, a finger pointed straight at his escaped pet smack in the center of the hallway.

Theodore held back a chuckle.

Coming from Mrs. Richardson were indecipherable noises that may have wished to become words. The nearly two-foot-wide tortoise remained still with its long claws reaching outward.

Theodore stepped off the final stair and walked over to it. "Slippers is very good-tempered, Mrs. Richardson." He was going to explain why he called her Slippers—she often found a way to slip out of her cage—but decided against it.

Mrs. Richardson's gasps grew explosive, combined with yowls of shock and fright. "Those is not slippers!" cried Mrs. Richardson, slamming both hands over her eyes, the broom's wooden handle nearly knocking her in the head. "Those is the largest claws on God's earth!"

He reached down to rub the animal's tan, bumpy shell. "Exactly what a *Gopherus agassizii* should have."

After a moment of breathlessness, she let one eye peek out. "What in tarnation are you talkin' 'bout? That ain't no gopher. That's the largest creature mine eyes have ever seen!"

He laughed. "She's a bit big for her type." He went down on his knees and peered squarely at Slippers's eyes. "She appears plunged in meditation, wouldn't you say?"

Quick puffs burst from the landlady.

"Or she may be thinking of absolutely nothing; who am I to assume what is going on in that glorious head of hers?"

"What the hey is it doin' here?"

"Slippers is my pet."

"A pet!"

"She's harmless. She spends much of her time worrying the ends of my trousers."

"Git this wicked stinkpot outta here right this minute!" Mrs. Richardson demanded, wrinkling her nose.

He braced his arms and picked up the reptile by its wide shell. "I rather think you would like her."

"Never again! I never wanna see this varmint again. You understand me?"

Theodore nodded, deciding it best to end the conversation here, being that he was in a rush.

"And Mister Theodore, put on some clothes. You can't be walkin' 'round like that."

Hurriedly he climbed the stairs, cautiously balancing concern for the towel and its one last fold hanging on and the tortoise, who was a heavyweight.

He held his breath, thinking it best to prevent any abdominal muscles from moving or else an unfortunate show might befall him in front of Mrs. Richardson. Making it to the top of the steps and his residence, Theodore kicked the door wider as the cloth surrendered to gravity. He put hip to knob, pushing the door shut, and moved quickly to place Slippers back into her enclosure. The lock clicked; he checked it twice.

He needed to prevent another escape, especially since Theodore had made plans to visit Chestnut Hill for the weekend. Who knew how Mrs. Richardson might react if Slippers slipped out again?

Chapter Four

————— ◦•◦ —————

The Clock Ticks

CHESTNUT HILL

*S*tanding alone in her bedchambers, Alice tugged at her dress. "Give this Roosevelt fellow a minute of amusement," she grumbled, thinking over the request laid out by her cousin Richard. She buttoned the twelfth and final silk button at the neck of the long black mourning dress that provided full coverage of her bosom. "Oh, I'll give him a minute of amusement."

The second hand clanked. Glancing over at the longcase clock in the right corner, she asked herself, What have you done between the clicks, Alice? She was disappointed with the answer. She knew her grandmother would have been, too, as she recalled one of Nana's maxims: *The clock ticks, the mind wastes, my dear granddaughter.*

Alice suddenly felt her stomach turn. She sat down on the edge of her generous-size bed with four posts that nearly touched the ceiling in the pretty-as-a-picture room highlighted by pooled silvery silk drapes designed to match the sophistication of the times. Now, silence left only the crackling from blazing logs in the marble-mantel fireplace in front of her. *Nana.* What a heartbreaking loss! Alice never had a chance to say goodbye, bedridden with fevers herself.

And when she finally got well, it was too late; her grandmother was gone from this world. She missed her. She missed her grit, determination, and courage. She missed those times she would sit with her here and point to the scenes of nature on the painted fabric wall coverings. This one that displayed a baby bird in a nest with the mother bird hovering, Nana loved most; she would say, "Alice, a baby bird can spread her wings, but the mother helps her fly."

Alice reached over to the stack of velvet cushions strewn atop the embroidered bed covering, brought the red one into her arms, and held it close.

"Your mind is in a fuss." Rose entered without knocking, as always. "What, pray tell, is swirling about inside that brain of yours?"

Alice sighed, feeling a bit fuzzy-headed.

"What is the matter with you, Al?" asked Rose. "Please do not tell me you have taken ill again."

"I miss Nana."

One brow lifted, as she inspected the dress. "Are you wearing her clothing?"

"The dressmaker adjusted the length"—Alice lifted the lace at the bottom—"with an additional inch of black lace. Do you think Nana would have liked it?"

"Your mother will despise it." She flashed a delighted smirk. "But I think you look dignified. Now, what did Hodges have to say to you after I saved you from the debate over the old maid and old bachelor? I attempted to eavesdrop but was unable to hear his whisper in your ear."

"Before I left your house, he told me my mouth was peculiarly charming."

"Charming? Isn't he the romantic?"

"*Peculiarly* charming. Whether he was referring to my actual mouth or the words that came from it, I am not certain."

"Yes, I did notice him drooling in your presence and then practically spitting as he left."

"Hodges makes me want to scream." Just the thought of him left a bitter taste in her mouth.

"How did you respond?"

"I graciously accepted his compliment," Alice lied.

Rose clearly did not believe her.

"'Expressions of such peculiarity reflect the underlying nature of the character from whom they emerge' is how I responded."

Rose hesitated. She often complained about "Alice-speak," as she called it, fancy language that she had no desire to use herself. "I'm curious about this athlete Richard is bringing here." Rose took a seat and rested her cheek on Alice's shoulder. "Mister Theodore Roosevelt is a prized athlete," Rose continued. "I hear he's an Adonis. And with trophies of all kinds, Richard says. I'm curious in which sport he excels. If he's a polo man, he's a horseman. If he's a crewman, he's a yacht man. If he's a football man, well then, Mister Roosevelt is perfection in my book."

Talk of boys was of no interest to Alice, especially today. She tried changing the subject. "Is that why you smell pretty?"

"I did dab on a drop of jessamine perfume."

"How are we getting on, girls?" a voice sounded by the door.

"Very well, Auntie Caroline." Rose's head lifted from Alice's shoulder, a wry smile crossing her face.

Not well. Alice rushed to arrange the pillows on her bed into neat formation, wanting to avoid hearing her mother's usual lesson in good manners, which often included some story of sorts:

There was once a girl who stowed all of her mess in her closet. When a noble gentleman came for the marrying, he opened the closet, was practically flattened by her belongings tumbling upon him, and nary a man called upon her again.

Mamma did not hesitate before talking, though not about the bed pillows, which Alice had placed in the straightest formation possible in the teensy time allotted. "Hair presents splendidly—and your gown, handsome, Rosie. Oh dear Alice, must you wear such a garment? This is unacceptable for an afternoon event. A black taffeta dress?" Her reproving tone and glare boded ill for Alice's choice. "You are aware of the story I have told you about the girl who chose to wear the wrong fashion."

Certainly, she knew that one, too:

There was once a girl who wore trousers to a ball. Under her gown the pants hid, until a noble gentleman spun her around, revealed her secret, and nary a man danced with her again.

"Why not wear that precious gown with the grand gigot sleeves— the white brocade one that makes the waist appear ever so tiny?" Mamma put her hands together around her own trim waistline.

"That poofed creation!" Alice despised the dress with arms fashioned so wide she could stuff a leg of mutton into each sleeve. She had hidden that one in case of a situation such as this.

"Hmmph." Her mother walked toward the tall-standing armoire in the corner of the room, large enough to hold Alice's many day dresses and dance dresses. "Every outing is a new chance to showcase your beauty, Alice. And as I understand it, there will be a gentleman of interest in attendance."

"We heard that, as well." Alice wanted to come across as matronly as possible for this Theodore Roosevelt. She wondered where she had put the one pair of trousers passed down from her grandmother.

Mamma spoke with her head in the gowns, her voice faint. "Rosie, 'tis true the cook is no longer with the Saltonstall household?"

"Yes, Auntie Caroline. My parents reckoned it wrong that she allowed Georgie to carry a tray of hot cross buns to us this morning, instead of doing it herself."

Mamma's head bolted out. "My George Cabot?"

Rose nodded.

"She allowed him to carry the tray to guests?"

Another nod came from Rose.

"Shameful!" gasped Alice's mother.

"Sad." Rose sighed. "Her hot cross buns were anything but cross."

Alice loved those buns. She regretted not having one on the veranda, and now she wondered whose fault it really was in regard to those buns; her little brother was known for his mischievous ways. "We do have space for one more cook, Mamma."

"Their business is none of ours, Alice. Is he a local boy, Rosie?"

"The Harvard boy?"

"Yes, the new gent."

"Far from it," Rose responded.

Mother groaned. "Please do not say New York."

"Yes, Mister Roosevelt resides in Manhattan."

"The island of portly hogs!"

"Mamma!"

"Thousands prowl the streets. Have you not read the articles? Tell Rosie about them, Alice."

"One article, Mamma, written ages ago."

She let out a huff of disapproval. "But, Alice darling, written by Charles Dickens."

Rose's eyes widened. "*The* Charles Dickens?"

"Yes," answered Alice. "You know the story, Rose. He wrote that they roamed New York City."

"By the scores," her mother said from among the dresses, voice coming through muffled. "Eating their way through Manhattan. Even the ladies, carrying their bright parasols, walking on Broadway had them trailing behind."

"Imagine the reaction to the grunting behind them." Rose let out a sound resembling a snort.

Alice tried a quiet one herself.

"I heard that, girls. Behave yourselves. Your granddad told the story many times, how he visited as a boy. Pigs found their way to his shoes—nearly ate them right off of his feet."

"But Ma, in what year?" A woozy feeling came upon her.

"What does it matter? I believe a New York boy should be off the list."

"Richard," chimed Rose, "tells me Mister Roosevelt has trophies of all kinds throughout his residence in Cambridge."

"Oh!" This seemed to pique the interest of Alice's mother, who backed out of the armoire. Alice knew her mother had been of the very certain view that her daughter ought to pair with not just any man, but a fine gentleman of good stock, great wealth, and high status, which often came along with a nudging toward Hodges. Mamma had made it quite clear all of this would have to wait until after her débutante ball when Alice turned eighteen years of age. "A residence full of trophies," Mamma noted. "Well, isn't that fascinating?" The shuffling stopped at the one dress hidden, as her mother brought the garment into the light.

Alice winced at the sight and her head suddenly began to ache.

AT THE WROUGHT-IRON gate separating the cousins' ornamental gardens, Alice attempted to avoid any glimpse of what she was wearing. Voluminous sleeves and brightly colored threads, "to give you an extra sparkle" as her mother suggested, adorned the pure white brocade gown. Paired with Rose, who dressed in a pale yellow flowing dress, they appeared as damsels awaiting princes to sweep them off their feet.

The black garment would have been a better choice, thought

Alice. She would have held her ground if not for the spell that had started to come over her. Rather than launch into a back and forth discussion with her mother over fashion, she changed into the dress then rushed herself to the kitchen for a slice of corn loaf to satisfy her stomach. She knew what could have come next: fainting onto the floor, being fanned and fussed over with that pungent-scented, camphor-clove, oil-acid elixir smacking her in the nostrils. The last thing she wanted was another stretch of time bedridden in ill health, with little explanation from the doctor as to the cause. Maybe failing to eat since the day prior had triggered that unsteady feeling, the one which often came and went.

By the gate Rose twirled in her ruffles, smelling more strongly of jessamine. "Is it just me, or do we appear as if we stepped out of a romance novel?"

Alice shrugged, wondering whether to inform her cousin of the overabundance of perfume.

"Dressed like this, we ought to play the part. Wouldn't you say?" Rose undid the latch. "My fairest cousin, please wait here." Rose's big eyes were alight with mischief. "If you would, please sashay with grace through the iron gate."

Alice was in no mood for her antics. "I will do no such thing."

"Oh, come on, Al."

"Absolutely not."

"If you do this, then I promise . . ."

Alice brought her large sleeve forward into her own face, hoping it would cover her cousin's abundantly fragrant smell. "No pledge will have me play this game of yours."

"What if . . ."

"What?"

"What if I promise that I will . . . ask the Harvard boy from New York about the swine."

Alice half-grinned, knowing that might give him a minute of amusement—different from the one requested by Richard, but a minute of amusement, nonetheless.

"Pause for a moment to imagine the look on our scholar's face as I ask so gently," Rose let out a full snort, "about pigs in his hometown."

Alice giggled.

"Please, Al."

"Fine. If you ask about the pigs, then yes, I will agree to partake in your silliness."

With a pat on Alice's back, Rose put on a thinking face and began one of her hammy narratives, those brief recitations by which she composed nonsensical dramas for her own enjoyment. "The mind rejoices as the enchanted one arrives. Miss Alice Lee enters through a garden's gate, exquisite in her gown, which glimmers from the sun's rays. The vision of her heightens the senses."

"Speaking of the senses, Ro. You have poured on far too much perfume, musky, medicinal, syrupy, all in one."

"Heavens!" she exclaimed, smelling herself. "'Tis true?"

"Yes. 'Tis true. Did you add more fragrance, maybe from my mother's collection?" Mamma was known to add too much jessamine to the water. "Add to that, hardly any sun is out, so 'glimmers from the sun's rays' should be dulled by the greyness."

"Oh, don't ruin my narration," Rose grunted, wiping her hand on her perfumed neck then on her dress. "Now, can you walk gracefully through the gate?"

Alice resisted for a moment but obliged, picturing the joy of seeing Richard's face when Rose asked Mister Roosevelt about portly pigs.

"He delights in the sight before him. She draws closer, carrying herself with the grace of a dancer."

"I play tennis."

"You take dance lessons every week." Rose cleared her throat and spoke theatrically: "She carries herself with the grace of a dancer and the gait of an athlete. She stands straight and tall."

"I feel my shoulders droop a bit."

"You stand straight as a board. It would be an impossibility to stand any straighter. Bring up your face a bit?"

Alice lifted her chin.

"She reaches high, all five foot five of her."

"You are five foot five. I'm five foot seven."

"I always wanted to be taller." Rose lifted onto her tippy-toes. "Please, continue your ever-so-elegant stroll; however, don't think I do not see your eye roll." She went on. "The way her hair falls and its movement in the wind . . ."

"My hair is tied tightly in an updo."

"Can't you bring it down? In every fanciful tale I've ever heard the heroine always has flowing locks."

"Bring it down? That would require me to remove the pins, and I would, with certainty, need a brush since, as you are well aware, my hair is never cooperative."

"Very well then." Rose's eyes gazed into the sky as they always did when thinking through her thoughts. "The gentlemen cannot help but admire our belle's hair in a beautiful updo, presenting a smooth, touchable neck."

"Has your story reached its end yet?"

"The end? I'm just getting to the good part." Rose lifted her voice an octave higher, adding a dramatic emphasis. "Her full lips make them irresistibly kissable."

Alice had to end this ridiculousness. "When will you ask about the swine?"

"My very first question, for certain." She used a singing, rhyming tone: "Mister Roosevelt, do oinkers roam free in New York City?"

"He will march right out."

Giggles came from both of them. Rose kept up her story. "Her almond-shaped eyes of ocean's blue outlined in black could hold a person prisoner; one could conclude them bewitching. Her heavy, curved lashes enhance the blush upon her cheeks." She gestured to have Alice continue onward. "Her sashay intoxicates even the most unsuspecting. She is, beyond doubt, the most captivating young woman ever to grace a Boston garden." Rose walked over to Alice and pinched both cheeks.

"Ouch."

"You always have a lovely glow to you, but today requires some blushing, which I assume you'll refuse."

Alice reached over and did the same to Rose.

"Ouch!"

Alice gave her another two-cheek pinch with a twist—"Being beautiful hurts."

"Well then." Rose rubbed her cheeks. "If I'm going to suffer through this agony, I expect to see the sashay upon Mister Roosevelt's arrival."

Chapter Five

Poetry Comes Alive

CHESTNUT HILL

The buggy bumped and thumped along narrow pebbled roads toward a welcoming countryside. Ahead of Theodore, evergreen trees towered. The ride with Richard from Cambridge to Chestnut Hill, crossing the river and heading west, lasted nearly two hours. The time moved swiftly for Theodore, being that he was in the company of a friend.

A fine chap, Richard played coachman in this small horse-drawn cart. The conversation between them focused on Theodore recounting each detail of how Slippers had terrorized the landlady that morning, as well as the story of how as a youngster Theodore had met an older woman in a streetcar and, on lifting his hat in recognition, to her shock, several frogs he had stored under his cap jumped gaily into her lap.

Hoots of laughter through bouts of wheezing came from Richard, not once but several times. "The Saltonstall home is up ahead." The road hooked left, then straightened, and at Richard's direction, the horse launched into a trot.

Theodore had developed a great respect for this man with ironclad qualities—resolution, strength, indomitable will, and maybe most of all, the power to do the rough work that must be done. Richard had been forced to drop out of Harvard his freshman year due to diphtheria, but when the cloud of ill health lifted, he returned to college and vowed to complete two years of work in one and was now a junior.

The rocky path up the private lane to the Saltonstalls' steepened, and the carriage slowed. The autumn breeze carried New England aromas: a mix of pinecones and a shot of chimney smoke. This was Theodore's first visit to the hillside estate and his first view of this enclave of the wealthy. Theodore counted only a handful of other houses, and across the sweeping properties, tall hardwood trees. He recognized the genus as *Castanea dentata*.

"Chestnut Road is notable for its chestnut trees, and notorious for its hill." Richard pointed ahead to where the road steepened. "A century ago, the Saltonstalls developed such a fondness for the house that they refused to part with it when moving. They cut the house in pieces, crated them, and brought them here. The only thing—the hill." The buggy lumbered. "Two oxen were used to drag up the loads. As the animals toiled, they tired." Richard urged the horse on. "How the laborers even expected they could complete the job with only two animals, I wonder to this day."

"The way I see it, whenever you are asked if you can do a job, tell them 'Certainly I can!'"

Richard's mouth widened into a grin.

"Then get busy and find out how to do it." Figuring out a way forward was built into Theodore's being. "Their solution?"

"They asked a neighbor for the use of their oxen."

Something a friend once told Theodore came to mind. "Do what you can, with what you have, where you are," he said.

"I do like the way you think, Mister Roosevelt." Richard gestured to the imposing dwelling. "We've arrived."

Set back on a mellow rise of land, the rambling three-floor Colonial home was painted yellow with green shutters and ornamented with elegant ivory moldings. How different from the way Theodore grew up. The four-story town house on East Twentieth Street lacked the bucolic magnificence of this place. He reflected on how in New York City one brownstone followed the next brownstone until a city block was full, and nature was sometimes only found when a redbud tree grew from a hole in the sidewalk. The Roosevelts did have a square patch of green in the back for some airy play. Altogether, he had always considered his city home as satisfactory as one could ask for in an urban setting.

Theodore took several short, quick breaths as he exited the buggy.

This was quintessential New England, a place that made one believe a flowery sonnet could come to life. An archway filled with honeysuckle blooms welcomed him. As they walked up the stone path, a most delicate, light fragrance floated his way. A single sunbeam fell onto a stream to the right of the house. Past that view, a row of quaking aspens presented golden leaves.

Without even entering the house, he had seen enough to call it homelike. It seemed an ideal place to settle down. A sentiment popped into Theodore's mind, one he found unexpected: *I so wonder who my wife will be.*

"My sister, Rose, and our cousin Alice." Richard led him up a mild slope to where the two young ladies appeared to frolic. "Alice spends as much time in our home as her own. She will have to show you the art of chestnutting. There's no one better than her. She can collect more chestnuts than any fellow can. " Richard moved toward a beautiful girl who came clearly into Theodore's view, an elegant figure gliding through a garden's gate. "Come meet them. They've been waiting to greet you."

Intrigued, Theodore gazed at beauty from a distance. She looked fair as a maiden stepping from the pages of literature. All four seasons collided within this lady of singular loveliness whose sway shifted gingerly like a falling leaf in autumn, whose gown shone brightly like shimmering flakes of winter snow, whose gait traveled lightly like the morning spring air, and whose aura glowed radiantly as summer rays off still waters. Watching grace from afar and thinking it wondrous, Theodore's heart tipped a beat faster.

A breeze lifted her dress to reveal the step of her leg.

He could feel galloping in his chest as if a herd of gazelle thundered in his direction, pounding. He did not care to move out of the way.

Richard spoke as they drew closer. "Mister Theodore Roosevelt, may I introduce to you my sister, Rose."

Richard's sister curtsied.

Theodore nodded.

"Mister Roosevelt, may I introduce my cousin."

Theodore could feel warmth cascade from the top of his head to his toes. She was alluring in a classical sort of way, perfectly symmetrical in shape, balanced between delicate and sharp. A button of a nose tilted up slightly, cheekbones sat high, and a small mouth had preciously plump lips on a face with dewy skin shimmering as if aglow from the inside.

"Alice Hathaway Lee, my classmate, Theodore Roosevelt."

Eyes the shade of a crystal clear ocean in which he wished to immerse himself froze him in place. Alice Hathaway Lee curtsied. The prosody of her name sounded heavenly—the assonance of the a's in Alice and Hathaway, the hard stress at the end of Lee, the consonance of l's in Alice and Lee, the trochaic pattern in the first two beats, like a pleasant fall, AL-ice HATH-a. Struck with such fervor, he was amazed his tongue found a way to form words. "A pleasure to meet you, Miss Alice Hathaway Lee." He waited for what seemed like an eternity to hear what voice came in return from artistry in human form.

"A pleasure to have you in Chestnut Hill." A melody to his ears. Her voice presented with a gentleness mixed with gravitas. She added his name, "Mister Roos-velt."

Richard stepped in closer to her. "Rose-uh-velt, not Roos-velt," he stressed.

Theodore listened more to her tone than her words, crisp with a distinct New England accent, like one would hear from a person focused on great pursuits.

"It is pronounced as if it were spelled R-o-s-A-v-e-l-t." Richard held up three fingers to her. "With three syllables."

"The first syllable"—Theodore nodded his head in a slight bow— "as if it were Rose."

"That will be impossible to forget," remarked Richard's sister.

Theodore watched Miss Lee wrap her arm around her cousin's and eye her with a heavy brow. He could see her hand yank at the dress of her cousin.

After a bit of silence, Miss Lee spoke. "Mister Rose-uh-velt."

The throbbing in Theodore's chest did not cease.

"Mister Roosevelt," she repeated, stressing "uh" in a much more meaningful, decided way.

A momentary stillness lingered as Miss Lee shifted a side-eye to her female cousin who inexplicably stared at him, then back at Richard, then back again at him, back at Richard, and back to him.

Beauty's face returned to his direction. A rush of words released from her heart-shaped lips: "We have a question you might be able to answer, Mister Roosevelt."

A question for him? What could it be? Maybe she would ask whether he enjoyed poetry. "I do," he would say. From classics to the moderns, he'd studied them. He could recite every word of Ralph Waldo Emerson's poems.

Give all to love;
Obey thy heart;

The romantic lines swirled about his head:

Leave all for love;
Yet, hear me, yet,
One word more thy heart behoved,
One pulse more of firm endeavor,—
Keep thee to-day,
To-morrow, forever.

Or perhaps she would ask if he'd traveled the world. "I have," would be his answer, describing how in the Netherlands, he had marveled at the arresting views of distant windmills. He'd been to Cairo and Athens, even journeyed on a saddle trip through Palestine, Damascus, and Beirut. The Italian monuments inspired him, as did the riverboat's cruise along the Danube to Vienna.

Just as the sound of a word began to release from Miss Lee, Richard interrupted: "Your question will have to wait. Mister Roosevelt and I are late in meeting the fellows. Our itinerary includes a stroll through the woods in the morning." He walked away briskly, throwing over his shoulder, "You are welcome to join us."

Theodore's feet followed Richard down the hill, though his mind stayed with Alice Hathaway Lee. He wondered what it was she wanted to ask. He stole another peek. Her figure was juxtaposed against the sunset with a sky of sweet pink folding into a fiery red, icy blue melting into deep cobalt, warm yellow blending into a bar of bright gold; slopes of color softly ascending and descending. Any being with a breath would be swallowed up by the vision, as was he.

Chapter Six

—◆◦◆—

The Insults of Shakespeare

CHESTNUT HILL

Her cousin had disappointed her, again.

"I couldn't ask it!" Rose cried out from behind her.

Alice marched out the gate. "I scorn you, scurvy companion." She shifted her footfall to avoid smashing a spray of wild violets.

"Hear me through. Please," Rose pleaded.

Picking up the pace, Alice set off for home, voicing her agitation with a good deal of force. "More of your conversation would infect my brain, you rampallian!"

The frustration from Rose's last reneged promise, the time before this one, still left her miffed. Alice recalled how Rose made her teach Shakespearean insults, with Richard out of the room, to his friends visiting from France who knew little English. In short order, the guests used the phrases quite proficiently. Alice felt an ounce of pride due to her success. But Rose failed to make good on her promise! She had pledged that during midday dinner she would roll her upper lip under and keep it there so as to appear to the guests that she had the largest of teeth and gums.

"I could not ask about the portly sow." Rose exaggeratedly panted.

Alice stopped, let out a loud sigh, and turned to her cousin. She had to swat away her gown's voluminous mutton sleeve from her face to see. "I have no more faith in thee than in a stewed prune." She wanted to get in one last dig.

"Please be done with the Alice-speak and allow me a moment."

Noticing Rose's cheeks becoming flushed, Alice trudged back. "Fine. A moment. And it's portly swine, not portly sow."

Rose's hands moved to her hips. "Whatever is the difference?"

"Sows are female pigs. Swine are both male and female. In truth, we should probably name them boars—the males."

"Either which way, but listen, my genius of a cousin." Her voice sped up. "This Mister Roosevelt was quite darling, a smart-looking fellow, with his rounded spectacles and his three-piece suit. The tan color of his cutaway coat paired nicely with his blue tie. And that blue matching his eyes."

The large sleeve blew back into Alice's face; she had no desire to move it.

"Although his hair he parts to the side." Rose paused. "Anyhows, what I was saying is that, after this walk-whatever-thing in the woods tomorrow, there would likely be a visit to you-know-who's estate. As you are well aware, Richard takes every one of his fancy friends there."

Alice agreed Theodore Roosevelt was a gentleman of decided fashion. Add to that, the new boy did fit into the category and yes, she was right, he appeared intelligent and strong. His face showed toughness, not as in forceful, but unyielding, solid, secure. And, no matter Rose's opinion, she liked how his hair was parted differently from the usual set; she deemed the middle part an emblem of a coddled snob.

Rose moved the sleeve from Alice's face. "I dared not rile either of them and have Richard deny us a chance at the most delicious meal ever."

Alice's appetite suddenly awakened. "We could see Fannie!" The taste of her cooking could uplift even the worst of days.

"Being she is now the head chef at the estate of Hodges Chate, I am certain she will be cooking up something delectable!" Rose made circles with her hand, pretending to stir. "Maybe she could show us a new recipe."

Alice folded her arms. "Please tell me I will not be forced to sit next to Hodges."

"Very well."

"The boy irks me so."

"You can be assured." Rose rubbed her hands together, up and down. "Just think of the feast that will be in store for us!"

"I then have the ability, even at the most inopportune moment, to call upon you to ask about the boars in New York." She paused before tossing out her final Shakespearean slight: "My most notable coward, infinite and endless liar, hourly promise-breaker, and owner of no one good quality."

"I agree to your condition." Rose rolled her upper lip under. "My dear, starveling, you elf-skin . . . how does the rest of the verse go?"

Alice did the same with her lip. ". . . Dried neat's-tongue, bull's-pizzle stock-fish!"

Chapter Seven

———◆◦◆———

Toward Lofty Things

CHESTNUT HILL

So blue was the October sky, so crisp the morning air, that Theodore wanted to drink it in entirely. Rows of blueberry bushes along a neatly lined pebbled trail at the Saltonstall estate provided an idyllic setting as he waited to see her again.

From the moment they met a day earlier, her radiance absorbed Theodore's thoughts and drenched him in bliss, leading him to reach a conclusion drawn not from words on paper with a set of rules governing the count of syllables per line, nor ones strung together creating an interplay of rhymes, but rather from a divine place between the earthly and the celestial: if a poem could live and breathe, Alice Hathaway Lee would be its title.

Beauty arrived. "Good day." Only two words from her created in him a lingering serenity.

Could there be a more enchanting young lady? He knew the answer. Seal this moment to memory. "Good day," he returned.

Richard motioned for the ladies to advance. Miss Lee's gait differed today—confident and firm. Theodore liked that. She had long legs; he was sure of it, judging from her dress skirt's length. The fabric, deep blue nearly presenting black, clung, allowing a view of the outline of her thigh.

"Can you climb her?" Richard asked.

The ladies halted.

Words jumbled in Theodore's head.

"Can you climb her?" repeated Richard, gesturing to a fallen tree about thirty feet off the trail. The tulip poplar, at least seventy feet in height and angled at more than forty-five degrees, rested in the nook of a maple tree where its branches shaped a V.

Climb the trunk? Yes, he could climb the trunk. Theodore could tell him he felt more at ease in nature than in any other place. He knew the outdoors because life provided no other choice. His family planned every trip, every outing, every vacation out of doors and for one reason: Teedie needed to breathe.

Theodore removed his morning coat, folded it neatly, and placed it on top of a sturdy hedge. Any excuse to tackle such an adventure, he readily seized. He walked over, kicking dried leaves, hearing the crunch under his step. He placed his hands on the rough bark, getting a good handle on it, inhaled, braced himself, and jumped. Feet on the trunk, he raised himself slowly, steadily. For balance, he jutted out his arms straight.

One foot after the other, he stepped without any apprehension, being he considered himself an expert; he grew up moving higher at every opportunity, and not just on trees. He remembered that one time he made the five-hundred-foot ascent up Bald Mountain in the Adirondacks, the dawn-to-dusk hike that proved arduous and dangerous. But the most memorable climb he had ever made was as a child ascending Italy's Mount Vesuvius in the wintertime. That is when he decided that not trying was not an option. Be the person who at best finds triumph through hard work and who, at his worst, fails while daring greatly. The one place he never wanted to be was among those cold, timid souls who knew neither victory nor defeat.

Today, he triumphed, making it near the top. Like the glorious view of the Bay of Naples from atop Mount Vesuvius, the scenery here in Chestnut Hill, too, looked magnificent. As he turned, he could see a smile on Alice Hathaway Lee, one he figured could brighten the darkest of his nights. There again in his chest, that galloping.

"Did you hear that?" Her voice gave reason for his ears to hear. "The bird above your head."

Theodore listened.

"Mister Roosevelt can identify any bird, any bird at all, by its chirp," Richard said to the ladies.

Not every bird, he amended to himself, however most, at least those in the northeastern part of the country. He knew quite a good deal about the class, having studied and collected them from faraway places such as Asia, Africa, and Europe, and near home by the Hudson River, Long Island Sound, and in upstate New York.

"Then, Mister Roosevelt." The correct pronunciation of his name by her floated his way, giving him a tingle. "Do you know from which bird the glorious *churr* call emerging from the woods comes?"

He started down the mountain of a tree, happily considering the audible notes. This was a question he could undoubtedly answer. Maybe this is what she had wanted to ask that moment before they separated at the garden gate: if he could recognize a bird's call? He could identify such music, whether the low, bell-like *chupp* of the meadowlark, or the raspy rambling of the bobolink, or the bold, bright music of the robin, which was as bold and bright as the birds themselves, or the catbird, whose sound was so very attractive until the moment it interrupted the music to squeal. So yes, he knew birdsong. He meticulously wrote down the quality of every bird.

And because he knew those qualities, these sounds stopped him fast: chirp, cackle, and a hoarse *churr*. The last time he had heard this bird was in the winter of 1874. He was reminded of this because he had cataloged his observations in Franklin County, New York, for his book, *The Summer Birds of the Adirondacks*. And he recollected having possibly seen such a specimen in a museum collection once. Certainly, he could name the flier without any visual cue. "I believe, Miss Lee, the music we are hearing belongs to a bird of the *Picidae* family."

"And he knows the Latin term for each," raved Richard.

Her gesture skyward guided Rose and Richard. "A cherry-red head with a black and white body." How the word "body" came from her lips charmed Theodore, again her accent coming through.

He made a clean jump off the trunk, delighted. "Otherwise known as the *Melanerpes erythrocephalus.*"

"The charmer found a friend," Miss Lee said to him.

Theodore came face-to-face with bright cerulean eyes meeting his. *The charmer found a friend.* He hoped those words were true. She smiled, then broke from his gaze, and he followed her attention. There in a weeping willow, two red heads peeked through the lance-shaped leaves. He turned back to eyes half-lidded as she studied the birds. Such elegance. His brain became oddly muddled once again.

"I would imagine the colors make them easy prey," Loveliness added.

"Like a parrot?" asked Richard's sister.

"Or the red-winged blackbirds," voiced Richard.

Even the slightest inquisitiveness on the subject of birds thrilled Theodore, allowing an opportunity to divulge the facts that held a permanent place in the files of his brain. Today though, he searched through incoherent thoughts, failing to find the right one. He stayed quiet, angling his eyes again toward the bird that was definitely *Melanerpes erythrocephalus.*

"Isn't it the oriole which has a brilliant orange plumage?" asked Elegance.

Theodore knew this, but he found himself suddenly and awkwardly mum on the subject.

"The cardinals normally flying around here are pretty." Richard's sister flapped her hands a bit.

A gentle laugh came from Miss Lee. "I've seen a painting of a bird of blue feathers appearing to wear a white feathered bow tie."

"Possibly the tui bird." Had he said that out loud? His words came dreadfully slow, as though drawn from a store of information rarely used. "A New Zealand native."

"Oh!" Miss Lee and her perfectly arched brows responded.

Theodore regained his senses: "These all compare to many others. Thousands of species of birds, in fact, have these highly advertising colorations." He was glad for his restored clarity. "I've seen up close a most interesting-looking bird called a scarlet honeycreeper with vermilion plumage, black wings and tail, and a long decurved bill. And the Hudsonian Chickadee is one of my favorites of the avifauna, for it surrounds itself with a flock of friends. And if you could only hear an ibis. It can be nearly two feet tall and makes a fascinating sound that combines a grunt and a buzzing," which he imitated.

Miss Lee laughed. "May I ask, how do you recognize their songs?"

"I have often stopped and listened for many minutes. It is the most natural music I know."

Theodore went on now, for some time, too, describing sounds he'd recorded on his escapades into the woods and the wilds. "Once, I was captivated by large flocks of the beautiful Kavirondo crane flying by with a mournful, musical clangor." He spoke of the birdsongs he heard over the years, numbering, perhaps, in the thousands. His ears made for better record-keeping than his own hand, he told them. "A watcher has to get up close to some nests, otherwise they are inaccessible because they are rarely built near roads or wood-paths."

Miss Lee listened attentively as he acted out the homely call of the song-sparrow. This drew light tittering from her curved lips, which pleased him.

"Show us another!" voiced Richard's sister.

In an instant, he let out the scream of a red-tailed hawk.

Laughter burst from the group.

Theodore decided to perform one of his favorites and voiced a *chek-chek-chek* from the catbird which spoiled into an awful squeal. The ladies both tried to imitate the bird calls and did quite a good job, especially Richard's sister with the squealing.

What had been planned as a brief walk in the woods drifted into an hour's worth of birding.

"Shall we prepare for the Hodges Chate outing?" asked Richard, guiding them home.

Theodore could have never imagined a more pleasant morning amble, and he could not believe he would have another opportunity to witness poetry come alive.

Chapter Eight

The Island of Portly Hogs

CHESTNUT HILL

Seated on black leather seats in an elegantly fashioned enclosed buggy with its interior panels painted gold, Alice could not help but stare at the girl across from her. Two immense striped plumes jutted from the top of the bonnet she wore. Martha Cowdin, all upper-crust and pomp, joined Alice and Rose on the ride to Hodges's family estate as she was a cousin of Hodges's.

"I hear Mister Roosevelt is a bit bumptious," squawked Martha, her prickly voice grating.

"Have you been acquainted with Mister Roosevelt?" Alice asked, miffed, adjusting her lace gloves.

The hat's tall plumage angled left along with a tilt of Martha's head. "Miss Lee, I do not need to be acquainted with a Cambridge boy to know a Cambridge boy." Her words carried delicate scorn covered in an unpleasant giggle.

Rose placed a hand over Alice's. "I think he's quite nice."

"Roosevelt's older sister summers in Bar Harbor where we have our summer estate, as you are aware," Martha spoke with an air of boastfulness.

Alice was not aware, and now could not take her eyes off the drama happening at the tippy-top of Martha's velvet headdress, leaving her to wonder at the elasticity of feathers as they struck the ceiling with the buggy's oscillation. How could her hat's feathers spring back again even after several impacts with the roof? Come to think of it, Alice realized Martha herself resembled a bird with her pursed lips, beaked nose, and eyes rounded like an owl's. Those eyes stared at her as the buggy turned the corner to the path leading to the manor.

"A fine gal of old Knickerbocker stock, this Roosevelt gal," added Martha. "Bamie is her name."

Alice would have guessed he had a fine sister. He was quite fine himself, especially with those piercing blue eyes.

"She has no looks." Martha's nostrils flared and mouth pursed.

Anger began to boil as Alice exclaimed, "Miss Cowdin!"

"She is very nearly ugly. She is almost a cripple. No one for a moment thinks of such things however, when near her. One is only aware of her charm. But as for her brother . . ." Martha hesitated.

Alice turned to look out the window of the buggy to distract herself from the gnawing conversation.

"But as for her brother Theodore," Martha repeated, "as I understand it, he is a bit bumptious."

Alice found *her* bumptious, and her insults repulsive. Add to that, Martha was not much older than her and Rose, maybe by a few months, and yet she acted as if an elder.

Rose whipped her eyes over to Alice, presumably to warn her against any verbal outburst.

"I hear he's noisy in a way," blustered Martha.

What an unfair way to describe the man whom Alice found to be neither boisterous nor pretentious. She spoke up: "We, in fact, found him quite the opposite."

"I agree." Rose gave Alice a slight kick, though clearly Miss Cowdin was getting under her skin as well.

"But did you find him to be . . ." A sigh came from Martha, her purple hat bouncing from a bump in the road. ". . . Eccentric?"

Alice refused to respond, instead looking out at the estate that was colossal. The lawn seemed to run for a hundred acres. Its vastness covered much of the town of Milton.

"Miss Lee!" Martha snapped, adding an exasperated breath. "I repeat: Do you think eccentric is a fitting description?"

Eccentric was a fitting description for that plumaged hat, yes. And, more important, Alice wondered to which bird the feathers belonged; a turkey, possibly.

"What do you think?" Martha adjusted the feather, clear annoyance in her tone.

"Of your headwear . . ." Alice paused, wanting to say that the hat was hideous and that Martha smelled as if she had slathered herself in honey. Thoughts of Nana came to mind. What would Nana tell her? She would tell Martha the truth—that her hat looked hideous and that she smelled as if she had slathered herself in honey.

Rose filled the uncomfortable quiet. "It's unique."

The buggy came to a stop in front of the massive entry door to the enormous residence.

"Of course it's unique! It's custom-made. Would I wear anything else?" Martha burst out of the buggy, ordered the driver to get her overnight bags, and gave Alice and Rose just enough room to step off.

Alice carefully placed her ivory satin shoes on the stone path. She had not chosen to wear these shoes nor this outfit. Rose insisted that every event at the Chates' was a grand affair and fashion needed to follow suit. Alice wondered if this dress was too fancy with its tiers of teal satin, an overlay of lace cascading down the front, and the bodice, a new style called a cuirasse, which carried just below the waistline.

"Miss Lee, what are your impressions of the fellow?" Martha, nearly half a foot shorter, glared at Alice. "How did you find him to be, Miss Lee?"

"Mister Roosevelt?" Alice replied, maintaining her composure. "Yes!"

"What I think is this." Alice figured she would be honest. "The new Harvard boy knows more about the bird species than anyone we have ever met." She appreciated his love for nature.

Martha's eyes nearly popped from her face. "He knows about birds, Miss Lee?"

"Outside that topic, we know too little to make a judgment."

"Birds?"

"We did thoroughly enjoy his interpretation of a hawk's scream. Didn't we, Al?" Rose grinned at Alice.

"He's a birder?"

Rose sounded the shrill call, causing Martha to jump.

"Ha!" shouted Martha. "Well, he's certainly not the sort to appeal to one at first."

Her feathered hat was not the sort to appeal at all. Martha thankfully left it with the attendant upon entering the mansion. Scanning the foyer, Alice decided the room was more elaborate than necessary, with its gilded moldings reaching high to a ceiling painted as the sky. Being a guest at such an affair had its privileges. The Chates made even a Saturday midday dinner feel like the gala of the century.

Martha guided Alice and Rose straight to the kitchen, putting a hip to the swinging door.

As she took in the exquisite scents of sweet and savory, Alice noticed a little jeweled pouch hanging from Rose's waist.

"My mischief purse," whispered her cousin, tapping it.

Alice instantly knew what Rose was planning.

"Fannie, look who I've invited for a visit," Martha announced, her voice piercing.

Alice raced to give the chef they had known since childhood the biggest of hugs. "We missed you, dear Fannie!" Alice and Rose wrapped their arms around Fannie Merritt Farmer, whose right arm was raised as she held a spatula full of pink frosting in the air.

"Soon, you'll despise me should my fluff drop on your perfectly coiffed hairdos."

"I've always wanted pink hair, Fannie."

"Oh, Alice!" Fannie's joyous whoop echoed through the kitchen and caught everyone up in it.

"How do you get it pink, Fannie?" Rose reached for a taste.

Fannie handed Rose the spatula. "It's my very own marshmallow frosting mixed with maraschino cherries."

Upon tasting the mixture, a wild smile appeared on Rose's face.

"Come, ladies, allow me to provide a preview of this afternoon's banquet." Fannie walked to the cooking station with a heavy limp on the right. Alice remembered how Fannie had suffered so after a paralytic stroke when she was only sixteen. Ever since, the only activity that kept up her spirits was cooking. Years of perfecting recipes had led to one job, then another, and now chef at the estate. Alice was so delighted for her.

"A bitty bit of refreshment, ladies." Fannie poured each a small glass of nectar as well as one for herself. "A cup and a welcome to the most fashionable ladies of Boston."

They clinked glasses and Alice sipped the drink, which was nicely flavored with cinnamon.

"My dear friends"—Fannie poured her a wee more—"I am at your service."

"Fannie, I do have a request."

"What is it, Alice?"

"Is there any space for one more cook in the kitchen?"

"Too many cooks in the kitchen is not a good thing. However, I did lose one of my favorite assistants to Boston."

"Ro and I know of a cook who makes the most perfect hot cross buns."

"Send him over."

"Her," corrected Alice.

"Even better."

"I'll be sure to have her pay you a visit, Fannie," Rose pledged. "On the quiet."

Fannie reached over to a silver tray filled with cookies. "Now taste these beauties. I call them Harvard wafers. They're made with butter, sugar, eggs, flour, baking powder, some flavoring, and then I roll all of that deliciousness into one-eighth-inch thickness. Shape it with a heart cookie cutter and bake them for about eight minutes. While in the oven, I sprinkle them with shaved almonds."

Even in Alice's small sampling, the combination of soft, buttery savoriness combined supremely. She considered it a triumph of a dessert as a note of anise awakened her appetite.

"I'm only telling you these recipe details up front because I know you both will ask me repeatedly."

"Fannie, it's perfection! As for the recipes, we inquire, but we fail to remember the ingredients. Ro and I attempted to bake a cake we tasted the last time, and it came out like a pancake."

"A delicious pancake, I might add." Rose snuck another wafer into her hand, wrapped both in a napkin, and slipped them into her mischief purse.

Fannie smirked. "I saw that, Rosie."

Martha put down her half-eaten wafer. "We've been in here long enough!" she whined, grabbing the gals by their arms. "And enough with the cooking class, as if this was the Harvard Women's School."

"If they'd teach cooking, it could be!"

"Cooking would be useful, Fannie, but as I understand, they're considering some unknown subject called quaternions," snickered Martha.

"Quad-what?" questioned Fannie.

"That Miss Abigail Leach," Martha snipped, "has been talking up something called quaternions or some such."

"The term sounds to me like something good for breakfast," laughed Fannie.

A disdainful chuckle emerged from Martha. "We should have our dinner enriched with that new edible, if edible it be."

"If you get the recipe, I can make 'em," added Fannie.

"Miss Cowdin, you are acquainted with Miss Abigail Leach?" Alice was stunned as she contemplated whether to explain that quaternions were not breakfast food.

"I am acquainted with her, yes, as with every other person of importance that steps foot in Cambridge."

Rose rolled her eyes, clearly in view of Martha.

Alice wanted to know more but first could not help but explain: "A quaternion is a mathematical quotient that's quite useful. The person who made the discovery realized there'd need to be a fourth dimension of space to calculate with triples."

They stared at her, blank.

Realizing there would be no interest from this group on the subject, she stopped her "Alice-speak." "The man who discovered the formula carved it into a stone in Dublin when he figured it out."

"Ah, Dublin," remarked Fannie. "I've never been, but I hear there are many fine taverns."

Alice wondered now whether Martha really knew Miss Leach or just knew *of* her.

"You'd best be heading to the dining room," Fannie said, shooing them away. "You wouldn't want to keep the boys waiting."

"You never did tell us, Fannie, what that pink frosting is for?" Rose got in one more lick.

"Git to the dining room, all of you. What would a dining experience be, my dearies, without some surprises, especially one for you, Alice?"

THE CENTERPIECE, A tall vase with fully bloomed red roses, sat on a round table set for six with a lace covering. Silverware etched with gold swirls, crystal glassware, and gilded porcelain china made for a highly ornate display—this, too, more decorative than necessary, decided Alice. As she stepped nearer, place cards adorned with purple hand-painted pansies at the corners identified the seating assignments. She found her name, then saw the one next to her. Hodges! He would be seated adjacent to her. Rose promised! Why she ever listened to Cousin Rose, she had no idea.

As Alice uncomfortably sat on a chair with a velvet cushion, she glanced across to see an already seated Theodore Roosevelt. Through the center portion of the glass vase, his face appeared distorted, with his nose elongated at one nostril, then the other when he shifted. His mouth looked even wider than usual and in a permanent smile. She wished she was next to him, instead.

The elegantly crafted menu did make her mouth water, though:

Chate Estate
Saturday Afternoon Banquet
1878
Thorndike Canapé
Chicken Soufflé
Mashed Potato Medley
Dessert
Fancy Cake with Crystallized Violets

Hodges approached and held a glass in the air, toasting, "We shall do nothing but eat and make good cheer." He spoke with the typical drawl of the Harvard set, which sounded something close to a yawn.

The guests responded with huzzahs.

"The words of Shakespeare, Miss Lee." Hodges found his seat, eyeing her up and down.

As if she hadn't read Shakespeare. She held back from engaging. She recited the next lines in her head:

And praise God for the merry year;
When flesh is cheap and females dear,
And lusty lads roam here and there
So merrily,
And ever among so merrily.

The recitation left her far from merry, especially the "flesh is cheap" part of it. She distracted herself by focusing on the first dish: thorndike canapés. The first bite was creamy, buttery, cheesy, and topped with a most precious red heart-shaped sweet pepper.

"Have I told you about my success at the Beacon Park Foot Race?" Hodges's unattractive voice was in her ear.

Alice leaned away, continuing to chew and taste the delightful crunch from the toasted bread. She could feel him seeming to survey her interest in his story, which was none. She swallowed. "I don't believe so." It irked her when he lauded his success in one thing or another.

"I didn't achieve a medal; however, I beat my record by nearly a second in the hundred-yard dash."

Nearly a second did not sound like much.

"Hope to beat Bob Bacon next time."

Rose leaned over Hodges toward Alice. "That boy Bacon is handsome."

"Handsome of face as an Adonis." Martha leaned over Richard to speak to Alice. "And very Apollo in physique."

Alice tried to jump in to ask a question of Martha about Miss Abigail Leach, but Hodges put down his fork onto the plate with a clang. "Bob Bacon needs to get off the track and focus on football."

"Bob Bacon is the best athlete at Harvard," Richard interjected. "I can attest to that."

Alice looked up at the sound of Theodore's voice. From her angle, his face remained skewed through the vase.

"And how was your run-in with Bacon?" baited Hodges.

"Uh-oh," Martha murmured.

Hodges muttered under his breath, "Four-eyes."

Theodore paid no mind to the insult.

Alice watched through the vase as Theodore's mouth moved. "Bacon rather used me up in a sparring match," he admitted, his voice clear in diction, suave.

Boxing. He was a boxer.

Theodore's grin grew even wider from Alice's view through the center of the vase as he continued. "I would have landed him if only my arms had been longer and Bacon's not so long."

Martha and Rose found this amusing, as did the rest. As for Alice, she found his reaction unexpected. Meanwhile, "Bacon" put a notion into her head. She leaned behind Hodges and, with her finger, lifted the tip of her nose at Rose, who still owed her the question for the new fellow.

Fannie Farmer's serving crew interrupted with the next course of chicken soufflé, topped in a buttered pudding with white mushrooms.

Alice stared down Rose and once again raised the tip of her nose with her pointer finger. This caught Theodore's attention, the corner of his mouth twitching into a smile. Alice saw him glance at Rose with a side-eye, back at Alice, back to Rose.

Rose cleared her throat. "May I ask a question, Mister Roosevelt?" She took a drink with a loud swallow. "Please don't take this the wrong way."

The guests stopped chewing.

Alice noticed Richard begin to drum the table with his fingers, appearing none too pleased.

"We are ever so curious in regard to an article written about Manhattan Island. We realize this must be an untruth." Rose sipped again from her glass.

Oh, get on with it, thought Alice, at least before Richard puts a halt to it.

Theodore peered straight at Alice and gave her a side smile.

"Do hogs run free in New York City?" Her cousin spurted the question in rhyming fashion.

Martha nearly spit out her food.

Richard glowered at his sister, then Alice.

Theodore made no response.

Martha raised her head high. "What a hideous question!"

"Charles Dickens wrote about it," Alice jumped in to defend Rose.

Hodges appeared quite interested. "*The* Charles Dickens?"

"They nearly ate my granddad's shoes right off of him when he was a boy," Alice explained.

Theodore adjusted his spectacles. He leaned right and looked straight at Alice. "I can tell you that when they did wander free on New York's streets, my grandfather once told me a story of them, as well." His voice came with a teasing note.

"You must tell me the details, Mister Theodore." Martha

positioned her elbows on the table, put her face with fluttering eye-lashes in her hands, and changed her tone to vivacious inquisitiveness.

Theodore glanced at Martha for a moment before returning to Alice. "This happened one summer afternoon after my grandfather had listened to an unusually long Dutch Reformed sermon. It was the second one on the same day."

"Those sermons can drag on for quite some time," acknowledged Richard.

"My grandfather darted for home before the congregation had dispersed," he smiled wide, "and ran into a party of pigs."

"Free-roaming swine?" asked Hodges with a scowl.

Theodore dipped his head and closed his eyes. "He promptly mounted a big boar."

Martha's birdlike eyes grew larger. "Your grandad did?!"

Theodore was quiet until the roar at the table settled down. "The biggest boar," his hand pushed forward, "which no less promptly bolted."

Richard's grin showed all of his teeth. "With him on it?"

"Yes! The pig carried him at full speed!"

Sounds of hilarity came from the lot, except for Hodges.

"At full speed . . ." Theodore's body lifted a bit from his seat. "And returned him into the church!"

"Oh, no!" Alice found the story beyond enjoyable.

"A church with an outraged congregation, I might add. Ladies leaping from their pews. Men running through the aisle to stop the boy on the pig!"

"I would reckon so," howled Richard.

"I cannot even imagine!" sang Rose.

"They roam free in New York no more, Miss Saltonstall. Though," added Theodore, taking his seat, "I would be quite content to have one as a pet."

Martha tapped his hand. "Mister Theodore, you jest."

Theodore continued. "In truth, if given the choice, I would be much amused with a big corral and animals 'round a ranch."

"How delightful!" Martha touched his hand a second time. "You are filled with an abundance of good humor, Mister Theodore."

"I'd choose the largest hog of the lot and name it Maud and house her behind a garden's gate."

Alice wondered out loud about the name. "As in Tennyson's Maud?" She knew every line of his poetry, especially being that Alfred, Lord Tennyson hailed from the same part of England as her family. The poem was the only time she had ever heard the name Maud.

"'Come into the garden, Maud, I am here at the gate alone,'" Theodore recited to her, without even taking a beat to think, "'and the woodbine spices are wafted abroad, and the musk of the rose is blown.'"

As Alice was about to continue, Martha jumped in: "'For a breeze of morning moves.'" Her voice became louder. "'And the planet of Love is on high.'"

Everyone harmonized through the next stanza:

Beginning to faint in the light that she loves
In a bed of daffodil sky,
To faint in the light of the sun she loves,
To faint in his light, and to die.

"And die? Oh, please don't leave us, Maud! Please," Rose cried, and pretended to faint.

Theodore laughed out loud. The entire table joined in the merriment of the moment.

The dessert arrived. Servers offered the guests cherry sherbet,

Alice's favorite. How she adored Fannie! A three-tier cake with a frosting of pink fluff and what looked like a string of pearls falling from the top to the base was placed in the center of the table, the icing's crystallized violets in purples and yellows with sugar coats glistening.

Alice dug into the sherbet, focused on Theodore's face. She was left shocked, shocked indeed, at how such a handsome fellow acted with such self-deprecation. The question had the opposite effect from what she would have imagined. She was taken aback by his unchastened eagerness in being chaffed. Mister Roosevelt was able to take a joke, even one squarely against him. He wore a boyish positiveness that she found refreshing, one of those rare countenances that displayed a sense of confidence combined with humility.

"Let us have our cake and eat it too," announced Hodges as he was served a piece. "But before we begin," his finger settled across his upper lip: "I mustache my friend a question?"

Martha yelled out, "Ha!"

"I think it best to shave it for later," Richard added with a grand smile.

All eyed the beardless Theodore, who was the only fellow at the table to wear just a mustache.

"My great, stalwart, bearded boys, I know you've been pleased to see me, even beardless."

Alice liked his face just fine.

Hodges put a fork into the cake. "I'm not saying your smooth face makes you less of a man."

"You just present like less of a man," teased Richard.

"I have heard your suggestion, gentlemen." Theodore laughed. "And I must say I wholeheartedly agree. I will grant the whiskers a return."

Self-deprecation, again, left Alice fascinated.

"Since we are all in agreement that beards are better," added Richard, "let's get on with the eating."

"After dessert, we move into the ballroom. Music is calling us to the dance floor. Will you join me, Miss Lee?"

Hodges's request made Alice cringe.

Chapter Nine

A Fellow Conspirator

CHESTNUT HILL

Miss Alice Lee's figure whirled like the green dance of summer, floating as tall grasses would in a gentle breeze, shifting with a weightless quality and with perfect fluidity. At the moment of still-ness at the end of the musical bar, when the rhythm arrived at its final beat, she held for a second, maybe a millisecond, but she held on to that beat as if holding firm in the fiercest of winds, and it was magical.

Never more than at this moment had Theodore wished his feet cooperated. A dancer, he was not. So, he leaned against a wall in the Chate ballroom as he watched her waltz with Hodges.

Beauty danced differently from any girl he had seen before, or maybe he failed to notice any girl dance before. The expression on her face, however, evoked pure disinterest, or perhaps no emotion at all. Maybe a rehearsed expression achieved through abundant training, he surmised.

Theodore kept his eyes on this lovely conspirator. That is who she was, he realized. He assumed she had plotted with her cousin to ask the question about free-roaming pigs in New York City. Maybe they expected him to tear off in a huff. Little did they know who they were dealing with. What would Miss Lee think of him if she knew he, too, was a rascal? He could tell tales from his past. He wasn't called "little berserker" for nothing.

Tomfoolery ran through his genes, even on the dance floor, way back to the day he learned to waltz when he was eight years of age. It may have been considered an unconventional dance. Theodore remembered the evening:

The time was midnight. He had been given a dispensation to stay up late. The adults danced rounds and a Virginia Reel. Mother announced, "A new waltz will be danced tonight!" Father tried to coax Teedie to join the dance floor: "Use your wings. You may fall by the wayside should they prove inadequate for your adventures, but you must try." His father even took to performing a galop with another fellow to make Teedie laugh. His sister Bamie giggled as she watched with Teedie, commenting, "Father is acting like a lady—a rather large one, is he not?" Bamie pulled him onto the dance floor, and they galloped their way around.

So Theodore did know that one dance. Whether his wings proved inadequate, he would soon find out.

As the song ended, he approached Hodges to suggest a change in tempo and the new dance. He seemed stunned by the suggestion. "The galop?"

"As in a horse?" yelled Miss Cowdin from across the room, rushing closer to them.

"The galop?" Richard walked over. "I hear it's in vogue." He threw Theodore a nod.

Theodore appreciated Richard even more.

"Very well," Hodges conceded.

Theodore walked to the center of the floor. He reviewed the movements in his head. The dance that derived its name from a horse's gait was the most basic in the ballroom. He explained to all the eight counts, a turn, and back to eight counts. The music should carry a 2/4 time signature, he suggested.

Miss Cowdin raced across the floor. "Let me try!" She grabbed Theodore by the hand and positioned herself in a waltz pose. "Strike up the band, Hodgie!"

As the music began to play, Theodore breathed in before galloping for eight counts, changing direction, and galloping for eight counts more. He kept his head and tail straight as he had been taught. He hoped his dancing came across as a first-class galop rather than a lumbering one. He counted the steps in his head, trying to get through the song to swap partners and finally have the chance to dance with her. When the song concluded, he put his hands on his head for a moment to give his ribs room to expand; this helped steady his breathing.

In those seconds, a missed chance, as *Hodgie!* butted in to dance with Miss Lee. The galloping started up again with Theodore paired with Richard's sister. Eight counts. A pivot. Eight counts. He concentrated on uniform breathing.

The song ended.

Without an instant's hesitation, Theodore approached Alice Hathaway Lee. Time slowed to a crawl as he neared her. He studied her graceful neck, smooth and arched, resting upon squared, pulled back shoulders. Beats pounded hard in his chest. He examined her face and cataloged two tiny freckles: one above her right arched brow, the other to the left of her nose.

Their hands came together, touching gently, leaving him bubbling inside. Awaiting the music, he breathed in her scent with a deep inhale. Lavender. A flower she was. A pure blossom. Trying to forcibly control his exterior, his interior trembled.

Gentle, dovelike eyes locked on his. "Theodore." She curtsied.

Theodore, she called him Theodore. Hearing her say just his first name left him weak at the knees. "Alice," he whispered.

"Miss Lee, if you would." She smiled wider through delicate lips, and even her eyes shone happiness, curved at the edges oh so slightly.

This caused him to pause.

"I jest, Theodore; Alice is fine."

How intimate to be able to call her by her first name.

Alice.

Alice.

Alice.

He could say her name forever.

"Now, Theodore, do we have to gallop like a horse, or might we prance as a deer?" Her words sounded delightful, but what did they mean? "Deer and their big horns strike at other deer," came her voice through a sideways smile, not failing to surprise him. Behind those eyes he saw certainty, courage, and an accomplice.

Oh, he could step up to her prankster ways. "Shall we begin with the white-tailed or black-tailed?" he questioned, ready to collude.

"What would be the difference?"

The first notes played. "The gaits of the two animals are quite distinct from one another," he told her as they began to move. "The white-tailed makes off at a great rate." They moved fast. "The head is carried low and well forward in running." He kept his head low as they changed direction and galloped again.

"I suggest just enough peril to make it exciting."

Theodore sped up the next counts of eight to double time and led the way right toward Miss Saltonstall and Hodges.

"Pardon us!" shouted Theodore.

Hodges huffed as the couple bumped into them.

"Our apologies!" Alice laughed loudly.

Theodore maneuvered her back to correct timing, waltzing again to the count of eight, the change, and the count of eight in succession.

Ocean's blue looked straight into his eyes. "Since we've experienced the white-tailed deer, may I ask about the black-tailed?"

"The black-tailed deer"—Theodore straightened his posture—"holds its head higher than the white-tailed."

She mirrored his steps.

"And progresses with a series of prodigious bounds." He had her leap with him for the change in direction. He went on, "Rapidly succeeding bounds enable the deer to cover more ground, more quickly." He moved her along to double time for the next eight counts. After the leap at the change in direction, a quick gait had them rushing right toward Richard and Miss Cowdin whose eyes went wide; she hollered just as Theodore and Alice struck. This led Richard's sister and Hodges to follow along. Soon the galloping regressed into mayhem, with each couple charging at the other with a nice amount of force.

Miss Cowdin gave up and bent over gasping, stertorous.

Quite surprised was Theodore that his own lungs had not given him any trouble. He hurriedly walked with Alice to check on her.

"I am fine. I am fine," she expressed dramatically. She put out her hand to have Theodore help her stand upright.

"Violent exertions can tire a deer sooner," whispered Theodore, leaning toward Alice.

"They can indeed," responded Alice. "But how to explain Miss Cowdin?"

Miss Cowdin leaned her head on Theodore. "You saved me, Mister Theodore." She grabbed a hold of him at the elbow. "And shouldn't you two be off by now?" She glared at Alice and her cousin.

Theodore tried to release himself, but to no avail.

Miss Cowdin giggled rather loudly and batted her eyes at him.

Richard's sister interrupted. "Mister Roosevelt, Mister Roosevelt. I wanted to speak with you about something."

He paused, still in the young lady's grasp.

"I must apologize for the question I asked earlier, about the hogs in Manhattan," continued Miss Rose. "I must make this up to you."

"No need for an apology."

"Please, Mister Roosevelt, I know a way," she added. "You must try chestnutting in our garden. Please, allow Alice to show you the art."

Alice whipped her head toward her cousin.

Elated, Theodore listened intently.

"There is no one better at chestnutting than Miss Lee." She grinned her way before turning back to him. "Have you been chest-nutting before?"

He could not believe his ears. Of course, he knew the art of chest-nutting. He had collected them with his siblings when they were children, usually trying to sell them to patient parents. He did not mention this.

"At dawn tomorrow?" suggested Miss Rose. "The garden's gate?"

Theodore nodded.

"But. . . ." Alice started to say, a stunned look on her face.

Miss Cowdin interrupted. "Are you certain, Mister Theodore?"

Wanting to go chestnutting with Alice was not in doubt.

"I'm sure Hodgie has a full day planned and, girls," she said as she released Theodore and grabbed hold of the gals by their elbows, "I hope you realize it's near ten o'clock!" She headed toward the door with them, her voice scolding. "Did you not know the time?"

He watched them walk away.

"It is scheduled then," Miss Saltonstall sang from a distance.

He was sorry to see the night coming to an end. But waking up to collect chestnuts sounded divine. His feet started galloping toward the fellows. At each beat, her name repeated in his head.

Chapter Ten

———◄•►———

The Art of Chestnutting

CHESTNUT HILL

Her arm tangled up in Martha's grasp, Alice could not have been angrier.

Martha led them into the foyer. "Mister Theodore dances as I expect he would."

Rose rolled her eyes. "Whatever do you mean, Miss Cowdin?"

"He hops!" Martha let them go and jumped up, nearly losing her footing as she landed, paying her awkwardness no mind. "He hops through a waltz!"

"Is that not what the dance calls for?" Alice asked, annoyed at the implication, and for many other reasons, most notably Rose's offer of chestnutting.

"I've never witnessed such a thing in my life!" Martha's birdlike eyes opened wide as she tapped her temple. "I wonder if he is truly the bundle of eccentricities that he appears. I must find out."

Alice needed to put aside her frustration for the moment to ask on the subject that remained on her mind since their time in the kitchen. "May I ask about Miss Abigail Leach?"

"Miss Leach?" Her face scrunched up.

"Have you been acquainted with her?"

"Why would you want to ask about her?"

"Why? Because, she is who we all should be talking about. Brave, smart, determined, and has an ambitious thirst for knowledge."

"Well yes, I know of her, but Father and Mother know the woman hoping to launch the Harvard School for Women more intimately, although they speak highly of Miss Leach." She pranced away, continuing a discussion with herself, then turned back to them. "And you both should be off. Shouldn't you?" She hurried back to the ballroom, tossing over her shoulder, "I'll be staying 'til morning, being it is my cousins' estate."

Rose grunted. "She irks me so."

"I can't believe her parents know the founder."

"I think she likes the fellow. Did you see how she was dancing about, giggling and all?"

Alice did not respond.

"Whatever is the matter with you?"

"Me?"

"Yes, you. Your brows are knitted. I know what that means."

Alice glared at her cousin. "I cannot go chestnutting with Theodore Roosevelt."

"We cannot allow Miss Cowdin to get her hands on such a fellow, Al." Rose imitated the screech of Martha's voice: "'And you both should be off. Shouldn't you?'"

"Dancing is one thing, prancing into the woods alone, another. Besides, I had plans for myself before church in the morning."

"Plans? Please do not tell me to study again, and on Sunday?"

"Reading, yes, Mary Wollstonecraft, *A Vindication of the Rights of Woman,* and you should, too."

"Upon this, we disagree. And chestnutting is a friendly pastime."

Alice placed her hands onto her hips. "How do you expect me to go alone with him? My mother will refuse. You know she is making me wait until the débutante ball."

"I would have offered to go alone with him, but he's been gazing at you all evening."

"I cannot go alone."

"Fine, then I will join you. Now, what do you think is the meaning of that surname anyway—Cowdin?"

"You know what it means, Ro."

"I don't."

"Din is an unpleasant, prolonged noise."

"Her voice is like lemon on a paper cut."

THE MORNING FOG clung to the long waves of Alice's hair that she did not care to tame. *Glorious dawns birth beautiful adventures,* Nana used to say. Today was anything but. Though the sun was rising, there was no view of it. The heavy greyness matched her mood as she was not fond of waking up this early. Muttering complaints under her breath, she should have been starting the book she had by her bedside; instead, she was walking through wet grass, grateful, at least, for her boots. The rest of her was dressed in the fashion of the day, a red Garibaldi shirt embroidered with a golden thread paired with a belted skirt that fell wide to the mid-calf. Except for the footwear, she'd wear the same clothes to church.

Through the mist, the figure of a broad-shouldered man moved sure-footed toward her. Even Theodore's walking tempo differed from the usual Harvard meandering sway. She pulled fingers through her hair to make it look somewhat presentable and smoothed her skirt. He neared the garden's gate alone wearing a white sweater with an "H" in dark red at its center. His high black leather boots reached to his knees, and his elegantly styled pants were loose and hung just over the boots.

She wanted to believe that she had begrudgingly followed Rose's request to join him this morning, but if she was honest with herself, she would decide that she found Theodore quite knowledgeable and, in actuality, to be just what Miss Cowdin considered him: a bundle of eccentricities. Alice found him an engaging bundle. With his comments and questionings, the most mundane of things could be livened up. Most Harvard friends were discreet, even strict, about showing a detached interest in most things. He, on the other hand, displayed a type of zest for living she had not witnessed before.

"Alice, good morning."

She enjoyed hearing the intimacy of her first name coming from his lips, but now wondered whether her offer may have been too soon. "To you, too."

There was no sign of Rose.

"It's pretty well filled with wild violets around these parts." His voice sounded pleasant and upbeat.

'Twas true. Their purple color appeared like puddles. "This is the best time of year for wildflowers, especially violets."

"I should be sure not to trample upon them. It seemed too bad to crush the life out of the dainty little flowers that hold up their heads to sunrise." Theodore stepped carefully. "They grow in great profusion here."

"They do. And they give off the sweetest smell." She focused her attention toward the Saltonstall house, waiting for the ever-late third party.

"Like powder."

"But the smell is quite temporary," she added, laughing to herself about the odor they would soon experience from the chestnut trees. "Take it in now, because once the nose gets used to it, it disappears."

His chest expanded as he drew a deep breath.

"The scent lasts for only a few moments. After that, people go anosmic to it." She tried taking in the smell again, but only notes of mossy earth came through. "Did Miss Rose not come with you?"

He shook his head. "I was told Miss Saltonstall would be unavailable to join us."

"Oh?" Her cousin displeased her, so often, she wondered how she continued to be related to her. Disowning a cousin seemed a likely next step if that was permissible.

He tried to take in the violets' scent. "You are correct. Now I smell nothing of them."

Going unaccompanied into the woods with Theodore Roosevelt, what was she to do? Nana would tell her, *If you start a project, finish it.* Leading the way, Alice moved along the path toward the forest, which was lined by bushes and branches and changing leaves, with him close behind. The only noise came from their shoes stepping atop the carpet of eastern white pine needles inches thick and her impatient breaths. She was worried her mother would see her. She sped up.

They passed a tangle of speckled alder which would soon bloom bright red berries in a dense thicket. Shifting as she went, sprigs caught her hair and tree cones stuck on her skirt. She realized she must appear as messy as the jumbled twigs.

An abrupt right led to a zigzag of large, round rocks upon the ground, which she used to jump about on one foot, side to side, as a child. She did it again. Theodore followed in similar fashion. This took them to the great, big pine, and a left turn hit them smack in the face with an awful robust stench. Alice flung her fingers over her nose. The chestnut trees were the foulest smelling of all arbors. A clearing emerged, chestnuts making their appearance in burrs on the ground. "Shall we begin?" she asked, nose pinched. She got down on her knees and spread out her skirt with one hand. Theodore followed her to the ground, knelt across from her, closer than she would have expected. He did not begin; instead, he stared at her long hair. She released her nose and brushed her fingers through the mess that cascaded to her waist.

"May I?" he asked with a tremble in his voice.

She gently nodded, even though she did not know to what he was referring.

He reached ever so slowly to remove tiny tree cones from her hair, his breath hitching each time, three in total. A palm brushed her shoulder at the last. Warmth rushed to her face; she could not recall such a feeling of heat on her cheeks. His eyes, brilliant, intense, rose to meet hers. She took notice of a chiseled jaw, and straight, thick brows that led to prominent temples.

"Shall we begin Mister Roos-velt?" Hadn't she asked that already? She could not now recall. And had she mispronounced his name, again?

"Hardly anyone can get my name correct," he chuckled, "except as Rosy." He flashed a wider grin. "Better than the pronunciation I usually receive. My professor calls me Rusce-felt during Latin recitations."

"Paenitet me," fell from her lips.

He reached down to the ground, picked up a few chestnuts, and placed them in her skirt. "Ah. You speak Latin." Theodore's big teeth filled a wide mouth that appeared most comfortable in a smile.

"Not very much." She shook her head, surprised at her initial willingness to show off in front of the new boy. She only knew a few phrases, one being "I'm sorry."

"My first knowledge of the Latin language was obtained by learning the scientific names of birds."

She pushed loose hair behind her ear and bent over to pick another burr, interested. "And on the subject of binomial nomenclature, I know very little." If she was honest, she would have told him she knew nothing, other than the one he taught her: *Melanerpes erythrocephalus,* if she recalled correctly.

One chestnut after the next fell into her open skirt, mostly from Theodore's adept skill. She wondered if he had experience in collecting chestnuts. Alice reached for a twig by her with ten small burrs. She added them to the growing pile on her skirt.

He suddenly halted his collecting, raising his face to the sky. Under his gold-framed rounded spectacles, she could see his eyelids close. "Did you hear that?" He kept them shut.

She listened.

He lifted his head higher, concentrating.

"What should I be hearing?"

"The birdsong."

Alice leaned a bit forward, lifted her head higher, and heard her own breathing, and his.

"Can you hear it now?" His head tilted, a dreamy expression on his face as his eyes met hers.

She could not.

Warm hands took hold of hers. Her heart leaped from the sensation. His palms were rough, his touch light. He moved her hands to her knees.

"Remain still," he whispered, his tone calm and soothing, his hands covering hers.

She focused, though it was challenging.

"The sound is like a *tu-a-wee.* Close your eyes to hear."

She calmed the thoughts swimming through her brain. Her body followed his suggestion. Sounds normally hidden came through: a rustling leaf, a gentle breeze, and then a low, slow pitch. A whistle, followed by short notes of a couple of beats, and another whistle. The sound was just as he related, *tu-a-wee.* The tune was crystal clear, each note going through her, echoing inside her head. "Yes!

I hear it!" The emotion in her voice surprised her: excitement. She opened her eyes to find his, not large but passionate, staring at her. Long blond lashes, blue speckled with grey, and maybe a bit of green. She had not realized he had such full lips under that tamed mustache. She wanted to keep staring right back at him.

The bird's call changed from a whistle to a querulous sound.

"Testy, isn't it?"

He chuckled. "You have now been introduced to *Sialia sialis,* otherwise known as the Eastern bluebird."

She looked up, then straight down at her dress skirt, trying to avoid another lock on his eyes. The burrs pretty well covered the fabric; not another one could fit. She wrapped the edges of her skirt around the burrs and held the cloth with one hand. They must have collected fifty or more. She should be leaving, she knew this. The time, it must have been late; she had completely lost any sense. Sunday service was approaching. Her mother would certainly start searching for her. As she rose from the ground, a tingling sensation climbed up from foot to ankle, arousing her nerves. She stomped on the ground to get rid of the vibration that started to journey up her legs.

Theodore continued listening for birdcalls as they moved up the path.

She kept up the quickened pace, making a right turn at the great, big pine, following the zigzag formation of large, round rocks; she jumped on one foot, side to side, to bring life back to her leg. Out of the stench, she knew they were almost by the garden's gate.

"Perhaps the sweetest bird music I ever heard was uttered in the dark of night while I was on a small lake in the heart of the wilderness," he explained as they went. "The moon had not yet risen. The surface of the water was perfectly silent. I could distinguish dimly the outlines of a gloomy pine forest." He stopped his speaking, took several deep breaths, and moved forward to reach her. "For two to three hours, I rowed in the quiet."

Beginning to feel a bit fuzzy in the head, with sprinkles of light appearing before her eyes, her movement resisted any stoppage.

"Nothing otherwise broke the death-like stillness of the night; not even a breath of air stirring among the tops of the tall pine trees," he continued, jutting forward to catch up to her.

She didn't respond.

"Suddenly, birdsong broke through. The song of the hermit thrush—dulcet, sad music filled the very air. Louder and clearer, it sang from the depths of the grim and rugged woods. It conquered for the moment the gloom of the night." His low, pleasant voice went on as they arrived at the garden's gate. "Perhaps the song would have seemed less sweet in the daytime. . . ."

She wanted to hear more, but instead, placed the chestnuts in a basket that she had left by the garden's gate.

". . . But uttered as it was, with such surroundings, sounding so strange and so beautiful amid the grand, desolate wilds, I shall never forget it." His story ended.

She would have enjoyed it more if not for the dizziness combined with a light sweat forming on her forehead. Not a word came from her lips as a pain in her head flashed hard and heavy. She finished adding the last few stray chestnuts to the basket, which she handed to Theodore.

Accepting the pile of nuts, he looked straight at her.

She avoided reciprocating, feeling as if she were coming apart. "Have a good day, Mister Roos-velt." She wandered away from him, needing to get out of there as quickly as possible, knowing as she did what could come next.

Chapter Eleven

———◆◆◆———

Simple Endearments

What had he said to offend her? Did he talk too much? He was known to talk too much. The rest of his Sunday back at his residence was preoccupied with thoughts of why Alice had hurried from him without explanation.

Their conversation did flow easily, effortlessly, a wonderful turn of events. The more he settled on it, the more he realized just basking in her presence, even for one morning of chestnutting, was enough. What a dreamy journey with the most captivating girl he had ever known!

Alone with Alice.

He would be forever grateful to Richard for introducing him to the treasure of a gal. And now worrying thoughts entered his mind. He had touched her. He had touched her thick, shiny, wavy hair. His hand had fallen upon her shoulder. His hands had laid on her hands. Was it too much? Theodore!

From a drawer at his desk he forcefully pulled out his diary, with an embossed leaf and "excelsior" written on the front. It had some heavy creasing along the spine from overuse and these tiny tears from shifting the pages too quickly when reading back his lines.

How many years had he written in a diary? He must have been five or six years old when he started. Six, yes, six, when all he had to write was "nothing happened worth mentioning." And then there were other days he liked best, when he wrote about playing in brooks with crayfish, eels, minnow, salamanders, water spiders, water bugs.

He arrived at a blank page and stared at it. Today felt much different. He wanted to write about what had transpired on Friday, Saturday, and Sunday, and without extravagance, he told himself, just the facts. He would keep it simple, although he could write an entire book about it. He began with Friday:

> Richard Saltonstall drove me in a buggy over
> to his house on Chestnut Hill, where I enjoyed
> myself to the utmost. All his family are just
> too sweet to me for anything, and the whole house
> is so homelike.

Then Saturday:

> Spent the morning walking through the woods with
> Richard, his sister Miss Rose and their cousin,
> Miss Alice Lee—

He thoroughly enjoyed having his pen write her name and added a dash followed by the words,

> a very sweet pretty girl.

The endearments that came into his mind were simple, short-syllable words. Sweet. Pretty. But when describing her, they were statements of genuine affirmation.

About midday we drove over to where
we took dinner and tea. We spent the evening
dancing, driving back about 11 o'clock.

He wanted to write how he knew what love at first sight felt like. He now knew what the arrow could do in the paintings of Cupid. He now knew what all of those dime novels were about. He had always believed such stories were not possible in real life.

Of course, there were other friendships with girls. Miss Edith Carow, his sister's babyhood friend. And then there was Miss Frances Theodora Smith for whom he had such an affectionate appreciation.

This time, however, was not the same. He busily continued writing about the following morning:

I went chestnutting with Miss Alice Lee.

The memory left him feeling weak. At the corner of his desk sat a basket full of chestnuts. Theodore wondered if there was a way to preserve chestnuts, keep them with him forever.

He wanted to keep her with him forever. But how?

A notion popped into his head, and he muttered to himself: "Thank Heaven I am at least perfectly pure."

Part II

—◆—

My happiness is so great it makes me afraid.

—THEODORE ROOSEVELT

Chapter Twelve

———◆•◆———

Here Roams Theodore

COWBOY LAND, NORTH DAKOTA

SUMMER 1885

THE PRESENT

Nowhere, not even at sea, does a man feel lonelier than when riding over these far-reaching, monotonous, never-ending plains. Here, I am isolated, feeling abandoned. Months into my stay, I have become restless and enraged, like a caged wolf.

Only dust churns in the wind as I urge my horse across this granite, scorched to dullness, and smelling of shriveled earth. Riding albeit slowly as day breaks in a cloudless sky, each of Manitou's steps thuds the hard-packed dirt. My heart thuds, too, blunt, bitter. What I thought would change in me for the better has instead become worse.

I should find food; I have not eaten much, and my body is wasting away, my waist itself thin enough to encircle with two thumbs and fingers. The only living beings I see, though, on today's journey are prairie rattlesnakes, and of these, I have never elsewhere noticed as many. One or two of them coil and rattle menacingly as I draw nearer. A third basks in the morning sun, stretching out to its full length, mottled brown and yellow. Another lies half-dead under stones, partially twined in the roots of the brush. This last one focuses straight at me with that strange, sullen, evil gaze, never shifting or moving—that is the property of only serpents and certain men.

One such man told me this place is hell with the fire gone out. Maybe that man was right—I am in hell, and I, along with the lands around me, am broken.

What can a person do when there is nothing? There is one thing I will continue to do. Each day, I look for a sign. Some days, she arrives without any searching on my part. On others, I have to fight to find her. That one day in winter comes to mind when the temperature dropped down to well below zero and I nearly froze to death trying to hear elegant notes amid ice-covered pines plinking in the gorges. The wind cut through me that night like a keen knife, and then the tip of my nose, one cheek, and both ears at the lobes suffered frostbite. Ice chips formed on my beard by the time I arrived back at the cabin. That entire next day it took for my skin to finally regain its color, after being wrapped in a big buffalo robe, sewed up at the sides. The pain was worth it. Just as I had hoped the gusts tunneled through, the pines shook, and I heard music again. She was back and it was captivating.

Now, from the empty air, quick, tinkling notes trickle. The hair at the back of my neck stands. I press my seat into the saddle, slowing Manitou, and I listen hard. Lovely single notes, a short *chek,* followed by melodic warbling and a change in pitch. Clear and tender, the music rises. I recognize the birdsong. Perhaps the sweetest euphony that can be comes from the queen of all singers, the *Sturnella neglecta*. From a distance off another meadowlark answers the call, and the two soar into view, mounting in whimsical curves.

The birds swoosh nearer to me, singing in unison, an unyielding harmony. A minute goes by, more follow. Such a willing and glorious journey they take. The sound of one completes the other and back again. My senses, numbed from long days in the barren plains, return. Their silhouettes, against the dawning sky with faded color of purple and orange, appear as love cometh to life. Has the duo ever known disillusionment or disappointment? I think not.

The birds travel away, distant, becoming visible only as dark specks. Their melody thins to a whisper.

The patter of Manitou's unshod hoofs over the turf makes little noise as our pace moves to a gallop, one at a good speed. The hot wind blows in my face as we travel fast, tracking the fliers.

The birds come back into view. I am not ready to let her go.

Chapter Thirteen

———◈◆◈———

A Hot Clean

CHESTNUT HILL

OCTOBER 27, 1878

THE PAST

Alice lost direction in the murky night. Her nightdress dripped wet from the vapored chill. Far in the distance, a clock clanked. She leaped from her pillow, perspiring and trembling. Every night, the same nightmare of a dream, over and over again, with her, lost in the fog of some moor.

The room sat dark except for the flame burning in a candle next to her bed. Light danced, spreading out as it reached the ceiling, moving its brightness back and forth, slowly, smoothly.

She was sick. Anytime she tried to find out precisely what caused her to feel so very tired with headaches, dizziness, and a pounding in her chest, those same blank stares came in return. Even from Doctor Francis who had made house calls twice that week, she received few answers. He said her ill health was not a physical condition but a state of mind: "A symptom of rhythm disruption in the brain which can alter internal manifestations." Mamma interrupted him, voicing her own diagnosis: "Too much thinking makes the brain go to mush."

The doctor agreed, stating, "The influence of severe intellectual exertion in women is found to produce physiological effects." What reading and studying had to do with internal rhythms Alice could not fathom. Add to that, immersing herself in a good book calmed her. Mamma made a suggestion for treatment after Doctor Francis picked up his medical bag, put on his hat and coat, and left. "You must stop all this thinking of yours, Alice." And she added, "You are tearing my nerves into little pieces."

How would Mamma react when Alice told her what her future would hold—continue her studies? Tutors once a week were not enough. She needed to learn from the learned, like Abigail Leach and the women who might one day attend Harvard. Her mother would never agree to such a path. Mamma had a plan for her: marriage. Maybe there was a way to try to convince her. Make an effort. Do something. Nana would have understood. Without education, without good health, without Nana, what would become of her?

Alice set a hot bath in the middle of the night, sprinkling the water with marigold blooms. She slowly climbed inside. Her skin needed time to appreciate the heat. She laid her body in without waiting for comfort to settle in.

"Be still," Alice whispered to herself. Fingers submerged under the water. Swirls of mist dissipated. Her head slowly dropped back onto the tub's metal surface. Serenity took time in reaching her. Concentrating, she first relaxed the muscles in her neck, moved to her shoulders, and did the same with her arms and hands. To her abdomen, she tried calming her stomach, her hips, legs, and down to the tips of her toes.

"Be soft and tranquil like the water." She closed her eyes. She needed the bath hot, very hot; it was the only way for her to find calm. "Be soft and tranquil like the water," she repeated. "And in time, what is soft will become strong; what is tranquil will become resilient." These were words of inspiration she had written down once, but the muffled sound of the clock handle clanking in the other room distracted her, and her mind kept thinking of her grandmother's maxim: *the clock ticks, the mind wastes.*

She wondered if she would see him again, Theodore Roosevelt. Rose had sent word that Mister Roosevelt had sent word that he would be interested in another visit. What a ruckus that caused! Alice had doubted he would want to see her again due to her awkward departure after chestnutting. Then, Alice's mother sent regrets that Alice was not up to a visit from friends. Alice was surprised Mamma was willing to call him a "friend." Rose sent word to Alice that she sent word through Richard to leave out the part that Alice was not up to a visit, and instead tell Mister Roosevelt that Richard was bogged down in studying for his exams, which is in the end what Theodore was told, and a truth, in part.

The marigold blooms wilted as they floated. Was their scent attractive or unpleasant? Maybe a little of both. Either way, the sharp smell failed to calm her. The flower petals contained an essential oil that was supposedly useful for a condition like hers. As a side note, she was once told that marigold petals helped relieve rashes on babies' bums. Luckily her bum was not in any peril.

She slid her fingers up her shoulder, lifting her long hair out of the wet heat, and thought of Theodore. Yes, being with him, alone, especially in the woods that day a week ago, it felt nice, as did settling her view on his chiseled jawline, on a face lit with passion. And that one wayward curl settling on his forehead; she wanted to swirl it around her finger. The way Theodore had brushed her shoulder when he reached over to her, so gently, left a tingle. Imagine if he were here, reaching for her, moving from her shoulders to her naked neck, hands caressing her sore muscles, leaving her in a state of bliss.

And his eyes, when she opened hers, were ablaze with longing and tenderness, and for the first time in her life she did not cringe at the sight of a man showing her interest in that way. So many other men's eyes had looked at her. But his gaze was different; it was real, authentic, accepting.

He was the most original boy she had ever met, but how could she see him again? The sickness that day chestnutting crept up on her with little warning. Palms started to tingle, legs felt like jelly, head went dizzy, and bones cold. Nerves took over and she figured she might scream. What if she had fainted right there in front of him? An uncomfortable end to what may have been something, maybe more.

The slow clean was not helping to soothe Alice's tattered nerves. That brief plunge into cold water the doctor had often advised might have been better. Taking even a dip in a steaming bath was considered a no-no. She once read if the water temperature rose above tepid, the oil would instead strip away a person's beauty. What good was beauty anyhow when there was nothing else but an empty shell? Alice immersed herself entirely, face and all; she wanted to be ugly.

A clank from the clock caused her to lift her head from the water. She needed to get out of this room. Do something, Alice.

Chapter Fourteen

The Burning

CAMBRIDGE

1878

Theodore appreciated receiving the fine news; he was invited to join one of the most prestigious organizations at Harvard, the A.D. But, as he walked down the stairs inside the boardinghouse, his mind was on something else, conceptualizing the idea that after spending time with Alice, something in him had changed, crystallized, put things in some happy order that ultimately could lead him on the journey of life.

On this chilly afternoon, Theodore plopped himself right atop the wide-planked floor of the crowded gathering room by the large coal-burning fire. A log snapped. The scent of embers combined with the smell of old books, volumes crammed on a nearby bookcase.

A group of fellows snickered about some such behind him, Theodore resisted even a glance that way. He had to study like a Trojan this week and for a good reason. An average B man he considered himself, and his grades proved it so. In no way distinguished on the intellectual scale among his classmates, putting in the extra work was essential, especially with philosophy, political economy, Italian literature, natural history, and his most challenging, the one he failed last year: German.

He needed to bury himself in reading, though his imagination soared. This moment would have been a dream with Alice sitting by his side. His mind had not departed from her since their morning in the chestnut forest last week. She had left so abruptly, nervous even, and called him by his full name, and pronounced it incorrectly at that. He hinted at another visit, but Richard was bogged down in studies as he had double the classwork of the usual student. Add to this, they were in the midst of examinations, so a trip to Chestnut Hill would have to wait. Today, Theodore had little choice than to be paired with a book written in German which placed a good amount of weight on his thighs.

He read and paused here and there due to the loud, unceasing debate behind him pitting housemates against guests on a very particular subject: whether women should be allowed admission to Harvard.

On the one side, those in favor: "The world moves, and Harvard College must move with it."

"Sufferance!" came from the opposition led by Hodges Chate. Theodore recognized his distinct voice but now could spare no time to join in the discussion.

"At present, it exists only by sufferance," asserted Hodges with a locution that sounded as if it were emerging from a locked jaw. "Now, as there are no ladies present for I should hardly dare to speak my mind fully in their presence and to say all I think of them face-to-face, I shall endeavor to speak my mind freely."

The verbal match persisted with supporters of the women's school. "We are not the first to discover that women have brains."

Theodore could hear a fellow jump on a chair with a thump. "This invention of a Harvard education for women is a contrivance," exclaimed Hodges with a flair of dramatics. "A contrivance, as I understand it, devised for the purpose of mitigating the austerities of college life—that is, for the college man."

Guffaws came in response, as well as a stern "Git down from that chair!" from Mrs. Richardson.

Hodges jumped down and continued his remarks: "At present, Miss Abigail Leach and her delicate damsels are to be admitted only to the outskirts of the temple of learning, but surrounding it nevertheless with a galaxy of beauty, and poetry, and sentiment, which will inevitably reach and pervade its most secret cloisters."

Theodore wondered whether Alice would be interested in studying at Harvard. She would be in favor of the school itself, he imagined.

The fellows continued fooling about, gradually getting noisier, sometimes bumping into his back, the wafting of brandy fumes in the room about him.

"Just think what this would have done for some of the graduates," Hodges cleared his throat, rather randy in tone, "if they had only enjoyed such gentle privileges!"

Theodore did not even turn around.

"Ah, yes," averred Hodges, pouring a liquid, likely more whiskey. "Suppose such a tender and soothing intercourse was possible in the college days of the men before us. What different men they would have been if, instead of spending their evenings in the rude and crude dissipations of the undergraduates, they had been soothed and softened by sharing with some fair sisters in the pursuit of learning the innocent cup that cheers but not inebriates!"

"Hear, hear!" Men on both sides whooped.

Theodore felt a tap on his shoulder, and a harder one. The landlady poked him again—"Somethin' wrong with you?"

"I'm fine, Mrs. Richardson."

"Why aren't you speaking up?"

"Too much on my plate."

"And where is your plate? You look flushed. What you doin' close to the fire anyhows? Maybe you need some food. Would you be liking some prunes, Mister Roosevelt?"

"No, thank you, Mrs. Richardson."

"You don't like prunes?"

Wondering how anyone could appreciate them, he told her kindly, "Not particularly." He simply could not enjoy prunes, and there was no changing that. The times he tried them, his tongue quickly felt the need to expectorate. In truth, he despised shriveled old fruit as much as shriveled old thinking.

"Some cut-up apples then?"

"Yes. Thank you." Apples he liked. Likes and dislikes fell upon strict lines. But he knew in eating, as with reading, it was all a matter of personal preference.

His eyes scanned the heavy science book written in German, pleased that at least he could study the language in a subject he enjoyed. If all went as planned, he would make science his life's work. Not as in a scientist in a laboratory; he had less interest in that than in being a financier, although he did have interest in political economy. After college, he decided, he would embark on a career as a faunal naturalist.

How he could convince the Harvard establishment that such a curious profession was genuinely possible was another story. He knew professors eschewed even the word "naturalist" as archaic, especially the college's biologists. It frustrated him that not only did they discourage the work of the field naturalist, but they also treated the work as of negligible value. By their accepted doctrine, a true scientist meant being a section cutter of tissue and spending time studying that cut tissue under a microscope. And he would certainly have to study for three years abroad where his choice of study was taught. That stopped Theodore's thoughts right there. He would have to be away from Alice Hathaway Lee for three years. Being away from her for just days proved difficult. He shook his head, realizing his thoughts were taking him too far. One day of chestnutting did not a courtship make. Still, three years overseas made him blue just to think of it.

The roisterers kept up their roughhousing behind him.

Flames picked up strength, roaring. Beads of sweat started to form on his forehead, much like that moment when he reached over to place his hands on top of Alice's while chestnutting. A clear image of her emerged, not a picture of the particulars of her beautiful face or the movement of her shapely figure, no, this was one of color—a pink glow, the one that appeared on her blushing cheeks when his hands touched hers, the one that seemed to come from deep inside of her, the one that appeared like the beam of an angel spreading light to the world.

Alice Hathaway Lee.

Three words he treasured. Three words he would always treasure. Her name happily jumped about his head.

Way down to the depths of his soul, he could feel her glow making a permanent mark on his heart. He imagined a soothing embrace, eyes locked on hers, arms entwined around each other, caressing her lengthy locks down her back. He breathed in deeply and leaned his cheek on her moist skin. The softness left him warm all over; actually, come to think of it, it made him hot.

The back and forth continued until Mrs. Richardson shouted an ominous question: "What's burnin'?"

Theodore turned around.

Hodges yelled: "Roosevelt's boots are on fire!"

CHARRED BOOTS IN hand, one of them with a hole right through, Theodore traipsed into his residence. Recklessness on his part, sitting too close to the fire, chiefly his very own fault, and now he would have to toss them away, or maybe he should continue wearing them to remind himself of his foolishness. Mrs. Richardson had nearly lost her head screaming, "He's on fire!" and pointing a finger at Hodges, blaming him for putting too many coals in the fireplace. Thankfully the flames quelled after Theodore rolled on the floor and Hodges hit his boots with the big German book.

Theodore dropped the soon-to-be discarded boots by the door, and his sock-covered feet shuffled over to the desk. He took a seat, sighed, and rubbed them. No sting meant no burn; there was not a mark on his socks. Theodore felt fortunate not to have suffered any burns, although he did have a few bruises from Hodges's strikes.

He opened his diary to today's date:

October 27

He drew a deep breath and sank into thought. This date which had so often brought great joy now instead ushered in a melancholy rare to his spirit. How could he celebrate today? He began to read his writings, one page back after another, until he reached that fateful one when the sharpness of despair struck so hard he did not think he could go on. All that filled his mind was what he had lost in the past year. It seemed impossible to realize. Down the margin of the journal on that day, he had drawn a wide black slash, then these words:

My dear Father. Born 1831. Died 1878.

It seemed utterly impossible to realize he would never see his father again. The following pages in his journal were blank. During those two days, he was unable to put pen to paper. The next days proceeding had proved to be the most distressing of his life:

I shall never forget these terrible three days; the hideous suspense of the ride on; the dull, inert Sorrow, during which I felt as if I had been stunned, or as if part of my life had been taken away; and the two moments of sharp, bitter agony, when I kissed the dear, dead face and realized that he would never again on this earth speak to me or greet me with his loving smile, and then when I heard the sound of the first clod dropping on the coffin holding the one I loved dearest on earth.

That sound was one he could never get out of his mind, and the hurt to his heart over the loss never stopped from that day forward. He moved to the next page:

He was the most wise and loving father that ever lived; I owe everything to him.

Guilt crept in as he considered all that Father had given him. What had he provided in return, especially during those trying hours when the man was so mad with pain, groaning, writhing, and twisting? There a son stood watching, helpless:

And oh how my heart pains me when I think that I never was able to do anything for him during his last illness!

Then the disease worsened rapidly. The doctors diagnosed it as a malignant fibrous tumor that strangled the intestines. And then hearing there was no cure . . . He read on:

It is terrible to think I have never done anything for him, not even during his sickness. I never had an unkind word from him; though I was always promptly punished if I did wrong. For the last five years he has scarcely spoken to me reprovingly. He was so unselfish, and was so continually making others happy that he was always happy himself; his 46 years of life were, excepting the last two months, very happy ones.

Sometimes when I think of my terrible loss it seems as if my heart would break; he shared all my joys, and in sharing doubled them, and soothed all the few sorrows I ever had. Sometimes, when I by accident think of him it seems utterly impossible to realize that I shall never see him again, till we meet in that Better Land. It is as if part of myself had been taken away. Every event of my life is bound up with him.

How could he find the strength to write a thing for today's calendar date? Theodore did not want to spew his feelings and was certainly incapable of celebrating; he could not even think of celebrating. This day would have to be different from every other one in years past, when his father would take him on hunting trips, spending most of their time talking, and Theodore listening to wise advice on every aspect of life:

"*You need to make your own way in the world, son. Find a career worthy of you.*"

Does this mean a career in finance? thought Theodore, because he had no interest in the field. "I'd like to become, in essence, an observer of nature," he admitted the truth.

"*If you wish to become a scientific man, do it,*" *his father spoke with an energy that was strong yet cheerful. "But only if you have an intense desire to do scientific work.*"

"*I intend to, Father.*"

"If you enter this field, you must make it a serious career and do remunerative work of value."

Theodore planned to.

"Only enter such a field if you intend to do the very best work that is in you. Do not dream of taking this up as a dilettante." His father smiled at him; his expression told Theodore that he accepted his choice.

Now, these conversations were only memories. "Oh, Father, no words can tell how I shall miss your counsel and advice," Theodore voiced to himself. "How bitterly I miss you." The diary closed. Theodore left his desk for the closet. His father had never judged him; he accepted the child for who he was, damaged and all.

Opening the closet door, Theodore reached up to the top shelf, removing a breech-loading, pinfire double-barrel pistol. He loaded it. He slid the weapon into his waistband and put on shoes.

"How I wish I could do something to keep up his name," he whispered aloud, moving briskly out the door and down the stairs, exiting the boardinghouse. The cold chilled his skin as he headed for the woods.

THEODORE COULD SEE the Charles River ahead. Off the road, he walked blindly into the groupings of trees. Theodore went deeper and deeper, ignoring the density and the fallen logs and rocks in his path; he wanted to slip away. A chill blew into his face. He did not care the temperature.

Before, he had always carried troubles and triumphs to his father. The vividness with which he could recall his words and actions was sometimes really startling. His father had once given him a piece of advice he had followed since. That talk came so very clear to his mind:

"If you aren't going to earn a significant salary, you must even things up."

Theodore was confused.

"By not spending," Father expressed this firmly, "the fraction has to remain constant, and if you are not able to increase the numerator, you must reduce the denominator."

Theodore understood.

"In other words, if you want to enter into a scientific career, you must abandon all thought of the fanciful enjoyments that could accompany a moneymaking career and must find simple pleasures elsewhere."

Theodore took a brief rest and leaned against an elm now, feeling its hard surface against his back. He shut his eyes for a moment. A most devastating experience it was to see the person you love best in the world in such agony, and be powerless to rescue him from the terrible pain.

Since that cruel day, his father's last, Theodore felt he had aged very much, now having to rely on himself in difficulties. Were it not for the certainty that as his father himself had so often said, "He is not dead but gone before," Theodore would almost perish.

The more time he gave himself to think, the more he believed he should almost go crazy. "Such a wonderful man as Father should not have had a son of so little worth as I am," he spoke aloud. Raspy breaths came from his throat, shaky and shallow. He needed a minute to calm himself.

Breathing in and out, he thought about his sheer inability, not because of lack of perseverance or lack of good intent, just plain inferiority to his father, morally, mentally, physically. "How little use I am or ever shall be in the world," he mumbled to himself.

Theodore moved until he hunkered in the shadow of a pine

grove, being even quieter than the trees themselves. He removed the gun from his waistband and waited. He kept still, slowly taking a long, deep breath, feeling the air go through his mouth and into his lungs.

It was time.

He focused his attention, steadied his stand, and listened, hearing leaves rustling in a breeze, a twig cracking, the quiet skitter of a small animal from a tree up ahead. Theodore stepped forward on his right, the loud pang of his shot sounded, and he wished himself a happy birthday.

Chapter Fifteen

———◦•◦———

Something's Cooking

A light rap at the door to Alice's bedchambers, a slow-turning handle, footsteps tiptoeing on the floorboards. A gentle tug came at her nightdress. "Sister." She felt another pull. "Sister."

She lifted her head to see her little brother's big green eyes staring at her.

"Are you gonna come out of here? Ever?" asked George, his voice sounding desperate. "Pa took Ma out, and I'm just here. They told me to watch after you, and I have been watching by the closed door nearly all of the morning, and then Cousin Rosie came over, and now I don't know what I should do."

Alice propped herself up, putting a pillow behind her head.

"Rosie's downstairs in the kitchen trying to cook up somethin' and I don't suppose she knows how to cook."

INTO THE KITCHEN Alice went, holding George's hand and wondering what her cousin was planning this time.

He led the way. "I have my sister, but she hasn't talked yet, Rosie, and I don't really know if she can."

Rose looked forlorn with paper in one hand. "Of course she can talk, Georgie. She just doesn't like waking up."

Alice hugged her little brother. "You are the finest brother a sister could ask for, Georgie. Thank you for looking after me."

"She can talk," George assured Rose.

"Very well, Georgie, now bring me a bowl, would you, darlin'? If you could believe it, Al, I already dissolved a yeast cake for the recipe."

When George was farther from them, Rose whispered to her, "I have some news to tell."

Alice forced her eyelids to open some more.

"From what I have learned, Theodore was at the dorm house yesterday with Hodges and friends, reading by the fire, a large fire."

"Roosevelt?"

"Yes, Theodore Roosevelt was sitting next to the fireplace, and someone yelled, 'Something's a burnin'!' and right there in front of them, Roosevelt's boots lit up in flames."

"For heavens no."

"They had him roll around the floor. A woman was screaming and hollering at Hodges who was visiting that day and lit the fire which grew way larger than a fire should in a fireplace. Apparently, from what I've been told, Roosevelt, he was sitting next to the fire, and the flames just ate up his shoes, just ate them up! Hodges slammed the flames with some huge book of some sort to put them out!"

"Oh no, is he hurt?"

"Just his boots."

"Are you sure?"

"Yes. Yes. Just the boots."

"Thank heavens. How did it happen?"

"Too many coals in the fire or some such." Rose stared at her. "You seem better, Al."

Metal bowls clanked about until George brought one over to them. "This good?"

"Perfect," responded Rose.

Steam rose from a pot on the stove.

"Georgie, check the pot. Is the milk scalding?" asked Rose.

George got on his tippy-toes to examine the pot. "How am I supposed to know what scalding milk looks like? I can't even reach in it to see."

"Don't touch it, Georgie." Alice walked over to inspect. "Are you certain, Ro? Scalding?"

"That's what Fannie Farmer wrote down for us, after—" She gave Alice a big smile. "After hiring the cook who makes the most perfect buns."

"Fannie hired her?"

"She sure did."

Fannie. She always came through in making Alice feel better. "How much milk, Ro?"

"One cup."

Alice poured the scalding milk into a cup measurer. "Done. What are we making?"

"A surprise." Rose read off the paper, "Now add two tablespoons of butter to it and a one-quarter cup of sugar." Rose pointed at George. "Bring us a tablespoon."

"In the drawer, there, next to the sink," advised Alice. She smiled, just thinking of George waiting by the door. He was just too cute for anything. "On the right side, Georgie."

Rose pulled Alice aside. "Oh, and something even more tantalizing about our dear Mister Roosevelt."

"More tantalizing than boots on fire?"

"Last night in the Yard."

"The yard?"

"Harvard Yard. Last night in Harvard Yard, a Porcellian man told an A.D. man that Theodore Roosevelt, given the chance, would have chosen his club first. The A.D. offered Theodore a spot, as you are aware."

"I wasn't."

"Well, they did. It's unheard of for a man to be confronted with such a unique distinction of an offer of membership from both the A.D. and the Porcellian."

"What are those?" asked George as he opened the drawer, pulling out two different-sized spoons. "And which one is the correct one?"

"Secret societies, Georgie."

"What's it mean, A.D.?"

"They are Harvard's most exclusive clubs, Georgie. Every man wants to be in one of them."

"Oh!" he exclaimed. "And which one's the tablespoon?"

"The larger one, Georgie," Alice answered.

"Anyways, it was a drunken quarrel," continued Rose in a whisper to Alice. "And the two of them argued that Mister Roosevelt favored their club best. Then the A.D. announced that as its newest member had not yet signed officially, he would be free to reconsider his acceptance and choose which club he liked best."

"Was Roosevelt drunk?" Alice asked, hoping for a "no."

"No. No. He wasn't even there. Richard told me they couldn't locate him." George gave Rose the spoon.

"Couldn't find him?"

Rose measured two tablespoons of butter and mixed them with the milk. "Now bring us a teaspoon, Georgie."

"Where do they think he was?" asked Alice.

Rose shrugged again. "But you can ask him yourself as Richard told me he is paying us a visit next door tomorrow."

"Roosevelt?"

"Yes, Mister Roosevelt."

George handed a spoon to Rose; it was another tablespoon. Rose kept talking: "I hope Roosevelt chooses the A.D. because Bacon is in the A.D."

"You need bacon?" asked George.

"No, Georgie, but we do need salt."

"Where's your loyalty, Ro?" asked Alice. Both of their fathers, and even Richard, were members of the Porc. "Once a Porcellian, always a Porcellian, as goes the motto, or something like that."

Rose turned to Alice. "Yes, of course, but being around Bacon would be much more agreeable." Rose proceeded with the salt after George handed it to her. She dumped the spoonful into the mixture.

"I thought salt was half of a teaspoon. Was that a tablespoon that you used?" asked Alice.

"Whatever is the difference?"

"You used a tablespoon, Ro."

"It is done."

"And a full one."

"What's next?"

"The difference is, what you are making will taste like a pile of salt. That's what the difference is. And what are we making?"

"Hush, hush." Rose peered back at the paper and started to read again. "Add the dissolved half of a yeast cake. Woo-hoo, I have that. Then, fold in three cups of flour and the egg." Rose added dissolved yeast.

George helped Alice put in the three cups of flour, some scattering onto the table.

"Crack an egg, Georgie," said Rose, leaning her hand on the table.

Alice helped, holding the egg with him as he tapped it at the corner of a bowl, trying to avoid a further mess in the kitchen. If

Mamma came home to this, Alice would certainly have to hear another one of her tales. Alice knew exactly which one:

There was once a girl who failed to wipe flour off the kitchen table. When a noble gentleman came for the marrying, he leaned his hand on the table, put his hand through his hair, studied his reflection in the mirror, and thinking the sight of her had aged him, ran from the house and nary a gentleman came calling again.

Alice found a cloth and wiped the table clean around the bowl.

"Then add raisins and currants and cover."

George, about to add some, was stopped by Rose's hand.

"Oh, no." A sudden puzzled expression appeared on Rose's face.

"Oh no, what?" questioned Alice.

"It has to sit for an entire night," responded Rose, floured fingers scratching her head.

"Really?" Alice, not surprised in the least, knew this was not going to end well, as per usual.

"Look!" cried Rose, eyes wide open staring at the paper, a white patch in her hair. "It says it right here. Allow to rise overnight."

"Allow to rise overnight." Alice read it herself.

"Written right here." She pointed again.

"Ro!"

"What's the matter?" asked George.

Rose crumpled the recipe in her hand. "Well, I'm hungry, and I cannot wait till the morning for hot cross buns."

"We are making hot cross buns!" George clapped his hands, clearly excited.

"We were," answered Rose, tossing the scrunched ball into the trash box at the corner of the room. She missed. Alice rushed to pick up the crumpled paper.

"You will be joining us tomorrow," said Rose to her.

"Me?" asked George.

"Not you, Georgie, your sister."

George marched out of the room.

"I don't think so, Ro."

"What do you possibly mean, you don't think so?"

"Last time I saw him, I started seeing stars and almost fainted right there in front of him. Maybe I should stay in my room tomorrow."

"How long are you going to remain in that room? And enough with this fainting. You've got to live, Al."

So they sat and ate the raisins and the currants—after Rose added a pinch of sugar for some extra taste—and invited George back in to share the bowl.

Chapter Sixteen

---◆◇◆---

Life Lessons

CAMBRIDGE

Theodore worked on a corner table inside his residence where a hint of toxicity lingered like a whiff of green corn due to the open bottle of arsenic powder. He removed a sturdy wooden ruler from a left-side drawer to measure the squirrel carcass laid out before him. Measurements down to the millimeter he was looking to get, until he realized his vision was not quite right. He had forgotten to remove his spectacles. He did, and placed them in the metal eyeglass case closing with a clack. Theodore chose a metal one to protect his rounded gold-rimmed spectacles, never wanting them to fall or even be hit with a bullet. Those glasses changed his life.

He had always considered himself a clumsy boy, and while much of that may have been due to his natural awkwardness, some may have been the result of failing to see clearly, and having no idea of his inability. Then one day, and he remembered it well, it was during the summer spent in Dobbs Ferry when he turned fourteen. Friends read aloud an advertisement from a billboard a ways ahead of them. Theodore realized at that moment that something was wrong with his eyes, for not only was he unable to read it, he could hardly make out the letters. He admitted this to his father that night, and soon his father purchased him his first pair of spectacles. The gift opened up a new world to him.

"I had no idea how beautiful the world was until I got those spectacles," he now said aloud to himself.

Before, especially in the outdoors, nature appeared blurry in the distance. Wasn't that how everyone saw things? That season proved memorable for several reasons, one being the glasses, and the other the gift of his first gun from his father.

"Eleven inches, two millimeters." He wrote down the length, as he did for a second specimen, and classified them appropriately in his journal; he kept copious notes.

He learned the technique of taxidermy many years back and had since spent time perfecting the craft: capturing the moment, ennobling and honoring nature, stuffing and modeling. However a person put it, being meticulous in the artistry was essential. Otherwise, all of this was a waste of time.

"*Melanerpes erythrocephalus!*" Theodore recalled. Yes, that had been the first time he had seen the redheaded bird, which at that moment years back was stuffed and not yet mounted. That one day he must have seen hundreds of the four thousand birds in the collection of specimens from the museum of Prince Maximilian on the Rhine. The prince had spent many years exploring the remotest parts of South America from Rio to Bahia and obtained specimens of mammals, birds, reptiles, and fishes that had never before been seen. Theodore's father, being one of the founders of the American Museum of Natural History, had allowed young Theodore a view of the recently purchased collection.

Theodore continued his work with the sharpening of the scalpel blade. "Careful," he reminded himself, knowing he had cut himself before.

Those lessons as a teen from a dour-appearing tall figure of a man had helped in the early days of his vocational study. That Manhattan fellow, with a shock of white hair who always wore a black frock coat, had the hands of a surgeon, working endlessly in a little corner shop, a sharp smell of poison hanging in the air.

Theodore now painted the fur with a brush dipped in the arsenic powder that he had recently purchased from a Mister Bisbee who manned a taxidermy shop in town and had that same dour look.

Since the powder needed time to absorb, he walked over to his desk and decided to write in his journal.

He opened to a crisp new page to write about yesterday. He was not up to detailing such events the prior evening:

27

My twentieth birthday. I cannot help having some very sad thoughts about my beloved Father. Oh, Father, sometimes I feel as though I would give up all my life to see you but for a moment! Oh, what loving memories I have of you!
2 gray squirrel

A knock came at the door. Theodore was not expecting anyone.

"One moment," he responded loud enough for the guest to hear as he rushed to change his shirt, wash the toxic smell off of his hands, and place a cover over the specimens.

On the other side of the door, his Harvard classmates greeted him with broad smiles. Theodore's spirit lifted upon seeing these fine chaps; good friends always seemed to do that for him. These were fellows he would not describe as brilliant, but they were plucky and honorable, and he could not ask for more than that for comradery. Richard stood there along with classmate Minot Weld, with whom

Theodore was well acquainted and who could be described as manly and gentlemanly at the same time.

"Grand news, Mister Roosevelt," Richard announced.

"The A.D. men have decided to allow you the opportunity to choose which of the clubs you'd like to join at Harvard," conveyed Minot. "Now, we are aware of the news that the A.D. offered you an invitation first, however since you have not signed the constitution for the A.D. nor possessed yet any voting powers . . ."

"You are not a member," continued Richard, "which means you have every right to accept our invitation to the Porcellian."

A folded handwritten note with the boar's head on the seal was passed to Theodore. He opened it. He'd been punched for the most venerable of the final clubs.

"What capital news!" Theodore was delighted.

"Certainly is," added Minot.

Offered the Porcellian and now free to accept the invitation to the finest society in all of Harvard. The fellows were correct: he had never been in the A.D. rooms, had not signed a contract—thus not possessing any power—and in fact was not officially a member. He did hate to hurt anybody's feelings. He was fond, too, of the gents in the A.D., including Bob Bacon. To be honest, Theodore was quite surprised to have been elected into the A.D. club to begin with—a totally unexpected social success, and now the Porc! They were such fine fellows in front of him, and both pig men.

"May I ask, what is that smell?" Minot inquired.

"You must see this," added Richard.

"Please come in."

The two removed their shoes and Minot walked over to the mounts, stopping at the hedgehog and giving it a good, long stare, touching the pointed claws on the specimen. "It's like a museum in here."

"My father was one of the founders of the American Museum of Natural History in New York."

"A founder?" questioned Minot, moving from one stuffed trophy to the next.

"I hope to follow in his footsteps as one who preserves and treasures nature."

Richard turned to Theodore with an outstretched hand. "Welcome to the Porcellian."

He hardly styled himself an esteemed club man, though as he had heard it, the Porc sought out candidates not with a checklist of accomplishments but with the elusive qualities of virtue and charm, a circle of friends one would want to spend time with. "I accept."

Both gents gave him a slap on the back.

"Celebrations are in order, then," exclaimed Minot, until becoming distracted by the vivarium. "Snakes?" He approached the two large animal pens. "Aren't they dangerous?"

"Garter snakes," answered Theodore, matter-of-factly. "They're only mildy venomous. And would need to repeatedly chew on you to deliver any poison at all."

Minot squatted down to the other pen. "And what's supposed to be in this one, the empty cage?"

DOWN THE STAIRS their shoeless feet scurried, first Theodore, followed by Minot, and a few steps behind, Richard.

Theodore gave them a hush sign with pointer finger to his mouth as he saw what he expected. Slippers had escaped and again filled half the hallway's width, claws reaching out from its shell.

"Who is there?" The landlady's voice echoed from the kitchen.

"It's me, Mrs. Richardson, Theodore."

"Mister Roosevelt?"

Reaching the reptile, Theodore squatted down and rubbed Slippers's shell. "Yes, Mrs. Richardson," he answered hesitantly.

Richard quietly shuffled closer to the ground to assist.

Theodore whispered to the fellows, anxiously, "Mrs. Richardson will toss me out of this place if she sees Slippers!" Theodore spread his arms wide to pick her up.

"Slippers?" asked Minot, confused.

"The name of the giant tortoise or, as Mrs. Richardson calls her, a wicked stinkpot." Richard laughed quietly as he reached down to help.

"Could Slippers be any bigger?" Minot joined in the lifting.

Mrs. Richardson's footsteps sounded. "Will you be joining us for dinner?" She neared the doorway to the hall. "Terrapin will be served."

They moved the creature toward the front door, the nearest escape.

"Mister Roosevelt?" came from the kitchen again.

"Yes, yes, Mrs. Richardson. I'm just leaving but will be back for dinner. And certainly, add a plate for me."

"Well, would you be likin' terrapin?"

His classmates shot him a look. He reciprocated. "I really must be leaving," Theodore said, raising his volume for her to hear.

Minot opened the front door.

"Very well, have a nice day, Mister Roosevelt."

They ducked out the front door with the immense animal in hand, the three of them only in socks.

"And what is that wretched smell?" Theodore could hear her say as the door shut.

Chapter Seventeen

———◈———

The Invitation

CHESTNUT HILL

"You are leaving the house in that? No future débutante would dare wear such a thing!" Those were the last of Mamma's words to reach Alice's ears as she rushed out the back door. It slammed shut behind her.

"We've another year before the coming out ball!" said Alice, but not loud enough for her mother to hear. The day dress of a taupe shade with plain buttons down the front presented not at all fancy, with no embroidery or embellishments, just simple fabric with a brown belt.

Without the sun, without rain, without even a whisper of wind, the day was as dull as Alice's mood. Her walk had altered from her usual, becoming slower. Her legs moved, although with a weary step. The head pain had dissipated, the legs-like-jelly feeling disappeared. Yet, she was not altogether herself. Alice contemplated not going next door to the Saltonstalls' at all, but she had promised Rose yesterday that she would get out of the house; it had been nearly two weeks since being in the open air.

Her lace-up boots crunched through dying leaves, and that hint of the decomposing matter struck her nose. A rustle came from the maple trees. Alice raised her half-open eyes upward. A leaf broke from its branch, dancing in the air. She eyed it, swaying and falling, and ultimately lying among the motionless. So unfortunate to lose something at the height of its beauty, she thought.

Another noise from the trees. A bird's wings flitted. And again, wings flapped. She could hear a *churr* sound. She narrowed her vision to where the call emerged. A cherry-colored head with black and white feathers appeared. That burst of red flew past her. "You're back!" she exclaimed. Her flying friend flew out from the tree and toward her cousin's house up ahead.

Roars of laughter sounded from the side porch. She could make out Hodges seated next to Richard, plus Theodore Roosevelt, who was wildly gesticulating, seeming to tell a story of some sort. Was that a "har-de-har" coming from Hodges? She'd never heard the curmudgeon chuckle with such intensity before. The men cachinnated with such force she was certain the whole neighborhood could hear them.

Rose was not with them. Alice wondered whether she should return home; she had no interest in joining a comedic hour with Hodges, but with Theodore, maybe.

The redhead distracted her as it made its birdcall from the trees ahead.

She turned her sights toward Theodore whose face brightened upon spotting her. He was waving to her and talking to the fellows at the same time. She raised her hand ever so slightly in a gesture of response and watched something completely unexpected happen: Theodore Roosevelt rose from his seat, stepped back behind the line of men's chairs, and picked up a vacant chair. He carried it forward and placed it to his right, in the same row as the men's seats. She and Rose always sat behind the fellows on the Saltonstall porch, listening to their discussions and chiming in every now and then with some type of drivel.

Alice's pace picked up with a firmer step. It would be the first time she would be invited to sit with the gentlemen.

Theodore shifted his chair left in order to make a bit more room and nudged the others to do the same.

She watched Rose leap from the porch door.

All the while, Theodore continued telling his story. Richard falling out of his chair in laughter. Hodges in tears.

"What in the name of chestnuts is going on here?" asked Rose, shifting her look to Alice, who was nearing the porch.

Richard clutched his side, barely able to put words together. "Slippers slickly slipped out of its cage . . ."

Hodges finished his sentence in half-choked mirth, ". . . and sluggishly slithered down the steps."

"Mister Slick here," Richard pointed to Theodore, "saved her from becoming turtle soup."

Alice could not understand a word of it.

Rose's brow lifted.

Alice shrugged.

Theodore retrieved a second chair from behind the men, urging Hodges as well as Richard to move their chairs, and placed one between them, where Rose planted herself. Theodore went on to tell the ladies the story of how his giant pet tortoise escaped its cage to enjoy the luxury of the boardinghouse first-floor hallway and how, to prevent being caught by a disapproving landlady, he, classmate Minot Weld, and Richard quietly carried Slippers outside the front door, leaving them stuck with no place to put the large reptile. And now, Minot had a pet turtle in his dorm room taking up half the space, leaving him to climb over the cage ever so carefully to get about.

"Minot's in fear of getting a toe eaten off every time he sneakily does the climb!" Richard howled.

"He's a good man, Mister Weld," acclaimed Hodges.

Alice reached her seat.

"And it feels good to have shoes on again!"

"We had to carry her out in only our socks. It was a quick exit." Theodore was quite the attention grabber, thought Alice, like a spinning sphere with his audience following his gravitational pull.

"And Mister Theodore Roosevelt, I understand congratulations are in order," Rose sang out.

She was surprised Rose held back from questioning him about the turtle; she could not imagine a reptile in a residence as a pet!

Richard lifted his head higher, reaching over her to shake Theodore's hand. "The Porcellian club has enjoyed generation after generation of the Saltonstalls."

Rose added, "And now the first tortoise owner."

"I am delighted to be one." Theodore inclined his head affably.

"A tortoise man or a pig man?" joked Richard.

Peals of laughter sounded from Theodore as he declared, "Both!"

Hodges returned to a polished seated stance as he gave Alice a good long ogling up and down.

She cringed.

His long stare lingered.

She thought about exiting.

"You are one of the lucky ones, Mister Roosevelt," opined Hodges, all entitled and haughty. "There was a time Harvard College prohibited New Yorkers."

"Like a hundred years ago, Hodges," interrupted Richard.

"What about women?" Alice muttered under her breath, frustrated to even think of it.

Everyone's eyes fell on her. Alice quickly regretted coming

over, for she knew the hullabaloo was about to begin. She looked around—could she just get up and go? The female ban remains, a voice in her head reminded her. The female ban remains, sounded in her head again. Why only sometimes had she the nerve to speak out for what was right and other times she did not. She voiced it out loud: "The female ban remains."

Hodges rolled his eyes.

"Women are just as capable of the finer work of the human brain as any man," Alice could not help but go on.

Hodges was silent, except for a mild harumph.

"Our English friends have already provided the footprint," Theodore stated, surprising Alice with his defense.

Hodges stared off, brow furrowed, clearly irked.

"The University of Cambridge," explained Theodore, "has already closely connected with its two colleges for the education of women."

Alas, a supporter, thought Alice.

He went on. "Girton College and Newnham are now allowing the young women of England a better education than Englishwomen have enjoyed before."

"Oh!" Rose entered the conversation with nothing more.

Hodges rose from his seat. "I must be leaving."

"So soon?" snipped Alice.

Adjusting his jacket straight, Hodges turned to Richard. "Please excuse me for I must be attending to Sunday school. I have the privilege of moderating the next group."

"Glad you could come by," responded Richard.

Hodges gave Alice a wink. "A pleasure to see you, Miss Lee."

She saw this and was disgusted by it, her fist in a ball.

"Enjoy Sunday school." Richard turned to Theodore. "Unlike those who skip it."

"Only the second time that I've missed," Theodore told Alice. "I teach Sunday school, but when the day is as glorious as this, I like now and then to instead spend Sunday . . . with a friend."

A friend, noted Alice. Her fist released, while thinking to herself that the day's weather was not glorious in the least.

"What do you think of it, Mister Roosevelt?" asked Rose, sitting up tall. "The Porcellian."

"No more should be spoken regarding gentlemen clubs," scolded Hodges from afar. Alice knew he had not been invited into the Porc.

"Is there nothing you can tell us about the club?" Rose urged on Theodore. "And Richard, might we want to remove the empty seat?" she suggested, which he then did, and all formed a semicircle of chairs to continue the discussion.

"Of him, they think highly," remarked Richard. "The Porcellian took in only eight men from the junior class."

"What I can say about the Porc is that my best friends are in it. Oh, and there's a billiard table. A magnificent library, too."

Richard chimed in, "And don't forget about the punch room."

Rose's whole body practically floated when discussing a topic that excited her. "I hear many pleasant suppers are served there."

Alice's interest was piqued, too; enticing food always did that. But she added nothing to this conversation. Women were never allowed in the club's inner sanctum or even the front door, so what did it matter to Alice?

"Chief items of the bill of fare are often partridges," Richard held up his hand to appear he was holding a wine glass, "and burgundy."

"I'll confine myself to the partridges," laughed Theodore.

"The name, Porcellian, is quite refined," Rose said and looked over at Alice. "Don't you think?"

"It used to be called just the Pig Club." Now Richard had his eyes planted on her. "A fitting name, wouldn't you say, Alice?"

She knew this was about the earlier pig question of Theodore—*do hogs run free?* That was done and over with. And the reality was the "Pig" name came from years back. Little had changed at the august society since being formed in 1791. Her father did tell her how the club got its name: from a student who had an animus relationship with the proctor living below him at Hollis Hall. When this said monitor was engaged in the studying of the classics, a student had a pet pig and would squeeze its ears to make it squeal in an effort to frustrate the proctor one floor below. When this person raced upstairs, the student would place the porker below a window seat, hiding him from view. Other students found this great fun and thought a club should be formed to provide regular entertainment of the like.

"To ask a new friend such a question about pigs in their hometown could not have been ruder of me," Rose said with a tune in her voice.

"I didn't mind, Miss Saltonstall."

"Why would you ask such a thing?" Richard tossed Rose a look.

"Ro owed me," Alice added quietly, deciding she might as well say what she had to say, otherwise they would keep on with their nonsense. "Ro owed me for a pledge she agreed to but never made good on."

"My sister's a welcher?"

"A welcher I am not! And my apologies, Mister Roosevelt, for paying the penalty on you. But a bet is a bet."

"Might it have been over Shakespearean insults?" asked Richard, knowing the answer.

Theodore's head tilted.

Alice made no comment. Here they go with the nonsense, she thought.

Richard went on. "A group of my acquaintants had been visiting from France. Alice decided when she was alone with them to teach them English, albeit in a Shakespearean tongue and only insults."

"I made her do it," Rose defended Alice. "It was my doing."

"Starveling bull's-pizzle, stock-fish!" A French accent came along with Richard's imitation of his friends. "Alice is a fine teacher of insults. They copied her perfectly."

Theodore smiled with a laugh.

"After her success," Rose rolled her upper lip under, "Alice told me to appear like this at midday dinner."

Theodore burst into a full, resounding guffaw.

Alice grinned, too; it was her most brilliant bet ever.

"Is there any worry your lip may remain permanently like that?" teased Theodore.

Rose released her lip. "Heavens, no!"

Richard now rolled his upper lip under. "Professor Lee, might you consider showing Mister Roosevelt your skill in Old English slang?"

Theodore wiped tears from under his glasses.

Richard sounded silly as he spoke like that, so much so that Alice decided to grant him a Shakespearean insult, her lip copying his. "My dear cousin Richard, go prick thy face, and over-red thy fear."

". . . Thou lily-liver'd boy," Theodore finished her sentence with a loud good humor, holding a hand over his belly.

Ah, he knew Macbeth's lines. Of course he did, thought Alice. What did the man not know? She figured very little.

Richard caught his breath. "But my dear friends, as you know, I am already pigeon-liver'd and lack gall."

Richard's quoting of Hamlet impressed Alice, although she had been quoting Macbeth. She let it be.

"I, too, happen to be devoted to Macbeth," acknowledged Theodore to Alice, his upper lip rolled under.

"Macbeth over Hamlet?" Alice was surprised.

"It would not do me any good to pretend that I like Hamlet as much as Macbeth when, as a matter of fact, I do not. While considered more thoughtful and poetic than Macbeth, I very seldom read Hamlet. Now, I am humbly and sincerely conscious that this is a demerit in me and not in Hamlet."

"How long will thou be stay-eth-ing with us, Mister Roosevelt? For the weekend?" asked Rose.

Alice felt giddy at the idea of a weekend with Theodore.

"And unfortunately, I am forced to be leaving shortly; the study of the German language calls."

Their lips all went back to normal.

Leaving already? she thought to herself. She was finally enjoying herself which surprised her—she had never enjoyed a conversation on this porch before.

"Then you must join us next week for our holiday dinner," pleaded Rose. "A spectacular feast will be served for Thanksgiving. 'Tis the Saltonstalls' favorite holiday. The turkey, the stuffing, the cakes. It's utterly fancyeth."

"And you can meet the randoms who join us every year," added Richard. "Our father won't allow anyone to spend Thanksgiving alone."

"Even that taxidermist bachelor from the musty shop in town will be here." Rose gave an eye roll.

"Mister Bisbee?" questioned Theodore.

"You know of him?" asked Rose, looking dumbfounded.

"Certainly."

"Then you've no other choice than to join us. Please, Theodore, grant us your presence for the holiday. We will need all the friends we can get. Please cometh."

"Thou must." Alice placed a hand on Theodore's knee.

Chapter Eighteen

———◆◆———

A Feast for the Eyes

Theodore had written to his mother to give her the news. He
hoped she would accept it kindly:

> I have begun studying fairly hard now, and shall keep it
> up until Christmas. I am afraid I shall not be able to come
> home for Thanksgiving.

Never before had he spent a holiday away from his family. Never
before had he met the girl of his dreams. Now here he was, at the
Saltonstall home to enjoy a feast with the first gal he ever cared a
snap of a finger for.

Theodore leaned against the fireplace mantle inside the large
foyer, shoes away from the fire. He tried to relax his shoulders. The
last thing he wanted was to seem tense. Dashing is how he hoped
she would see him. When he thought his life through, he really had
no boyhood crushes or romantic victories or defeats. Women interested him little, until now. His younger brother, Elliott, was more of

a ladies' man and social leader; that limerick he had written about Theodore always got under his skin:

> There was an old fellow named Teedie,
> Whose clothes at best looked so seedy,
> That his friends in dismay hollered out, "Oh I say!"
> At this dirty old fellow named Teedie.

Seedy? Theodore inspected his clothing, glad of his upgrade. What would Elliott think of him now? A three-piece suit with a cut-away coat in a deep shade of brown seemed the proper choice. His polished Madison boots were considered high fashion being that they were two-tone, brown at the base, tan at the top, and embellished with six brown metal buttons running down the side. A gold pocket watch with a chain completed the look.

Relatives of Richard walked by, here and there, giving him a nod. Alice was not among them. How splendid of the Saltonstalls to invite him. If he were ever to find a place that made him feel like home, it would be here. The smells alone—the wafting of the savory meal, roasting turkey, and baked pumpkin pie—gave him a cozy feeling.

His only problem today: his lungs. A deep inhale had a hard time finding its way. In and out is all he asked for, yet the simple things proved not so simple, so he widened his mouth and took a breath in and out and in and out. The specter of the disease affected him less frequently these days, although it remained a lurking menace. A little asthma, as he would refer to it now, still dogged him, and at the most inopportune times. This would be one of those times. He needed to breathe.

He shifted one shoulder against the wall and placed his hand in his pocket. More relatives, no Alice. He concentrated on his breathing. The numerous days since last seeing Alice should have occupied his thoughts with other matters. The night of his initiation into the Porcellian Club was triumphant. Oysters and mongrel goose and larded quail were served. He was higher with wine that night than he had ever been before, but still he could wind up his watch, which gave him a bit of pride. He was not planning to drink like that again. Truth be told, wine always made him awfully fighty. The beginning of the ritual had him dressed in a green jockey uniform, then led blindfolded all about the town, taken to the clubhouse, and recommended to kiss the snout of a roasted boar. The final event had him reciting quotes of the value of friendship in an ancient text before taking the sacred oath. This was a club for life—once a Porcellian, always a Porcellian. And for much of the time, Alice lingered about his mind, enveloping his senses. He had been thinking of the words he should say to her, words that expressed his true feelings.

Suddenly, warmth touched him from his head down to his feet as he watched the rare, radiant maiden enter the room. She was as unique as a radiant maiden could be. She leaned with a refined posture to kiss the elders hello.

Poetic verse bloomed as she drew nearer, the girl with whom he shared lines of Shakespeare. A verse from Hamlet he mouthed this time without a sound releasing from his lips:

Doubt thou the stars are fire;
Doubt that the sun doth move;
Doubt truth to be a liar;
But never doubt I love.

Her hand reached out to Theodore's, and everything around him went quiet. Watching the prettiest girl in the world offer him her hand, as he took her dainty fingers in his and felt the silkiness of her skin, energy grew within him; not loud or booming energy, but an intimate one that made him realize her hand was the only one he would ever want to hold. He kept her in his grasp longer than he should have, bent down, and lifted her hand. Her softness graced his lips.

"Good afternoon, Theodore." She curtsied.

He adored hearing her say his name.

"You look quite dashing."

She thought him dashing! Just as he had hoped. Her words touched him to his belly. After six weeks' acquaintance with her, he decided, win her, I will . . . if it is possible.

"Hello, Alice." He could say her name over and over and over again. He released her hand.

"My parents, George and Caroline Lee," she introduced them as they neared. "And Grandpa Lee."

Theodore reached out to shake her father's hand. He was about five foot nine, he figured, being that Theodore was five ten. Mister Lee had greying hair, beard and mustache, bright blue eyes like his daughter, rounded spectacles, and was dapperly dressed.

"A pleasure to meet you," Theodore said to them.

"Good to meet you, Mister Roosevelt." Mister Lee's voice possessed a ring of authority, as did her grandfather's, who greeted him similarly.

Mrs. Lee had light brown hair, brown eyes, a long thin nose, and a frame more petite than her daughter. She nodded politely.

"And my little brother, George Cabot," Alice added, proudly giving her brother a tight squeeze. The boy tossed out his hand to shake Theodore's.

"I'm hungry as a moose!" George shouted to Theodore. "Aren't you?"

"I sure am," he responded.

"Let's go eat!" The boy grabbed ahold of Theodore's hand and they walked together to the dining room, perfectly timed as *clang, clang* went the bell that Mamie Saltonstall, Richard's mother, swung. The cloth-covered table extended into the hallway to fit all of the guests. George sat at the end, followed by Richard and Theodore on one side, Alice and Richard's sister across from them. The elders sat at the other end with relatives in between, an uncle here, an aunt there, and at least a half dozen others that Theodore had not yet met, the randoms he guessed. One sat beside him, a hint of arsenic wafting from the man. He recognized him, the man from the taxidermist shop.

"Good to see you again, Mister Bisbee," he greeted the man, noticing a nearly empty whiskey tumbler in front of him.

"I'd like to keep the turkey carcass," announced Bisbee to the elders, and an awkward silence followed as the full table shot him a look.

"What in the world does someone do with a turkey carcass?" asked Alice under her breath.

Theodore understood, for measuring.

"This and that," Bisbee remarked to a shocked group of faces, including that of Alice, who grimaced.

"For anatomical measurements," Theodore assured her.

Now, Theodore scanned the long table filled with food, thinking of how grateful he was to be here. He eyed the handwritten menu in calligraphy, the linen paper set on his plate:

Thanksgiving

1878

Clam Chowder

Roast Turkey with Chestnut Stuffing

Cranberry Jelly

Sweet Potato Croquettes

Mashed Potatoes with Chestnut Puree

Dessert Feast

While he was famished, he couldn't help but keep his focus on her.

Miss Rose interrupted. "Theodore, Alice and I created the menu."

"The actual paper menu," Alice clarified.

"You can see she has much better handwriting than me. I decided we should write dessert feast rather than list all of the pies and cakes and cookies and such. Alice thought we should add them."

Theodore glanced again at the paper; her handwriting was indeed beautiful with the capitals penned in an ornate fashion.

"I just love maple and apple and pecan pies," Alice said with a twinkle, "so I thought it would be nice to savor the idea of dessert as we enjoy our meal."

Theodore had always hoped he would find a girl who was as delightful as she was wise. But her mind . . . he may have been in love with her mind as much as all of her. She sat across from him and looked lovely.

Richard's father, Mister Leverett Saltonstall, rose to say grace; he was one of the best examples of a true gentleman of the old school that Theodore had ever met. He began:

Gracious God,

Today we thank you for gathering us together.

Bless all of those, people and animals, responsible for our feast,

and we remember those without, without food, without shelter, without love.

We ask that you soften our hearts on this Thanksgiving Day.

A flurry of activity burst forth: glasses clinked, plates clanked, talk grew louder. All the while, Theodore felt like he was in a world separated from the others, except for her. He tried to avoid staring, but this proved difficult as her hands reached for a crystal glass and drew it to her lips. Pink with a full lower lip, curved at the corners—her mouth, he imagined, would be delicious to the taste. The thought of a first kiss popped into his mind.

(The whisper of ecstasy surrounds him in bliss. She shudders, a quick breath, and he searches her face, waiting. Her head tips back, resting on the palm of his hand, and eyelids close as he nears his face to hers. Lips almost touching. He will wait . . . for as long as it takes, until her eyes open and her gaze returns to him, until he sees the heat bloom in her cheeks, the pink glow of acceptance. Then, he will know.)

"Pass the potatoes," yelled the other side of the table.

He sucked in a breath and leaned back in his chair. He could hardly handle it. What would it be like?

"Potatoes?" Richard pointed in front of Theodore.

Oh, the potatoes. Theodore passed them.

"These potatoes remind me of the moment Harvard first became acquainted with Theodore Roosevelt," said Richard. "Shall we inform them?"

Theodore laughed and nodded; it had turned into a night of amusement, one in which he probably should have acted differently than he did, but it was his freshman year, and he had only been at school for a month at that point. Besides, he refused to let anyone get away with things like that again; he had been bullied before, and pledged to himself that he would never allow it to happen again.

Theodore recalled the potato situation which occurred the night before his eighteenth birthday. The Harvard freshmen had set out for Boston that night, a crowd of them, quite noisily, with torches upon their shoulders, dusty paths underfoot. The quaint streets were brightened by torchlight and awakened with "Huzzah for Hayes!"

Many carried banners; one crookedly designed one read, FREE TRADE, FREE PRESS, and FREE BEER.

"Is this the night you howled about the wax in your hair?" interjected Richard's sister.

Richard stroked the back of his hair and exchanged a complicitous grin with Theodore, who had experienced the same. "Those high hats of paper with lighted candles inside were a brilliant success."

Theodore had proudly painted the year "1880" on his.

"Mother had to comb that wax out," Miss Saltonstall explained tartly. "She even had to cut some hairs off your head."

"You came home with holes in that coat," chimed in Mrs. Saltonstall, which drew a chuckle from the relatives. "I had to throw out that overcoat."

Theodore's luckily survived with his hair and coat intact; it was his reputation in question.

"Nobody can mend a coat with holes," added Alice's mother. Mrs. Saltonstall nodded.

"Now, how did you meet?" Alice brought the conversation back.

"Thank you, Alice. Anyhows, the Harvard freshmen paraded." Richard picked up the story.

"What was the procession for?" asked the taxidermist.

"In support of Rutherford B. Hayes," stated Richard, proudly and definitively.

"Hayes?" shouted the taxidermist, brows raised half up his forehead. "Hayes stole the presidency!" Mister Bisbee's fist pounded the table. "We all know Samuel Tilden had the votes."

"The popular vote doesn't win the presidency," Alice's father countered with an impatient glance.

"Makes no sense," Bisbee protested sharply, draining his glass. "He had the people's vote. Tilden shoulda' won."

"Mister Roosevelt lives just a block away from Samuel Tilden in

New York," Richard said a bit boastfully to Alice's father, glancing at Theodore, who nodded. It was the truth; Tilden lived on 20th Street between Park and 3rd, one block east of the Roosevelt home in Manhattan.

"As I understood it, Tilden resides in a mansion in the city of gracious living along the Hudson River," interrupted Mister Lee. "In Yonkers."

"Possibly, he has two residences," added Richard.

"The country wanted Tilden," Bisbee harrumphed. "Hail to Sam Tilden!"

"It's history now." Mister Saltonstall looked at the man squarely. "First time it's ever happened in this great country. Likely never to happen again."

Mister Lee appeared to try to settle the matter. "I remember Sam Tilden stating, 'I can retire to public life with the consciousness that I shall receive from posterity the credit of having been elected to the highest position in the gift of the people, without any of the cares and responsibilities of the office.'"

"History," Mister Saltonstall wrapped the debate.

"So anyways," Richard went on, "we were proceeding, with flickering oil torches in hand, and our group erupted in song, a fine song. Good, but rather loud. Then, from one of the windows came a yell—'Hush up, you bloomin' freshmen!'"

Theodore remembered the moment well. Obnoxious voices in the dark, anonymous, without the guts to come down.

"Every student there was profoundly indignant. I noticed one freshman slam the base of his torch onto the street." Richard mimicked the action with his hand. "We assumed that was the worst of it, with the hollerin' from the window and such, but then, someone threw a potato!" Richard's eyes opened wide. "A big ol' potato."

It *was* a big potato, recalled Theodore.

"A potato thrown right out of an upper floor window, straight for him." Richard pointed at Theodore's head. "Can you imagine? The fists of this freshman," he gestured toward Theodore, "quivered like steel springs and swished through the air as if plunging a hole through a mattress. I had never seen a man so angry before."

Theodore had been furious at such an act. However, he did not remember throwing his fists in the air.

"Then some kind of mucker on the sidewalk shouted something derogatory at Mister Roosevelt, which I can't say here, being that we're in a polite setting." Richard waited now for Theodore's approval before continuing to the next part of the story.

Theodore smiled.

"Would you believe this boy right next to me reached out and laid the mucker flat?" announced Richard. "Laid the mucker flat with just one punch. We all wondered who this freshman was, who it was that could take care of business, and then keep us moving without any kind of hesitation." Richard was in full smile. "Someone proclaimed, 'It is Roosevelt from New York.' And from then on, we made an effort to know Roosevelt from New York. The whole freshman class made an effort to get to know Roosevelt from New York."

"Hail to Roosevelt!" Bisbee raised a newly filled glass to him.

Even the ladies were chuckling. He laughed, too, at all the fuss being shown to him by the family.

"Hail to Roosevelt!" Alice raised her glass.

This made his heart jump.

"All hail Roosevelt!" came the calls from the wonderful group of people.

Theodore was not quite sure what to do.

"Speech! Speech!" yelled Mister Bisbee.

Theodore bowed, deciding it best to enjoy the moment and revel in the joy of this family. So having enjoyed their story through and through, and now understanding after two years why everyone seemed to know his name and made an effort to get to know him, he rose from his seat at the Saltonstall table. He took another bow to the continued applause of the Saltonstalls, noticing Alice was clapping, too.

"Now, pass the turkey, turkeys," Mister Saltonstall said to the bunch of them.

Chapter Nineteen

———◄•►———

Delectable Delights

CHESTNUT HILL

Alice had no plans to eat another thing being that she was stuffed like a turkey. The parlor, though, smelling of sweet nostalgia was ever so tempting. One long whiff left her wondering with which dessert to begin.

Theodore walked side by side with her.

A magnificent display: maple pie, pecan pie, mince pie, fancy cakes of all sorts; cinnamon bars, salted almonds, maple sugar candy, chocolate caramels. A large bowl of vanilla ice cream. A three-tier cake had icing drizzling down, and cream seeped from chocolate-coated round mini desserts. Some lifted high on stands, quite glorious. Upon a high silver cake stand the grand apple pie, already cut into perfect slices, steamed.

She could feel his eyes on her as he sipped from a gold-rimmed porcelain teacup, a hint of lemon drifting her way.

"With which should we begin?" he whispered.

"Let's start with one and then come back for more," she decided.

"Perfect."

Examining the many lavish choices, she chose the most appropriate first: a slice of apple pie. She scooped a piece from the high stand and placed it on an ivory dessert plate, offering him the same. "Would you care for one?"

He accepted the plate, and his face came ever so close to hers; the breath of citrus warmed her cheek. She plopped a spoonful of ice cream onto each, which made him smile, full and real.

She forked into the deliciousness on her plate and tasted it, feeling Theodore staring at her as if he had never seen someone eat pie before. A light buttery crunch enfolding gooey cinnamon-sugared apples tasted divine. When she glanced his way, he quickly turned to his dessert and cut into his slice.

"Delectable, isn't it?"

Theodore nodded in delight, although he hadn't eaten any.

She did have many questions for her new friend, not about pies but about pets. This idea of wild animals sharing a home with humans. She had heard of dogs and cats, but a tortoise, that was something she could not fathom.

The two of them walked nearer to the dining room to give relatives space around the desserts. It was crowded with "oohs" and "aahs" about the table.

"Have you always had pets?" she began the interrogation, albeit gently.

He was in the middle of a bite of pie, which he swallowed before giving an answer. "The house would seem very empty without them."

She wondered how that could be in the hustle and bustle of an urban setting such as Manhattan. "In New York City?"

He paused; a breath released. "We don't have as many in New York City as we do in our summer house in the country."

That explained things more clearly. She ate another smidge of pie, perfectly moist apple filling with the drippings of melting ice cream.

He set down his dish. "Growing up, we were always wildly eager to get to the country when spring came," he spoke with enthusiasm. "And very sad when in the late fall the family moved back to town. In the country, of course, we had all kinds of pets—cats, dogs, rabbits, a coon, and a sorrel Shetland pony."

"A pony?" she asked and continued eating.

"Yes, named General Grant," he grinned wide. "When my sister Bamie first heard of the real General Grant, she said to me, 'Teedie, someone named a general after our dear pony!'"

Alice found this quite funny. "They call you Teedie?"

"They did. As a child."

"And now?"

"Thee."

"Thee? As in thou?"

"No. Thee. As in Thee-odore."

"That fits you. Thee. I've always wanted a nickname." She finished one last bite of the slice of pie.

"And what would you like to be called?"

"Miss Lee is too formal. Alice sounds a bit too girlish. Ro calls me Al. I would rather have a more serious-sounding name. One that would confuse a person at first as to whether I should be dealt with more like a gentleman."

"Oh?"

"Hmmm. What about just initials? . . . A. H. L.?"

"How about A. H. Lee?"

"A. H. Lee." She liked the sound of that. "I agree. A. H. Lee is a fine name. Now tell me about this G.G. of yours." She figured this would give her time to get back for another dessert. Which one to choose this time?

"General Grant is very cunning . . . the pony, that is. He is a little pet, like a dog, but he'll buck a person over his head if they try to ride him. He's done it already."

"The general sounds crafty. Any other pets?" She reached for a heaven of a dessert—chocolate rounds with cream filling—and took a full-mouth bite. Divine.

"We do have a large blue macaw named Eli, a most gorgeous macaw who is very friendly but who makes curious noises."

She smiled with full cheeks, enjoying the taste too much to hurry the eating.

He made the squawking noise, screech, plus a long *rrrraaah* to her, quietly. "He eats bread, potatoes, and coffee grains and has a bill that I think could bite through a boilerplate. He crawls all over."

It surprised her to think that parents would allow a loud, giant bird in the house and permit it to crawl about freely. She had seen an image of such a bird, brightly colored like a huge parrot, but had never seen one in person; she imagined it a glorious sight. She let him continue to talk as she continued to eat.

"And a number of other pets. A horse, of course. A very good natured, well-behaved, gentle horse, but timid and not over-wise, and when in a panic, his great strength makes him neigh uncontrollably."

"Really?" She added a piece of cake to her plate.

"Accordingly, he is a bad horse to try to force by anything."

"Maybe he needs time."

"A little time, yes. When he behaves well, I lean forward and give him a lump of sugar, and now the old boy eagerly puts around his head when I stretch out my hand."

"A lump of sugar can make anyone behave, I think. I liked sneaking a lump of sugar from the kitchen as a child."

He laughed.

"And you have a tortoise, or Minot has a tortoise. Any other pets?"

"Jonathan, the piebald rat."

She put down her fork. "From years back, I remember blood-curdling screams from my mother when one whizzed by and my father chased it about the house."

Theodore's smile was infectious.

"It was a horrifying hour." She giggled as she spoke. "He never did find it."

"Well, I can tell you that Jonathan is a rat of the most friendly and affectionate nature, who also crawls all over everybody." He made the motion with his hands, crawling his fingers up her arms.

It tickled.

"And we do also have a flying squirrel."

"They fly?" she asked, stunned. She had never heard of such a thing.

"They do."

He continued to surprise her. Having a rat or squirrel, or a tortoise for that matter, in someone's abode seemed an impossibilty. Her mother would never agree to such a thing—a rodent as a pet in the house—never. "What about the usual?"

"The usual?"

"Dogs and cats."

"Always cats, yes. And dogs. One of them has just had a litter of puppies; you would love them, with their little wrinkled noses and squeaky voices."

She did adore puppies, as well as his love for animals.

Theodore broke out into full untamed laughter. Being their conversation was not so amusing as to trigger such a response, she realized his eyes watched over her shoulder. His breath caught in the middle, leaving him practically choking and wheezing. He folded over but held up his hand to gesture he needed no assistance. Authentic joy, she thought, may have been the greatest of his charms.

There was Rose approaching, cheeks full like a chipmunk.

Richard appeared the same, as did George. "Here's our instigator." Richard nodded over to George.

Alice joined in, filling her mouth with all that was left on her plate.

Theodore rose from his position, surprisingly presenting the same silliness, and went one step further. He walked over to the uncles and made sure they inspected him, most reacting with a questioning glare.

Before long, the appearance was repeated by quite a number of the guests who found Theodore to be quite delightful as he pranced around the room trying to get the folks to see him, which they did.

Rose brought them together in a huddle, Alice and Theodore. "Mister Roosevelt, you are the funniest Harvard classmate we've ever met. We need a photo of our newfound appearances." Rose made a suggestion, mouth still full: "What would you think of a professional tintype spree?"

"A tintype spree?

"On an upcoming Saturday?" he suggested.

"What a darling idea! And please call me Rose."

A darling idea it was not, thought Alice.

"Well, that would be wonderful with our new appearances," maintained Rose.

"Like this?" Alice added, then swallowed and continued laughing.

Rose swallowed. "A tintype!"

"A genteel photo of such a genteel group," Theodore made clear.

"With a genteel gentleman," Rose laughed at Theodore.

"And when would this take place?" questioned Alice, knowing full well that the only place to go on a tintype spree was to the photography studio on Main Street, in town, a place her mother would never let her go, especially on a Saturday.

"Which date would be preferred?" asked Theodore.

"A Saturday," suggested Rose.

"Sounds perfect," responded Theodore. "And which Saturday would you suppose, Rose? I will take care of the details."

Rose stayed mum, so did Alice.

Theodore rehearsed how he would pose—chin up, shoulders back, and a facial expression serious and cavalier. "We shall be quite the dapper group."

Alice knew the whole time that none of this would be possible. Firstly, going into town without their parents escorting them was not an option and secondly, a tintype spree with a boy would undoubtedly be vetoed, so how this at all would happen seemed beyond any reasonable possibility. But as she thought it through, she wondered if they could somehow make it happen, maybe without telling her mother. She liked the idea of having a photo with Thee looking quite darling.

"Alice, you must write to me and tell me which Saturday would be best," Theodore pleaded, and leaned into her ear. "I promise not to show your note."

Chapter Twenty

An Offer to Bestow

CAMBRIDGE

Theodore was hot with anticipation, pacing and impatient. He eagerly inspected all of the envelopes after breakfast. Nothing. Neither a letter from Alice nor Rose had arrived. It had been more than a week. So here he was, walking to and fro about his residence, though the apartment left not much free space for such. He did it anyway.

To take up some time, Theodore thought about what he could do to waste the minutes. What would take his mind off of Alice Hathaway Lee? Likely, nothing. And he was certain that he had no desire to work on his specimens today. He took a deep breath and headed for the desk, sat himself down, pulled out his journal, and wrote:

> I have gotten very well acquainted with both of them.
> Rose is a very pleasant girl, and as for pretty Alice Lee,
> I think her one of the sweetest, most ladylike girls I have
> ever met. They all call me by my first name now.

And Alice now called him "Thee." He adored the sound of her voice, especially when his name came from it. He reread his journal entry and realized it was pale and paltry language, but in truth, he could dare not write down his true feelings for her. He had no choice but to keep those concealed, for what if he revealed and she refused? No, he was not ready for a refusal from her. How could he win her heart? His mind pondered on this for a moment. Slow, systematic, planned, that's how.

He resumed his pacing, arms behind his back. Three steps to the fireplace, hurled himself around, and headed to the sofa and back again. He had to take his mind off of her. So, since he was most recently enjoying the writings of Charles Lamb, he picked up the book, placed himself on the couch, and opened to the essay entitled "Valentine's Day."

"Madam, my *liver* and fortune are entirely at your disposal," he read out loud and laughed. How brilliant that Lamb queries why the heart is the symbol of the day and not another organ, he thought. ". . . Have you a *midriff* to bestow?"

The latter part of the essay—when a valentine is sent to a young lady, not from a lover but an admirer, and she responds with pure joy—got Theodore thinking.

What if he were to write Alice first?

A gentle note of gratitude to which she would be required to respond and that would provide him with a forever momento of the beauty's handwriting. He placed the book down, got up quickly, and walked briskly over to the desk. Yes, that is what he would do. Imagine if she agreed to see him again, even possibly for the tintype spree. Well then, heaven would forever be in his pocket, for he would carry her with him everywhere. He had been hoping she would agree to pictures, maybe as soon as next weekend. He took a seat. He could only hope, for he hadn't seen her since Thanksgiving. And every day he waited was agony.

From his drawer, he removed a clean four-by-six-inch sheet from a short stack of ivory linen papers with the heading "Porcellian Club." He began with a deep breath and the date:

Dec. 6th, 1878

Keep the language simple, he told himself, then continued to write:

Dear Alice,

I have been anxiously expecting a letter from you and Rose for the last two or three days; but none has come. You <u>must</u> not forget our tintype spree; I have been dexterously avoiding forming any engagements for Saturday. I send this by Minot Weld—who knows nothing of the contents, whatever he may say. Tell Rose that I never passed a pleasanter Thanksgiving than at her house.

Your Fellow conspirator,
Thee

Fellow conspirator? Was that best? He figured she would enjoy reading that from him, for they were a team, together, conspirators. He reread the letter once, and read it through two more times, to be sure all was correct and appropriate.

Theodore sealed the letter.

Now for the name of the addressee. Rather than Miss Lee, maybe he should write something more.

Onto the envelope he decided to put A. H. Lee, hoping this would make her smile immediately.

He sealed the flap.

Now, he went back to pacing. The letter sat on his desk, and he stared at it each time his steps took him by.

How would she react to the letter?

Chapter Twenty-one

A Response to Offer

CHESTNUT HILL

How in the world was she to answer this? A tintype spree? Her mother would never allow it. Never. Although how splendid an idea. She imagined Theodore Roosevelt dressed up to the nines; what a fine tintype that would make.

She touched the paper again with both hands, her pointer finger taking a moment to rub down the linen paper, mind wandering, thinking of her fellow conspirator, a prankster in his own right.

Whether he used a ruler below each line came to mind, for each sentence appeared straight as could be, and the spacing between letters was exactly even. This may have been the neatest handwriting she had ever seen from a boy. Another lookover and she placed it back in the envelope, giggling to herself about the addressee, A. H. Lee. No boy had ever changed her name. A. H.—she liked it. He remembered their conversation over dessert. How dear of him.

Her thoughts sat on the dilemma of how to answer this in the nicest way possible without insulting him. Certainly, she wanted to go. She had been thinking of an answer since Minot brought the letter to her home the previous day.

She placed the letter back in the first drawer on the right where she kept all of the letters she received from boys, most never answered. The pile from Hodges grew by the week; his letters were one or two lines about him being pleased to see her. Athletes like Bob Bacon, too. She never did reveal this one fact to Rose, who would be so upset if she knew that Bacon sent her letters. Alice never thought much of Bacon, other than he showed patient humility on the outside with bottled up supreme egoism on the in.

"More letters? From whom this time?" Rose had a way of arriving without making a sound.

"Mister Roosevelt," she answered with a hint of excitement.

"Really!" Rose said, delighted. "Allow me to see."

Alice removed the letter from the drawer, double-checking that it was the correct one, and handed it to her.

She raised an eyebrow. "Who is A. H.?"

"Me, silly."

"Ooh. A nickname already. I like it."

Alice liked it, too. She retrieved a clean piece of ivory linen paper out of the left drawer and picked up a pen, as Rose read the letter.

"How are you going to answer it, Al?"

"Tell me how you think this sounds." Alice voiced the words aloud as she wrote:

Chestnut Hill
Dec. 8th, 1878

Dear Thee,

"Thee?" Rose asked, teasingly. "Your nickname for him?"

"Apparently everyone calls him that now."

"Is that so?"

Alice continued:

Minot brought me your letter yesterday morning.

She stopped.

"Is that all you're going to write?"

"Well, what should I say next? There is no way our mothers are going to allow us a tintype spree with the New Yorker."

"Not even with a Bostonian!"

"Why, Ro, would you tell him, as you did on Thanksgiving"— Alice changed her voice to a tune—"'What a darling idea!'"

"I get caught all up in these moments, you know me, Al."

"I'll just tell him the truth." Alice got right back to writing:

We have by no means forgotten our little spree, but as neither of our Mothers like us to go in town on Saturdays if we can possibly help it, we think it had better be put off until the spring when dancing school is done.

"How does that sound, Ro?"

"Perfect."

Alice wrote on, saying aloud what she put on paper:

Rose sends her regards to the <u>genteel</u> young man of Cambridge.

Rose chuckled as she, too, stressed the word "genteel."

> Sincerely yours,
> A H Lee

"Now tell me, A.H., how will you prevent him from showing your letter to every boy in Cambridge? You know that is what they all do."

Alice folded the paper and on the back side added a postscript:

Remember you said that you would not show this note.

Rose looked forlorn.

"What's the matter, Rose?"

"I wish I would receive such a letter from my dream of a man. You know who?"

Alice shut the drawer tighter.

"Well, Al, I should forget about Bacon. Now, my dear cousin, I have quite the surprise for you!"

"A surprise. Well, why didn't you reveal this upon entering?"

"Because it is the most exciting news that my Alice will possibly ever want to hear, ever, and you will scream for certain upon hearing it."

Part III

———◆◆◆———

My cup of happiness is almost too full.

—THEODORE ROOSEVELT

Chapter Twenty-two

Here Roams Theodore

I was not quick enough. A bronco balked and thrust himself backward with me on him. Now I am in the dirt; the point of my shoulder has snapped with no one to blame but myself. I should have been more patient, should have given the horse more time to trust me. Instead, pain shoots through me. Tears in my eyes. I should have known.

What if I screamed out, "Help!" A waste of breath, as there is not a soul within hearing. Besides, I will need all my air for the long walk back to the cabin, on foot. Alone. Ahead of me, far into the distance, there is no one, just a deathlike and measureless expanse. This country stretches into a billowy sea of dull-brown soil shaped into parallel furrows, and everywhere a dreary sameness.

Dust on my clothes. Dust in my mouth.

My predicament may be of my own making, choosing to live in the open with civilization remote. It is as if I were living in an age long past, tending my herd on horseback, thus simplifying my wants, and with only one need remaining: to breathe.

With my left hand holding my right shoulder in place, I try to sit up. The sting proves too much, a groan falls from my lips. I set myself back down.

Part of the grind of being a rancher in these lands is taming wild horses, and a man who is merely an ordinary rider is certain to have a pretty hard time. While some ranchers might consider me more experienced in this area of insanity than most, after these ten months, I still have not nearly reached the ranks of the broncobusters.

And here my body lies, writhing from the latest of my injuries.

There have been worse experiences. There was that roundup, my first, managing a string of nine broncos altogether, each having only just been broken, maybe saddled once or twice. Under my hand, I remember eight becoming perfectly quiet after a short time. The last one, though, that beauty named Blue, was just impossible to bridle or saddle single-handed; I could not even get on or off her without difficulty. I remember she became exceedingly agitated whenever I moved my hands or feet. She turned out to be the worst bucker on the ranch: when Blue tossed me off, I flew, and then came the landing on a stone and the cracking of a rib.

Today, I am hurt again. I say again, although torment follows me, my heart in particular. That ache never heals, doubt it ever will. I have taken to bargaining. Make me suffer a hundred broken bones to bring back my love.

I learned to subsist in a place so strangely cut off from the outside world. There was that time when I tried to carry on with a veneer of a life that remained in New York, but no, that was no longer my place. Of course, to leave a life is no easy thing, especially when others rely on you, truly rely on you. Yet to save yourself, you turn away from your own blood, and that, too, leaves a scar. But here, here is where I must be. I am incapable of existing anywhere else. Whatever I think is right for me to do here, I do. I do the things that I believe ought to be done. And when I make up my mind to do a thing, I act. As much a westerner as an easterner now. This rough country makes me hardy, self-reliant. In the duties of a cowboy, I concentrate and focus on every single moment to make instant decisions.

In all this space, there is less room for remembering.

Rising slowly, I grit my teeth and with force, steady myself to stand, that arm hanging helplessly by my side. It is a ways to my cabin, that shack made of logs and chinked clay, a roof of mud, and on the inside, a bunk, a chair, and a table looking as rough as the house itself, each homemade with the tools available, a spade and ax.

The strong stink of sulfur hangs in the air, still, sultry, as I begin the journey home. I round a corner by a ravine. Smoke lifts from a rift in the crags ahead, and for a moment it startles me. Sylphlike, a figure rises high, dissipating as it reaches the heavens. Motionless, I forget the agony, and my mind returns to a memory of a shapely figure juxtaposed against a boldly painted canvas of hues that lingers among timorous clouds, the length of her legs, the curve of her hips.

What I would give for a chance to take Alice in my arms again and place a kiss on her soft lips. What I would give to look into her eyes and tell her how my world changed because of her. For another chance, I would give anything. I would give everything.

My body remains still, my eyes to the sky. The smoke rises, again and again, taking on different shapes with the breeze. I watch them as they move. I see her in each of them. I gaze at her shifting with a weightless quality, then another as she stands tall, perfectly poised, still another of her gliding as if in a gown that sways with the soft wind.

One slow step, then another, and I track the smoke to its point of origin. A rifle shot away, I can see tongues of blue- and cherry-colored fire dancing to the surface here and there, the lurid glow of subterranean flames from burning mines—uncanny places where the earth crumbles and releases fiery heat through the clefts that form in it. Coal seams erupting is the cause. Some send up smoke columns that are visible miles away, while others are not noticeable a few rods off.

The fire's intensity compels me forward. I cannot help but bring myself closer. I have been burned worse before. If this time it devours me, I would accept my fate.

Chapter Twenty-three

The Movement

Alice, standing while nibbling daintily on a ginger finger sandwich, found herself feeling alone in a cloud of expensive perfume.
Not that she was not herself garnished in lace and pearls and a touch
of lavender, it's just that the fancy girls standing around her seemed
to be treating this event as just another courtly social gathering,
among them Martha and Rose.

"Boxing is not a real sport," Martha grumbled, quickly shifting
to Rose. The turkey feather adornment on Martha's hat swept across
Alice's face.

"Not a sport?" Rose snipped.

Martha harrumphed, nostrils flaring, mouth pursed, that tense
appearance of hers, the one that never quite went away.

Rose took a bite of cheese from a small plate she was holding.
"What would you call it then, Miss Cowdin?"

Martha ate some cheese, chewing with a smug look on her face,
without response. That same feather made another swipe at Alice's

cheek as Martha turned. "Some information for you, Miss Lee. Theodore Roosevelt is competing in the lightweight boxing tournament."

Alice moved the feather aside. She could not fathom how they could be speaking of sports at a time like this, although she did want to know more about Roosevelt and this tournament. Add to that, she would have much rather been standing with someone who understood the gravity of this announcement, someone like Theodore.

"Maybe against Bob." Martha cocked her head.

"Bacon?" asked Rose.

"Of course, Bob Bacon," yapped Martha. "Is there any other Bob that matters at Harvard?"

"So if boxing is not a real sport, then why would Bob Bacon participate?" Rose asked, taking a cracker from Alice's plate.

A hush fell over the room as the lady of the house walked to the front of the perfectly appointed parlor. She spoke without introduction. For Alice, she needed none.

"Our movement here is of the simplest nature." Elizabeth Cabot Agassiz, with a shiny updo and wearing a dark blue full gown that fell wide at the sleeves, spoke with a voice that sounded dignified, yet quietly steady. "And it seems strange that no one has made the proposal before."

Martha reached up and leaned nearer to Alice's ear, whispering, "Mrs. Agassiz used to run a school for young teenaged girls."

Alice did not know that. However, Alice had studied her work on the Thayer Expedition to Brazil, and the Hassler Expedition to the Strait of Magellan. She knew her as the author famous for writing books on natural history, specifically things alive below the water's surface. And now, she was something even more. In her, Alice could see her own hopes, dreams: her future.

Martha was in her ear again, cheese on her breath. "She mostly took notes of her husband's research," Martha whispered a bit too loudly, and Alice had to shush her gently, glad that they stood a few rows back. She had no reason to insult Martha; after all, she was the only reason Alice had gotten here. Two surprise invitations had arrived, one for Alice, one for Rose, since the Cowdin family knew Mrs. Agassiz quite well. "He has since passed. He discovered the age of ice, you know," Martha continued.

Yes, Alice knew. Louis Agassiz discovered the Ice Age and was the first naturalist, per se. "Please, this is important," Alice pleaded with Martha who now rolled her eyes and stuck her chin farther up into the air.

"Our sole and simple purpose is to give to women the same instruction that men have," Mrs. Agassiz explained her efforts. "That is, instruction of the same grade . . . in the same subjects . . . and by the same professors."

A pinch of a hoot came from Alice before Mrs. Agassiz continued:

"With your presence, on this occasion, I announce the Society for the Collegiate Instruction of Women, where the instruction is to be systematic—that is, it is to be the same which leads to the first collegiate degrees. I am engaged in perfecting a plan which shall afford women opportunities for carrying their studies systematically further than it is possible for them to do in this country. My objective is to get collegiate instruction for women . . . at Harvard."

Applause came from the surrounding girls, muted given gloved hands, though Alice had handed Rose her plate with two crackers and an untouched finger sandwich and removed her gloves to clap loudly.

"There never was a worse time for a boy to be in Harvard," Martha muttered, not even attempting to clap.

Rose took a bite of the sandwich from Alice's plate.

Martha interrupted the eating: "Harvard's president is in favor of this annex of sorts."

Rose finished off the sandwich.

Approval from the president? Alice had not known that, and how could Rose be eating at a moment like this, especially as Mrs. Agassiz went on with her speech: "It is necessary for our purpose that a group of ladies should be chosen to give the public confidence that if young women are sent to Cambridge, they would be cared for. There are a good many women who wish to get exactly the same course of study that is given at Harvard College."

Alice could only hope to be one of them.

"One of them has already proven it can be done by excelling in classes taught by individual Harvard professors. Her presence would certainly lead instructors to look favorably on the plan. Please welcome Miss Abigail Leach."

A thrill ran up Alice's arm. Abigail Leach! She had read everything Miss Leach had ever published and everything published about her, most of those critical of her attempts to equalize education. There was a rumor that she might speak at this event. Alice was elated.

Out walked her hero, dressed head to toe in a maroon gown with a matching silk ribbon at the neckline. In her loosely placed updo were orange wallflower blooms; fitting, for in the language of flowers the name meant "fidelity in adversity."

"The value of education is why we are here," she began, her voice light, gentle, yet properly serious. Miss Leach wore a locket that fell long. "Let us ask the question, 'What is education?'" Her hands remained at her side, her shoulders square. "Training . . . and discipline . . . however . . . those are of little value without a consenting will. The interest must be roused, the desire to know must be stimulated, that the pupil with an alert mind may set herself to learn, not counting the cost of effort, because she is eager for the result."

Alice led the clapping.

"While still a young girl, I began my studies in Latin, reading it for entertainment."

A titter came from the crowd.

"Fellow students considered it a burdensome task, the reading of Latin. Not me. Many would ask, 'But why, Abigail, would you read Latin for entertainment?' And I would tell them that, for me, knowledge should be wide and deep, knowledge loved for its own sake. I have hopes of gaining knowledge in other areas which my fellow classmates would have considered burdensome, subjects like Sanskrit, classes on Aeschylus, Pindar, and Aristotle."

Alice turned to the audience, wondering if others could feel the energy coming from Miss Leach.

Leach scanned the young ladies, her eyes settling on Alice. "That one should study for the mere pleasure of studying, that one should spend hours in pondering the thoughts of the great wise ones of other days, and should delight in learning languages for the deeper meaning to be gained, all this seems a sheer waste of effort to the majority who cannot understand it."

Alice agreed.

"And let me say this. We are the silent gender. We have no reason to remain so any longer. For every book, every lesson, every essay, moves us further."

Alice finished the sentence in her mind: And soon, silence will turn to action, action to change, and change to equality.

Mrs. Agassiz walked to the center of the room to say the final words. "Ladies, the time has come for women to have a place at Harvard."

AT THE POLITE reception, prim young ladies gracefully held their embossed teacups and spoke at a courteous level. Alice, a ball of excitement, wanted to shout. Knowledge for the sake of knowledge, so perfectly said. Knowledge purely for its own sake!

"Care for a crumpet?" Rose asked Alice, taking two from the server.

Alice could not eat a thing, caught up in her elation. She now focused on the decor of this room which seemed representative of Mrs. Agassiz's research. Markings of nature were displayed on the furniture, the window treatments, even down to the hand-painted wall coverings. Walking closer to them, Alice examined the underwater scenes with fantastically imaged coral reefs and tiny anemone.

"The Radiates," Mrs. Agassiz said as she approached her.

"Some are miniature little ones," responded Alice, before quickly realizing she should have greeted her first.

"Diminutive in size, yes. However, through investigation and insight into these complex worlds, one realizes the wonderful process of development in uniting the most dissimilar individuals into one cycle of growth. Those considered insignificant can bring together and elevate entire communities."

"How perfectly stated."

"Glad you could join us, Miss Lee," Mrs. Agassiz kindly added.

"The pleasure is all mine," Alice insisted, taken aback that Mrs. Agassiz knew her name.

Martha and Rose were in full conversation as Alice approached.

"It is a sport!" Rose exclaimed.

"It is not!" Martha barked.

"Hello, ladies," greeted Abigail Leach, joining their circle, taking them by surprise.

"Miss Leach, hello!" Alice's voice volume rose a bit too high.

"May I ask what you are discussing?"

As she was about to answer Miss Leach's question, Martha jumped in. "We were discussing," she said with a nasal tinge to her voice, "which sport would be considered more prized: Would it be football, crew, or could it possibly be"—she rolled her eyes—"boxing?"

Alice cringed. She knew this to be the truth as to what they were discussing, but still, couldn't Martha have come up with something else? Here was Abigail Leach before them. Alice's forehead started to perspire.

"I, then, have a question for the three of you." Miss Leach's tone changed from pleasant to stinging. "Who is the hero of the hour?"

Alice wished she had still been looking at the wallpaper, being she could foresee this not going well.

"The successful athlete?" asked Abigail Leach.

Martha and Rose nodded.

"This hero of yours will do nothing to inspire you. For certain, he has comrades ready to bear him on their shoulders, his little world at his feet." She opened the locket she was wearing and pointed to the picture. "I recommend you find a real hero. I find my inspiration from women who've come before me, such as my grandmother, who guided me into becoming the person I am and the person I strive to become."

Alice let out an excited breath. She, too, had a locket with her nana's picture and felt the very same way.

"You instead should show enthusiasm for the intellectually successful, whether it be a gifted grandmother or a gifted student. One who reads and studies because she delights to read and study is the new world, a world where sordidness and pettiness have no part. Her mind ranges freely and exults in its free-ranging. She is the person who should be considered the hero of the hour."

Snippy! thought Alice. Abigail Leach was snippy. The woman was a genius and able to put people in their place in one fell swoop.

Miss Leach walked away.

"Well, she certainly told you," Rose said, giving Martha a stern look.

"Me? She was talking to Alice the entire time. And I do need to get myself a locket with a picture of a nice old lady in it."

If only Alice had stayed away from these two a little longer.

Martha's mouth went crooked, pondering. "Can a person be considered equally gifted in athletics and academia? Bob Bacon, for example, or, I guess, Theodore Roosevelt. I wonder if we should ask Miss Leach if she is acquainted with them." Martha started to walk toward her.

Alice yanked her back. "Please don't, Martha. Of course, she is not acquainted with them."

"How could you be so sure?" questioned Martha. "Everyone knows Bacon, and if she doesn't, she should."

"And yes, a person can be both a successful athlete and student. However, the point Miss Leach was making is we should be enamored with a person's mind, brain over brawn."

Rose's head tilted. "Please do not tell me you are becoming one of them."

"One of whom, Rose?" This time Alice really thought she would disown Rose.

Rose mumbled something unintelligible.

And *becoming one of them* is exactly what Alice wished. She studied the crowd—well, none of them. These girls appeared like they did nothing between the clanks of the clock, other than try to present prettiness. Alice knew what needed to be done. Convince her parents of the necessity of a college education. Apply. Be accepted. Her mother would never be in favor. Her father, well, that might be a possibility.

"Speaking of brawn," Martha interrupted. "The entire group of them, Bacon, Roosevelt, Hodgie, and all, will be sleighing tomorrow on Chestnut Hill. They have invited us to join."

Chapter Twenty-four

———◄•►———

A Diamond in the Snow

CHESTNUT HILL

Theodore high-stepped through the drifts that must have been a foot and a half or more. It required some effort to walk, but the feeling was euphoric. He had experienced a sense of this in the winter, a flash of it at least, when he trekked the Adirondacks. Reaching the apex of a hill, he studied the evergreens laden in icy frost glistening like a forest of emeralds.

A higher bliss captured his attention today.

Through the trees with their icicles hanging like chandelier crystals was an opening, and through that opening, snowy puffs of bushes encircled a pristine bed of white. At its center, the sun's rays spotlighted the most radiant of gems spinning on her culet. Alice whirled, arms open wide, dressed in a white coat that swung out at the bottom with hat and gloves to match, and her smile, so bright, dispersed glee like a spectrum of color, flawless, brilliant.

What a beauty, he thought, who has no idea of it.

She looked his way. He waved. She did not wave back. He waved again, thinking maybe she failed to see him.

No response.

He moved closer and watched as she bent down into the snow. She stood back up, an arm appearing to stretch behind her, and in what felt like an instant, a snowball smacked Theodore right between the eyes.

"Ouch," he moaned.

She threw a second, clocking him on the side of his head.

Theodore wiped his spectacles, scooped up some snow, and missed Alice with his first throw as she darted away.

She pegged him again, this time on his coat at the spot where his heart was skipping.

Three for three. Theodore was downright impressed by the snowball prowess of his A.H.

Hullabaloo and frolicking followed, as much as hullabaloo and frolicking can when the snowfall is light, and spirits are high.

Another failed throw from him, and this made him realize that he missed this gal in another way, down deep into his core. He had not communicated with the charmer since December eighth, and weeks had passed since receiving a letter from her which stated their tintype spree would have to wait. His introspection took his mind off his feet and he tripped, his body falling fully into the snow. Loud laughter came in return from her, though it sounded muffled. His body could not move for a moment.

Hands reached in to grab him, his fellow classmate Bob Bacon's. "You're a lucky man, Mister Roosevelt."

Theodore shook snow from his head. "Did she leave a mark?" he asked, touching the spot between his eyes.

"Yes, siree, she sure did. One good strong smack can do that." Bob helped him up to stand with one hand. "Believe me, Roosevelt. Survey this group over here."

Upright, he did, after wiping smeared snow from his glasses.

"Don't think that every fellow here doesn't want to get pegged by a snowball thrown by Alice Hathaway Lee."

Theodore scanned the hill. Bacon was right: a crowd of fellows surrounded this gem. Smart, refined, and with perfect aim. What girl ever had all of those? Every person would admire her.

"I wouldn't mind being you right now," a smiling Bacon added. "Wear that shiner like a badge of honor, but next time, Mister Roosevelt, my friend—duck."

Oh, Theodore did not want to duck, but he did not say as much. He was perfectly content putting himself in the way of things happening so that they could happen. He moved quickly. None of these fellows were getting a chance with his girl, not today, not ever. He got hit with her snowballs, not them. She certainly was good at throwing, and now, he noticed, at dragging a toboggan.

He could see Alice start the climb up a snowy hill, alone, hands fisted around the rope of a highly varnished six-foot-long toboggan behind her. She moved sluggishly while fending off every gent leaping to give her a hand with the sled. Hodges seemed to not take no for an answer.

Theodore raced through the group of men. Direct and focused, he climbed. Without asking, he picked up the hardwood from the ground and swung it above his head.

She let go of the rope. "Ah, you made it out of the snow."

"Can I give you a hand? If you don't mind."

"I'd be glad of the company, Mister Roosevelt."

"I would rather you call me Thee."

"Thee." She sounded a bit flirtatious. "I was going to call you Mister Face with Dusted-white Mustache, Clouded Spectacles Awry.

He chuckled at Alice's ribbing and moved with swiftness for the footing was surprisingly good and the going easy.

"Isn't that too heavy to carry above your head like that?"

"Not in the least, A.H."

They continued to climb.

She halted mid-hill. "Thee." A nervous twitch emerged from her. Was she nervous? Or maybe she was nervously excited to be around him? He hoped for the latter.

"Yes?"

"Well, I feel terribly silly that you caught me spinning like some sort of snow ballerina, but it was Ro's suggestion. And in order to distract the situation, I struck you with those snowballs, and I do feel bad one left such a mark."

He let out a laugh so loud the whole group must have heard, because when he glanced back down, Hodges had his hands on his hips, frozen with envy. "First of all," he said to her, "you make a fine snow ballerina. And second, there's no one to blame but me—I should have ducked."

She smiled.

"Now let's take this hill by storm." Not a thing could make him happier than being with Alice.

Up and up they went until reaching the apex.

Theodore let down the toboggan onto the snow and took a long inhale, not because he could not breathe but because of the sight before him. A gloved hand above her eyes, she searched the distance. He watched her carefully as she bent down to adjust the toboggan, positioning the head of it so as to not travel back down the same path they climbed. "This side of the hill has long been off-limits, Thee. But today, what's off-limits appeals to me."

He liked her even more.

She pointed to the toboggan, giving him the lead position.

The grain of the hardwood sleigh was shinier than he had ever seen before, newly and heavily waxed; they would be moving fast.

"Well?"

There was a choice to be made here: either he could take the girl of his dreams into his arms, or he could do what she asked.

"Are you getting on or what?"

Onto the toboggan he climbed and braced himself, planting his feet in the snow. He scanned the hill's surface: a perfect new covering laid smooth and glistening, and steep.

She climbed close behind him, wrapping her arms around his waist, her legs snug against his hips, feet on the toboggan.

"Are you ready?"

"I am." She spoke quietly, her chin falling upon his right shoulder.

A lock of her hair was so close he could smell the lavender scent. He wasn't sure whether to hold this position forever or go.

"Go!" she yelled.

He lifted his feet and pushed off.

"Go, Thee! Go!"

Was ever a day more thrilling? As the descent began he felt himself ascending, for the girl of his dreams was on an adventure with him. How this ride would end did not matter. It was the going that mattered now.

Chapter Twenty-five

---◄•►---

Flying

CHESTNUT HILL

"Faster! Faster!" Alice roared.

Theodore leaned way back against her, complying with her request.

She was awfully glad to be on this adventure with Thee. With anyone else, she would be scared out of her wits. That toboggan ride with Hodges last year had been such a failure, and on a hill much less dangerous. He could hardly handle the sled. Shaky from the start, he shifted left when they should have gone right. Into the snow pile, she went headfirst. She swore from then on never to ride with that man again. And yet, Hodges was so pleased, he spoke of it as the most enjoyable one that had ever been.

A bump gave her ears an extra whoosh. She had never attempted to go down this side of the hill before. Now, she realized why. A big drop sent them zooming again.

A great whoop came from Thee.

The plunge made her scream out loud, not because she was frightened, but because she wanted more. She had not played in the snow all winter. Her mamma rejected the possibility given the bouts of illness now and then experienced. Today, Alice felt healthy and wonderful and she did not want anyone or anything to interrupt her joy.

"We've another one coming!" shouted Thee.

A crisp breeze slammed her in the face.

"This is it!"

She buried herself into his tan wool coat and hugged him tightly. She tried to wrap her arms all the way around him to clasp her hands together. His chest was just too wide for that. He felt very strong. She hadn't realized his mass before this. Sure, she knew he had a great breadth of shoulders. Anyone could see that from the fit of his suit jacket. But she hadn't envisioned he would be this full of muscle, like a real-life Adonis. Another steep drop and the toboggan flew.

"Almost there!" He leaned back into her chest, holding a tight grip on the reins. "Hold on!" His tone sounded dreamy. She obliged, bringing herself closer to him, legs firm against his, now feeling his powerful thighs through the wool of his pants. She imagined his masculinity would be even more apparent below the material. She tightened her position.

Theodore stretched out his left hand far and pressed his right leg against the wood. The toboggan shifted. He steered effortlessly, avoiding a crest in the snow right in front of them, possibly a rock.

"Phew!" he yelled, sitting up straight again. "Hang on, A.H.!"

The way he called her A.H. caused her breath to come up short.

Way back again he leaned, his handsome face toward hers, his cheek brushing hers. "This is a big one!"

Quickly she lost her breath again as the hill was about to give them another drop.

"Here it is!"

"I hope we make it down alive!"

"Don't let go."

Eyes upward, the sun's rays emerged from behind a curtain of puffy clouds, the sky a periwinkle blue. The toboggan lifted, going airborne. Her entire body felt the whoosh and inside her, it was like freedom awakened, a bird daring to fall before the moment of flight, her winged heart rising skyward, taking on the air without anyone's permission, soaring where she longed to go, into the unknown, onto a journey of her choosing.

The falling landed them hard with a thump yet added speed. Her hands had never clung to another person so intently before.

A bump at the bottom of the hill angled the toboggan right, tipped, and tossed them into the blanket of white. She found herself in the deep snow with her body atop Theodore's. Cold and fluffy to the left and right. Warm and strong beneath, facing her.

"Are you all right?" Strength asked.

Her mittened hands reached down to help lift his snow-covered head.

"Me? You're the one encased. At least I have a way out, Mister Face with Snow-packed Eyebrows, and a Little Pile of Snowflakes Sitting upon His Chin."

"Is that what you've transformed me into?"

"It seems I have turned you into a snowman."

"Will you kindly place two buttons on my eyes and add a carrot nose, then?"

He was a funny one, this Thee. She wiped her mittens together to remove the white chunks and got to work, enjoying the task of clearing the snow from his face, although he did look cute this way. A brush here and there revealed that red circle on his forehead, the result of her first throw. She caressed the spot. "Are you certain you are okay?"

"To be honest, I've never been better," he whispered these last words, eyes searching her face tenderly.

Her lips touched his reddened forehead, kissing the mark she had left on him.

Breath hitched—his and hers.

Intimacy. She knew the word because she had read the definition from that dictionary on her nightstand: a state marked by emotional closeness. But now, living the word, she let herself be lulled.

Was this his heartbeat she was feeling even through the heavy coats? She imagined it was, and her beat joined with his. She drew herself up, elbows against his hard chest, and stared at him. She watched his face rise ever so slightly from the bed of snow, his lips nearing hers, and there was nothing she could do but fall.

Chapter Twenty-six

A Heart Swells

CHESTNUT HILL

A pink glow upon her cheeks, her eyes gazing into his, her face drew nearer to him. Her lids dipped. His heart felt like it could leap from his chest. Their lips found each other. Brain fuzzed, toes tingly, he wondered whether they were on the ground or floating like a snowflake, guided by the air and its intensity, letting the air decide whether the flake should continue on. She was the air, choosing.

Here he was buried in the snow kissing Alice Hathaway Lee! His body could not move left or right. He was glad of it. His eyes stared dreamily at this utterly perfect girl as her face lifted from him. He could stay in this very spot, forever.

The chilliest nose he ever did feel rubbed his warm nose, then slid back and forth until Theodore could take the tickly feeling no more and he started to chuckle.

She hushed him with her lips, kissing him again, and he tasted sweetness, a wonderland of ecstasy. Seal the flavor of her kiss forever—mint—mint mixed with cornbread. He realized in this moment that nothing in the world really mattered but her. Her, whom he could not at this moment describe with any words, for any figure of speech would fall short.

Her, her, only her.

Back again came her lips and this time she removed her hat, letting her hair fall onto him, the tips with lacy snow brushing his cheek.

Theodore seized her by the waist and spun her into the snow. Being that she had the cutest pile of snowflakes perched on her nose, he kissed them off.

"Thee."

He waited for more words, so swept up in her awe. A blush appeared on her cheeks.

"Thee," she whispered again.

He hoped for the lines from Shakespeare: *Thee will I love, and with thee lead my life.* But she said nothing more, instead keeping her eyes on him.

Voices could be heard calling out for them.

He rose up to his knees, bent forward, and scooped her up with both arms. With her whole self in his arms, he did not want to let go, so he kept them wrapped around her, and she embraced him in return.

Did he have to move? Couldn't he stay here and turn their world into their own personal globe in the snow, waiting for the next adventure?

Again came voices from the wintry woods: "Alice!" "Theodore!"

He stood and placed her gently onto her feet. Their hands held one another, mitten on bare, as they walked back.

"That was quite something!" she said, then giggled.

He squeezed her hand.

People emerged from the trees, Rose and Richard and Bacon and the others. She released his hand and straightened her coat. "There was a moment," she said to him, "when we hit that great big dip and I wasn't sure how you were going to land us without flipping. Somehow, you did it! But the whole run, how you got us down in one piece I'll never know. Wait till I tell the others about this hill. They're never going to believe we rode it. Never going to believe you steered us the way you did. We've never been allowed to go down that way."

Rounding the hill, all eyes were on them as they came closer.

"Oh my!" cried Rose. "What has happened to you, Al? Your hair is in a bundle. And you seemed to have lost your hat."

Bacon gave Theodore a solid slap on the back while Hodges glared at him.

"No one's ever gone down that hill!" yelled Richard who came along with a good number of gents who grabbed ahold of Theodore, lifted him up on their shoulders, and headed back up the hill.

"We've got a plan," announced Bacon. "Us fellows on one toboggan, going down the hill of hell!"

"And Theodore Roosevelt takes the reins," shouted Richard, launching into song, the others joining in.

Hill of hell? A hill of dreams was more like it, and he could only hope for another chance at it, with Alice.

Chapter Twenty-seven

———◆•◆———

Oatmeal Soup

CHESTNUT HILL

So invigorated was Alice from the day's events, she resolved to find the courage to begin the conversation. The topic had been sitting like a weight upon her chest, nagging her. She just could not wait any longer. Besides, she was running out of time. *The clock ticks, the mind wastes,* Nana's words repeated in her head.

With Papa, Mamma, and George sitting down to dinner, she drew a few deep breaths and rushed out these words:

"Papa, I would be ever so grateful if you would be so kind as to consider the fact that I am very interested in the field of academia." The entire sentence came out in one long exhale.

Her father lifted his head from the bowl of soup in front of him. He had not taken even a spoonful, mostly stirring the mixture about.

"It strengthens the immune system," Mamma said, not even giving notice to Alice.

While waiting for a response, Alice took in a whiff. It smelled like oatmeal.

"You must eat all of it," came from her mother, now eyeing Alice's soup. "Good for the brain."

Alice stayed patient and put a spoonful in her mouth—definitely oatmeal. She swallowed, feeling its thickness take its time going down her throat. She continued. "And as you know, Papa, judging from my years working with tutors, I have endeavoured to study hard and do all that is possible to excel in the subject areas of most importance: English, history, and the sciences."

Her father nodded his agreement.

"And as you know, I allocate much of my time to reading and studying literature and linguistics."

"Are you going to try it?" her mother interrupted, zeroed in on her father.

Her father shifted to Mamma.

"The soup? Are you going to try it?"

He did, then grimaced before giving her a nod.

"Tastes like oatmeal," chimed in George.

Her mother shot him a stern grin. "George Cabot Lee, the chief ingredient in hygienic soup is oatmeal, yes. It's good for you."

"Are you sure we shouldn't be havin' it for breakfast?" her brother asked. "I think oatmeal is for breakfast, Mamma."

Her mother laughed a laugh that showed she had no desire to laugh. "We need to maintain steady health. And hygienic soup, I have been assured, can help to clear up Alice's brain, especially since finishing school will take all her focus soon."

"My brain?"

Mother flashed her a look, annoyed.

"My brain is fine."

Mamma whipped her head to her. "Alice, tell that to Doctor Francis. Do you recall the last time that brain of yours was thinking too much?"

"Mamma, I feel fine, and finishing school? You've sent me to lessons my entire life. I *am* finished."

"Alice, you were in bed for weeks with the chills." She put her hand over her heart quite dramatically. "My poor nerves cannot have such a scare again. Your débutante ball is approaching—you have no choice but to attend finishing school. So much to do! And the last thing my heart can take is a daughter in bed, violently ill again, and me able to offer nothing but tears at her door."

Alice could not recall once that her mother cried at her door. Remain composed, she told herself, this is not the time for a tiff.

"Georgie, finish your soup," her mother said, her voice sounding testy.

The boy pretended to take another spoonful, then reached over for a roll and handed it to Mamma who buttered it for him.

"Continue, Alice."

Thankful for Papa's hint of hope, she went on with a forced calmness: "So as I was saying, Papa—" Alice placed the spoon down and sat up straighter. "Young women are now being given an unprecedented opportunity to study the same subjects as men." She paused here, formulating how she would say the next words.

"She wants to go to Harvard!" George blurted out, mouth full.

"What!" Mamma removed the napkin from her lap and slammed it onto the table.

Father gave no reaction.

"Heaven forbid!" Mamma leaped from her chair. "Do you take delight in tormenting me?"

"Why would you say such a thing, Mamma?" asked Alice.

"Is this even allowed?" Mamma glared at Papa.

"Caroline, women will soon be allowed entrance into an annex of Harvard College," replied her father.

"Women deserve the right to an advanced education," Alice stated emphatically.

"In a college? Whatever would be the need?" Agitation becoming visible in her every feature.

"Harvard's president is in favor," Alice added calmly. "I heard the announcement of the collegiate instruction for women from Mrs. Agassiz herself."

"Mrs. Agassiz has been spearheading this for years, Caroline. It's finally come to pass. Alice, when does the acceptance period begin?"

"Or denial period," Alice replied. "June."

"Challenging subject matter to get through," he continued.

"On the linguistics side, I should be fine. Mathematics would be difficult, especially on the subject of quaternions."

"I cannot believe you, George Cabot Senior, that you are even consenting to this discussion. I will not partake in it." Her mother's words sounded as if they were being ripped from her through physical torture. "The last thing this family needs is a sickly girl in bed with an overtaxed brain, never married, and for what? A piece of paper saying you are smart!"

Alice tried to stay calm. "Mamma, knowledge should be wide, and deep."

"My daughter will never marry!" Her mother, still standing, sounded as if she was hyperventilating. "After all these years of etiquette lessons, and dance, and now you say it means nothing. And you will finally have your finishing school certificate this fall!"

Alice had to weigh her words now due to her mother's choking sobs. "No, Mamma, all of it has been wonderful, it's just that . . ."

"Just what?" Suddenly, her excess breathing subsided, making way for a furor in her tone. "Alice, no man of a good stock will marry a girl in her twenties." She fanned herself with her napkin. "I'm getting overheated." Mamma walked out of the room.

Papa abruptly rose from his seat and rushed from the room. "You mustn't fret yourself, Caroline," Alice could hear him saying.

Alice reached for one of the rolls, buttered it, and gave it to George. What was she to do without an education? She would have no purpose, no way toward true intellectual growth.

Fake cries from her mother sounded from the hallway. "What will become of her? She will become an old maid!"

"Don't you worry, Sister," said George with crumbs on his face, as he handed Alice half his roll. "If you become an old maid, I'll become an old bachelor."

Chapter Twenty-eight

Chapter Twenty-eight

———◦◦◦———

The Argument

CHESTNUT HILL

Cleaned up, smelling swell with a sprinkle of forest-scented cologne, Theodore shot a glance at himself in a hallway mirror at the
Saltonstall home, straightening his shirt sleeves and adjusting his
belt buckle. He smiled into his reflection; his forehead was finally
free of that red circle. It had taken a full week to disappear. He had
not minded, being that he figured nothing in this world is worth
having, or worth doing, unless it means a little pain, difficulty, and
effort. What an adventure, one like no other he had ever experienced. The sleighing gave him a thrill, especially with those legs of
hers snug up against his hips. He could not get the feeling out of his
body. And then, oh that kiss in the snow.

Today's tobogganing on Chestnut Hill had been filled with fun, but
it would have been capital had she been there. He had seen the beauty
in the distance while standing at the hill's apex. When he slid to the
bottom, she had vanished from sight. The fellows and he coasted on
double runners with a large sleighing party of about twenty-five classmates, singing songs for a great part of the time. At some points, nearly
all of them piled onto two large sleds, speeding down the off-limits

hill. That Hodges Chate gave Theodore plenty of trouble throughout. A number of times, sliding wildly, he had tried to outrun Theodore's toboggan, turning a day in the snow into some sort of competition. Theodore never minded competition—in fact, he relished in it. He could go plenty fast, too. And Hodges, red in the face, never did beat him down the slope. When the sled racing was done, Theodore put out a hand to him. Hodges paused on the return handshake, but Theodore waited, knowing well the most important single ingredient in the formula of success is knowing how to get along with people. Finally, a handshake that felt like a wilted petunia came in return.

And now Theodore looked forward to what was to come. She was expected at tea this late afternoon.

He practically skipped his way down the mahogany stairs at the Saltonstall home. With utter certainty he could say the more he saw of Alice Lee, the more he adored her. What would it take to make A.H. forever his girl? His brain swirled, thinking about it, so much of his day caught up in these thoughts. What would it take?

Friends were gathered in the parlor as Theodore entered, however there was no sign of her. Theodore walked from room to room in search, even to the kitchen where cooks and Mrs. Saltonstall were preparing the tea. They offered him a crumpet. It smelled wonderful, with a scent of cinnamon, but he was on a mission to locate Alice. He would have to be leaving in the next couple of hours as nightfall would come quickly and Bacon had promised him a lift back to campus, otherwise the ride on horseback would be a lengthy one through the snow.

Out of the fog-leaden window in the living room he caught a glimpse of Alice. Was she sitting on a rocking chair on the front veranda? In the freezing cold? He realized as he got closer that she was fully covered in winter clothing, coat, hat, and gloves. But who was she with? Hopefully not Hodges. No, no, not Hodges. He could hear the man blustering in the main room about the same subject, allowing women into Harvard:

"Artifice, I tell you, to allow these damsels in Harvard!" Hodges hollered. "What say you to this, gallants?"

Theodore moved quicker through the muffled cheers. Getting closer to the window, he noticed something quite awry; it did not appear Alice was with anyone. She was alone, seated on a rocking chair in temperatures so cold that a cloud of smoke released from her mouth as the chair moved backward and her breath flew back into her face as she rocked forth.

The unsettling picture made him worried for her well-being. He moved swiftly. No one should be sitting in the cold like that: she could freeze out there, especially being it was the close of day and not a ray of sunshine to help ease the weather's chill.

He launched out the door and the crispness smacked him in the face. He rushed toward her. "A.H.?"

Her rocking halted. Eyes rose to him, appearing puffy. "Thee," she spoke softly. Her gaze moved to a tree.

He slid an empty rocker close to her and quickly took a seat, wondering whatever was the matter.

"I thought I caught a glimpse of the redheaded bird."

He had not heard her speak in such a melancholic tone before. He reached over and placed his hand over hers; even with wool gloves, her hands were too cold.

"I'm beyond worried for it. It should have flown south for winter, shouldn't it have?" Her feet were firmly planted on the floor with no rocking. "Can they remain this far north if something goes wrong in their brains and they do not understand that they should fly with the other birds?"

Birds in the middle of winter in the north were an odd sight. "Most every migrant would be long gone from here."

"Oh, dear."

"But not all. Some species find a way to survive winters in New England."

"Really?"

Recalling what he had read about the *Picidae* family, he said, "If I remember correctly, the *Melanerpes erythrocephalus* is not truly migratory. Some even wander north of here. And that bill, like a chisel, would certainly help it make deep holes in tree trunks for shelter."

"What about food?"

"They have long sticky tongues." He stuck out his as far as he could.

She smiled.

Tongue still out, he continued as best he could: "The tongues help the bird reach into crevices for a delicacy." He would do anything he could to get her to laugh, which she did. And her chair began to rock forth and back and forth again. His joined hers in a harmony of smooth rhythms, the chairs' runners cracking a bit of ice on the porch's wooden boards.

She reached over and knocked on his head. "And it must have a strong head for all of that woodpecking."

He knocked on his own. "Not as hard as mine. So have you tried a birdcall?"

"I have not. It seems you are the expert on such matters."

He voiced a chirp, cackle, and a hoarse *churr*.

She tried the sounds herself and sounded quite good.

He eyed the trees, checking for the redhead that would stand out amid nature covered in white.

She kept her eyes forward. "I do feel better knowing it is where it is supposed to be."

"We will have to keep a lookout for it then. And Alice, we missed you on the hill today."

"I thought I could do it, then realized I just wasn't up to coasting with all the fellows."

"It would have been a fine affair if you were there." He wanted to ask why she appeared upset, but didn't want to pry.

"Thee?" came from between chattering teeth, the rocker not stopping. "Maybe you can answer a question for me."

"Anything."

"It's a complicated question."

"Yes?"

"Not complicated in the academia sense, complicated in a sociological sense, questioning people's perspective."

Complicated in its sociological perspective? He couldn't imagine what it was that she wanted to ask. He was fascinated to hear.

"In the structure of human society—" She paused.

He held his gaze on her.

"Well, do you think one should consider an old maid . . . and an old bachelor as the same?"

A question he had not expected nor had ever heard before. "An old maid versus an old bachelor?"

Alice nodded, her cheeks bright from the cold. He wondered whether he should get her inside. But she was awaiting an answer and he was not going to let her down. Her question was an interesting one. The query which he supposed was referring to an issue of rights. Certainly, he could offer his opinion on the matter.

She continued, steam coming from her mouth. "Most would say the old maid is the single woman *too old* to be asked to marry, whereas the old bachelor is the eligible man who *chooses* not to marry."

That was what most would assume.

"The assumption irks me so."

Society was a mess in some ways, he knew that for certain. "Society puts in place these rules, nonsensical rules, yet all follow along," he started.

She stopped rocking, interested.

"We all know, A.H., that we live in a sort of semi-barbarous state and these artificial rules are meaningless."

"Exactly."

"Old maid, old bachelor, I've never heard of such a comparison, but it's a valid argument."

"Thank you."

"They should be considered the same."

Her head tilted. "Do you really believe that?"

"I do."

Alice got up from the rocker at once, came around to the front of his rocker, staring down at him, and grabbed a hold of his ears. "Finally! Ears that hear me!"

"More like frozen ears that hear you." He reached up and touched her ears. "Yours too! And are you sure you don't mean the cold maid and the cold bachelor? Because if we stay out here any longer, ice may form on my mustache."

A nod came along with a faint smile across her face. "Forgive me, I hadn't even realized you stepped out without a coat."

Neither had he. "An old maid and an old bachelor. Had it not been taken into account that the woman chooses for good reason not to marry?"

She wrapped her arms right around his head. "And a brain that understands me."

"The way I see it, Alice, many women are superior to the general run of men," he said, his head in her arms.

"I have been thinking about how to convince others of this for a long time. A really long time! What if the old maid has no desire to marry? Or what if the old bachelor cannot seem to get anyone to say 'yes'?" She released his head. She stepped back and leaned against the post, arms crossed.

Old bachelor, he thought, there but for the grace of God go I. "Well, I think you may be onto something. If we could get rid of such a feeling that an old maid is more to be looked down upon than an old bachelor, we would advance our society."

She sighed as he rose from his chair. She approached him, and her arms reached around him in a tight embrace.

Words left him and he wondered what would be the appropriate action. With her so near, he had a hard time concentrating on anything other than the beauty that was Alice Hathaway Lee.

Being that she was cold and likely needed body heat to help her, he reciprocated, wrapping his arms around her. The sensation drove through the top of his head down into his core and all the way to his heels. She lifted her face to his. Her gloved hand stroked his cheek. He had to take a breath; her lips were calling him. He bent forward and closed his eyes. Her lips found his and his hers—a beautiful softness. Her heavenly kiss lifted him into such a euphoria he felt he could be the one flying, and in which direction mattered not. North or south, whatever be her pleasure would be his as well.

He rubbed his nose onto her chilly one. He pressed a kiss on the top of it. "Would you consider, Miss A. H. Lee, continuing our discussion over warm tea? It seems your nose might freeze off if we stay out here any longer."

"Mister Roosevelt, I think you are a very astute man, and a thoughtful one, to think of my well-being," she said as she walked with him toward the entrance.

The door flung open. It was Miss Cowdin. "You'll catch cold out here like this!" she interrupted. "Hodges has been searching everywhere for you, Alice . . . for you both." She stormed back inside.

"Me?" Alice appeared confused. "That Hodges Chate, a moss-grown holdover."

He laughed under his breath. He *was* a moss-grown holdover and not a particularly favorable specimen of humanity. "Tell me," he asked, "what is it that brought upon such an argument?"

"About the old maid and the old bachelor? Your classmate kept talking about Abigail Leach as a certain old maid. And I couldn't take hearing him say such things. The woman is brilliant and should be praised."

Which classmate? he wondered. Likely Hodges.

"And then I thought I saw the redhead fly by and *my* head just couldn't get off the fact that the bird might be in some sort of danger."

"Maybe we should stay by the window to keep a lookout for your feathered friend."

The door opened and he was glad of the warmth, not for him but for her. "And the old maid versus the old bachelor. A wonderful thesis could be made based on this." What a stunning debate for equal rights! Equal rights and the practicality of such should be at the forefront of discussions at Harvard, he thought.

"You will have to consider it then." Placing her winter coat, gloves, and hat into the closet, she guided him into the parlor where they found a seat by the fireplace.

He took her hands into his; they were much colder than was acceptable. He held them there.

"Now, may I ask, hasn't society placed too many a barrier for any of this old maid / old bachelor argument to change?" she asked.

He adored this woman before him. Her mind was lucid. Her point, clear. "Insuperable barriers," he answered.

"They *are* insuperable barriers."

Mrs. Saltonstall brought them cups of tea, the heat on their hands a pleasant change.

He watched her take a sip. He did the same before continuing with their discussion. "Alice, these barriers that you speak of may remain, unless, of course, a different state of society existed."

"And what would that be like?"

"A society where strict justice would be used to place both man and woman on an equal level."

"Wouldn't that be something? Man and woman on an equal plane. But practically speaking, it seems an impossibility, Thee."

"Why would you say that?"

"In the practical sense, females are considered physically inferior to males by nearly everyone. That alone puts any change at a halt."

"If you are saying we place men at a higher physical class than women, then all these objections should apply just as well if one caste of males were weaker than another caste."

"True."

"For example, a consumptive in the eye of the law is equal to the strongest athlete if we take physical superiority as the main consideration."

"You mean, Thee, a woman could be physically just as strong as a man."

"Or stronger. Take the Amazons."

"Ah yes, the fierce female warriors. The story of legends in Greek mythology."

"They are by no means creations of the fancy, but really existed."

"You do make a valid point that there are and have been many accounts of the physical strength of women in society."

Bob Bacon approached. "Sorry to be the interrupter. However, if we don't make an exit soon, Roosevelt, we won't get back to Cambridge."

"Just a few more minutes, please."

"Certainly."

"There never seems to be enough time," she said to him. "My grandmother used to tell me, do something between the clicks, or you'll find the clock stops, and you'll have nothing to show for it."

That gave Theodore an idea.

Bacon was hovering.

"I think your people are waiting," she said to him. "Before you go, would you consider it as the subject of a thesis?"

"I will."

"Truly?"

"Yes. Truly."

Hodges joined in the stare-down.

Theodore had no idea how long Hodges had been awkwardly looking at him and Alice but did not much care. He did have an idea about showing Alice something, something he thought she would find splendid. "We should continue this discussion. And I know the perfect place. Might you be available, A.H., say, a week from today?"

"Next Saturday is a tea party at Martha Cowdin's."

He had not heard.

"Are you not attending?" she asked.

He was not, in fact, as he had not received an invite. "I'm not, but I hope you have a wonderful time."

"My dance lessons take me to Cambridge on the following Saturday. I could be available in the late morning, maybe eleven thirty."

"Very well, I will make arrangements," he said, as he hoped those arrangements would include a way to win her heart, for good.

Chapter Twenty-nine

———◆◦◆———

While We Live, Let Us Live

CAMBRIDGE

The click of Alice's brown tie-up boots echoed on Harvard Street. Each of her steps tapped the wood planks laid out along several storefronts. Ever so curious about what Theodore wanted to show her, she moved eagerly along to their meeting point two streets up ahead. Catching her attention, the window display to her right with the words "C. D. Wright Boot and Shoe Shoppe" etched in the glass. Only men's shoes were showcased at the front. Too bad, she thought, for if the women's shoes were not relegated to the back, which she had to squint to see, the shop would sell more shoes.

Passing 8 Harvard Street now—Allnutt's Dining Room, considered the only first-class restaurant in Harvard Square—she read the sign at the front:

SINGLE MEALS AT 30 CENTS

MEALS FOR THE WEEK COSTING 4 DOLLARS (TABLE BOARD)

The sign should have added, "No meals for women." Females were never permitted in restaurants, unless in the company of a male escort. Some dining establishments had opened downtown in Boston, for women only, called ladies' ordinaries, but Alice thought that nonsensical, especially since they served only prim meals like light salads.

One street to go. Alice's plan had been to meet Theodore after her ballet lessons, which finished at eleven in the morning. She had told her mother she would need more time in town due to an important discussion after dance, which somehow worked. Having changed into her strolling attire after dance class, she found that her caramel-colored cool-weather walking suit, of velvet material, offered great mobility. Being two pieces, it allowed her to skip the tight bustier, and this skirt went wide at the bottom near her ankles. The high-fashion design was not in the outfit itself but in the lace flowing at the wrist and neckline. A cashmere overcoat, in a matching camel shade with twelve gold buttons down the front, completed the look.

Squeaking wheels sounded from a horse-drawn trolley running in the middle of the street. Several gents in top hats eyed her curiously. She understood why; it was not, after all, a usual sight to see a woman walking alone.

And there he was. Theodore Roosevelt gave her a wave from the end of the block. She noticed his garb. He was wearing a navy three-piece suit with a bow tie, and a newsboy hat. He certainly presented darling no matter what he wore, and he really did know how to dress. Each time she saw him he was head to toe a man of fashion.

First, she would have to thank him for the purple floral arrangement sent to her home, a glorious selection of fragrant alyssum and clematis. She never before received such a combination, clearly thought through on Theodore's part: every flower had a meaning. Most boys sent her roses or some such. Hodges always sent burgundy roses. Alice knew their meaning—"unconscious beauty"—a horrendous choice, especially if Hodges had understood her well enough. Theodore, on the other hand, obviously knew his flowers. Alyssum meant "worth beyond beauty" and clematis, "mental beauty."

She recalled the thank-you note she sent to him, hoping it was appropriate. Rose had helped her craft it:

Dear Thee,
Thanks for the lovely flowers, which you so kindly sent me. I assure you they were greatly enjoyed and the party was a very pleasant one, I only regret that you were not there with us to enjoy it. With again many thanks for your kind remembrance,

> Sincerely yours,
> Alice H. Lee

Those flowers did brighten her room and their scents, a pronounced almond combined with honey. It smelled nothing like that now on Harvard Street, just mostly of horses' business.

She assumed Theodore would start out by asking why she was walking alone, why she did not have an escort, why she had not mentioned that he should have picked her up from the dancing school. She sighed just thinking of all the time that would be taken up with explanations to the usual pointed questions, when they really required only the answer, "I felt like it."

A broad smile played over Theodore's face. She was happy to see him, too. There was so much she wanted to talk with him about.

His body moved toward her, and he waved again. "Alice H., you came!"

"I did, Thee." She paused, realizing he noticed her name after the salutation in the letter. She waited now for the grilling to start as it normally would when she traveled alone.

"Shall we start our journey here?"

Surprised, she agreed. "I hope you received my note."

"I did, and it certainly was not necessary. And I hope you enjoy this even more." Theodore stepped toward the black door with a boar's head over it. "Do I have plans for you today!"

Black door with a boar's head. The Porcellian? She remembered overhearing her father giving direction to some fellow about its location, referring to the black door with a boar's head. "Simply a man's place" is how her father referred to the club to her mother.

Mind swirling, she waited. No woman had ever entered this place, at least that is what she had always been told. The club seemed dark. The shades were not pulled, yet it seemed not a light was on.

He turned back with a great Theodore Roosevelt smile, full and beaming. He seemed to pay no mind to the violation he was committing, allowing her in. What would the other members think of this?

Alice had to take a deep, deep breath now.

He opened the door. "Miss Lee, will you lead the way?"

Never a day since its founding almost one hundred years prior had the Porcellian Club ever seen a lady trod through. Every hallowed tradition would be smashed today! Let the veil of secrecy be lifted! She knew the club's Latin motto, she had picked up snippets throughout her life—*Dum Vivimus Vivamus!* While we live, let us live!

One click of Alice's shoes and there she was, inside, with him.

"Welcome to the Porcellian Club," he said quietly.

She could not help but release a wondrous sigh. For years, she had imagined what the club might be like. It surprised her that the entry was not much to look at, containing an old bike rack against one wall, a stack of cane chairs, and a sign that read, "Booksellers, peddlers, and solicitors, are not allowed." They should add women to that list, thought Alice.

Theodore helped remove her overcoat. He reached around her shoulder and snuck a kiss onto her cheek. "This is what I wanted to show you." He pointed to the windup Tiffany clock on the wall above her, with the hands of time frozen. "Inside the club itself, time has no purpose. Tiffany's hands never move, many saying the Porcellian is 'The same yesterday. Today and Forever.' The specific time of day is actually not even available after entering these doors. If one needs to ask the actual hour, it is referred to as outside time. The hour matters not here, much like how I feel when I'm with you. Time has a way of standing still." He hugged her.

Those may have been the sweetest words anyone had ever said to her. She was left speechless.

He hung Alice's coat inside the closet and headed toward the next entryway door. The house was quiet, the only sounds came from the steps of her heels. She was so fascinated to see what was actually inside. A smell rushed her, a dusty note of yellowing pages, leather, and wood polish. The library, a long narrow room with a barrel-like ceiling, appeared on her left, and inside, at the end of it, a number of bookcases with a collection of hundreds of choices neatly displayed. The club's full collection neared ten thousand in number, she had once heard.

Young gentlemen sat within the atmosphere of learned opulence. Their faces shot up from their hardcovers. Theodore gave them a nod, but spoke to her. "So good of you to join me."

Her hand now wrapped around his elbow. "'Tis my pleasure, Thee," she replied, noticing one of the men leap from the couch, quickly rubbing his hip.

"They call that couch the Rockpile, it's so uncomfortable," Thee said to her.

She found this funny.

"Mister Roosevelt," the man snipped.

Theodore paused their movement.

"Mister Roosevelt," he repeated. From his watch chain a gold pig dangled, from his necktie a pig head emblem displayed.

"Good to see you," returned Theodore.

The man, appearing to be a graduate, maybe in his mid-twenties, glanced back at Alice, and then glared sternly at Theodore, speaking into his ear in a low volume, though loud enough for Alice to hear: "Since you are an immediate, you may not be aware as to the rule that only men are to be members of the Porcellian Club of Harvard."

"Miss Lee is not a member," answered Theodore. "She is my guest," he added with a pound of pride.

The man cleared his throat. "Meaning only men are to walk onto these premises." He gave Alice another look, this time a full stare from head to toe.

"It seems I've already done so." She spoke for herself in a light tone, giving this gent a curtsy.

No response came.

"'What's done cannot be undone.'" Her whispered ode to Shakespeare accomplished what she had hoped:

The fellow, without any further response, headed back from whence he came.

Let ancient prejudice be dug up root by root, she thought to herself.

Chapter Thirty

———◆◈◆———

A Filling Lunch

CAMBRIDGE

Theodore helped guide his literary goddess farther down the hall toward the small punch room. That mind of hers was beautiful—more beautiful than her beauty. Her words reaffirmed what Theodore already knew, that with this Alice Hathaway Lee, fair is foul, and foul is fair. He knew that gent could search the horizon for a reason to confront him and would realize any possible argument for her not to be allowed in as a guest today would be rendered a nullity when given proper thought.

At the club since the morning, Theodore had planned every detail of this luncheon, even down to the type of flowers at the table. He wanted everything to be perfect. He was glad she enjoyed the flowers which had been delivered to her. The florist had suggested he send burgundy roses to her, that they were the fashion of the day. Theodore decided against that. He had always thought the burgundy rose signified beauty without brains.

"I hope you didn't mind my words to your fellow member," stated she who looked like an innocent flower, but as in the verse from Macbeth, be a serpent under't.

"I especially enjoyed your homage to Shakespeare."

"I hoped you would." The pink lips of hers rose into a delightful curve. "'Do you not know I am a woman? When I think, I must speak.'"

"'Sweet, say on,'" he finished the poetic verse. How could he handle this queen, she did bring him out.

They took their seats across from each other at a finely decorated table for two with a white linen cloth and white porcelain dinnerware. Theodore's chair, he remembered, was named the H. H. Richardson for the famous architect Henry Hobson Richardson, who adored this chair while an undergraduate. Memorizing odd pieces of trivia, like the names of furniture pieces throughout the club, came along with initiation of the immediates.

Alice gracefully pointed to the vase at the center of the table filled with white eglantine blooms. "The flowers of poetry."

He was thrilled she noticed. Eglantine meant poetry in the language of flowers. Of course, she would notice such a detail.

Written in calligraphy on a rectangular linen paper was the menu he had planned for lunch:

Porcellian Club Lunch

Duchess Soup

Scalloped Lobster

Candied Fruit

"Such perfect choices." She placed the napkin on her lap.

He took a drink of Crew George, one more piece of Porc Club trivia that meant ginger ale.

Soup bowls awaited them at the table, and now she picked up her spoon. He watched her swirl the Duchess Soup so elegantly, the motion appeared almost poetic:

She blew, granting the air a touch of her. Another blow, giving the ingredients the pleasure of her company. The blade of mace was the first to follow her spoon's circular path, the carrots came next, and soon the onions respected her choice, everything accepting the course she laid out. The half-filled spoon lifted slowly, on a journey to her lips, the warmth steaming as it passed her bosom, and then her smooth neck, closing in on a slightly opened mouth. The silver sat on her lower lip, the top lip coming down to meet it. A tilt of the spoon gave the soup its wish. Oh, how he envied that spoon.

She gulped. "Thee?"

Was he staring? He hoped not.

"Thee, I have a question I wanted to ask of you."

He could not wait to hear what she had to say. With her, it could be anything. There was no telling.

"The woman we spoke of at the Saltonstalls': Abigail Leach, she being the first to gain instruction from Harvard professors."

He knew and had read her name in the newspaper.

"Well, her contention is that the hero of the hour has long been the athlete, whereas the student of intelligent mind should really be the one placed in the highest regard."

Her newest argument he had long believed. "Miss Leach is correct."

She put down her spoon. "But don't you compete in athletics?"

"I do."

She did not say anything further.

Was she testing him? Again? Over the equality issue? Fascinating, he thought, to discuss in this way, through ethical debate.

She continued spooning her soup, until she continued: "Miss Leach was speaking at the announcement for collegiate instruction for women at Harvard when she brought it up."

"In truth, athletic sport is often given improper prominence."

"You agree?"

"Certainly."

"Miss Leach was saying, 'There is no similar enthusiasm for the gifted student. The one who reads and studies because of the appreciation of reading or studying should be held in the highest regard.'"

"He or she, for that matter."

"He or she, you are correct, Thee."

"I feel the development of the body should come behind the development of the mind."

"The truth."

"Add to that, both athletics and education should come behind the development of those moral qualities which we sum up under the name, character."

The scalloped lobster arrived, cubed for easy handling, and layered in butter for easy tasting. She seemed to enjoy it immensely, along with freshly baked bread which he broke and buttered for her. She took a nice big bite, and ate all of it plus a second, even dipping the bread into the last drips of melted butter.

For Theodore, the feast was not in the food. He ate some but focused his attention on his treasured guest. "Since you bring up sport, I'd be honored to have you attend the annual boxing intramural competition the Saturday after next. I'll be competing."

"How wonderful. But I wasn't aware women were allowed in the gymnasium."

"That hasn't stopped you yet."

Finishing the lobster, she smiled delightfully, "I'd be glad to be there. I wouldn't want to see you injured, though."

He tilted his head, not understanding.

"In the boxing match, I wouldn't want to see you hurt."

"The men in these fights are hard as nails, and punishment they do not mind, nor do I."

She politely nodded.

"It's confirmed then. And now, I'm looking forward to dessert!"

"I haven't had candied fruit since I was a little girl."

He recalled summers at his family's getaway along the Hudson River. He told her, "Candied fruit had me and my siblings running for more."

"What type of fruit?" she asked with curiosity.

"We had candied cherries, then, and the same today." He made sure earlier that they did not serve prunes.

"I adore candied cherries, it's those candied prunes that my tongue cannot abide in the least."

This made him chuckle. "It seems we have something else in common."

"Not a fan of prunes?"

"That shriveled up ol' fruit? I abhor it. As with shriveled up ol' thinking."

"Same for me. I had rather live with cheese and garlic . . ." She paused, awaiting a response.

He knew it: "'I had rather live with cheese and garlic in a windmill.'" Shakespeare, again. "From *Henry IV*."

Her eyes lit up and she smiled, a dimpled cheek on display.

He figured he would try her Elizabethan skills with this one question: "And what if, Alice H., we were to serve you onion and garlic?"

"Onion and garlic, hmmm. . . ." She knew it, he could tell by her crooked smile. "I would eat no onion or garlic, Thee, 'for we are to utter sweet breath; and I do not doubt but to hear them say, it is a sweet comedy.'"

"'No more words. Away!'" he continued the verse from *A Midsummer Night's Dream*.

She completed it. "'Go, away!'"

"I hope you are reciting Shakespeare and not your true feelings for me," he pleaded, hoping for a certain response.

"Shakespeare. And yes, I would rather you stay, especially since I don't think your fellow Porcs would take kindly to me being here without you."

"I must say your Shakespearean prowess is impressive."

"As are you, Thee."

Her being impressed with him left him impressed with himself. Not only did he bring the first woman into the secret gentlemen's club, but he also brought *the* Alice Hathaway Lee, the woman Theodore considered the most perfect girl in all of Boston, or maybe anywhere on this fine earth.

Did she think her foot settled itself against the table leg? But it was not the table leg, it was his leg, and the brush of her shoe against it left him incapable of speaking. They shared the quiet but for the breath coming from her lips and his.

A server set down the tray of candied cherries.

Watching her lift one to her mouth, he had to keep silent or else profess his love to her, right there and then. Would that be such a bad thing? Maybe he should tell her his honest feelings of love. She was perfect from head to toe on the outside, but being pretty was the least of it. Her intellect and charm, that's what drew him to her. He could recite Shakespeare with her: With whom else in the world could he do that? He had attempted with other girls, but they just returned blank stares. He knew he wanted her, needed her, but could he be enough for her? Every fellow wanted to be with her. What was he? Mediocre in every sense of the word. Not enough, he knew that with certainty. He would have to change, be better, stronger, smarter, wittier, or maybe none of those: he needed to be whatever she needed him to be.

Chapter Thirty-one

---·◆·---

Fair Harvard

CAMBRIDGE

Light filtered through the branched canopy in Harvard Yard as Alice and Theodore walked over a thin layer of snow. She was glad for another Saturday spent with him. Their last day together had them lunching at the Porcellian! Never would she have imagined being granted entrance into the club. Maybe she was really the first?

It had taken nearly two years for her to get back here. On her sixteenth birthday, she had asked Papa to give her a tour as her gift. He kindly granted it. What she saw that day appeared the same as now: redbrick dormitories, ivy crawling up the sides though asleep with winter, a collegiate setting of perfection that sang out, "Fair Harvard!"

She began to hum the tune. Theodore grabbed hold of her hand and swung it to the rhythm, launching into the song with a baritone that was not quite ready for presentation. "'Thy sons to thy Jubilee throng, And with blessings surrender thee o'er / By these festival rites, from the age that is past, To the age that is waiting before.'"

She joined in, a little off-key, "'O relic and type of our ancestors' worth / That hast long kept their memory warm, First flow'r of their wilderness! Star of their night! Calm rising thro' change and thro' storm.'"

Theodore went full volume on the word "storm," which started her giggling.

"Mister Thee Roosevelt, you are quite something."

"'Quite something.'" He adjusted his collar, and she noticed his powerful neck holding up his fighter's head and heavy jaw. "I've been called worse."

"Now tell me about this boxing career of yours."

"What a fine career it has been!" he exclaimed, hands in the air, clearly joking. "Starting at fourteen years of age, I became a champion. I was entered in the lightweight contest, pitted in succession against a couple of reedy striplings who were even worse than I was. I punched and I punched, and to their surprise and my own, I won."

"Hooray for Roosevelt!"

"They handed me a pewter mug as my trophy."

"A pewter mug?"

"Became one of my most prized possessions. I'd imagine the mug might be worth around fifty cents, 'bout the same as my worth as a boxer."

"Ha!" She said this loudly, which caught her by surprise. "I must say, I am looking forward to seeing your match. I wonder if bringing Rose along would be best, with Richard, too."

"That would be capital!"

Now, she wanted to tell him something else. "I've been thinking, Thee, that—" Her breath hitched. "I might consider applying to Harvard."

"Brilliant!"

"Do you think so?"

"Certainly."

"I wish others felt the same; most people I know think it's pop-pycock for a woman to go to college."

"Not every woman is you."

"Harvard will welcome twenty-seven women this year, quite competitive I would imagine."

"Every woman who desires a higher education should have the right to one. And you should certainly apply," he tapped her hat, "especially with a brain like yours."

"Thank you." She was flattered.

Harvard Yard felt dreamlike with him so accepting of her. It felt right being with him here, walking within the Quadrangle, through the sun-dappled snow. The walk brought them to a row of ancient elms and he leaned back onto the bark of the first one, bringing her in close. They stood together, silent, only their breaths making a sound, harmoniously, in and out. She didn't want to move, and he didn't seem to either. They stayed this way, in an embrace, just holding on to each other.

He whispered into her ear, "'Doubt thou the stars are fire.'"

Hamlet's letter to Ophelia. She adored those lines.

"'Doubt that the sun doth move,'" he continued, then paused.

She waited, wanting to take it all in, every word of it.

"'Doubt truth to be a liar.'" He stopped here.

She mouthed the next line, without voice: "'But never doubt I love.'"

Did he see what she'd not spoken? He didn't say. He leaned against her cheek. She felt his finger caressing the side of her face, lightly, gently, slowly. He kissed the spot where his finger left. He kissed it again and again, moving to her other cheek, and her forehead.

She rubbed her cheek back and forth on his, feeling his rough growth. He was a man, a real man. She grabbed both sides of his face, firmly, and kissed him hard.

Theodore rested his forehead on hers and opened his eyes, waiting. He smiled wide. "Alice Hathaway Lee, will you be mine?"

"I will."

"Forever?"

What was she to say?

Chapter Thirty-two

---◆◆◆---

The Man in the Arena

CAMBRIDGE

Every man has a reason to knock the living block off another. So did Theodore. The thirst to fight, to win, came from deep within him, from even before winning his worthless pewter cup in his youth.

Today there was another reason: she was here.

The day of the Harvard Athletic Association's intramural boxing championship inside the old gym in Harvard Yard had the air thick with anticipation and sweat. Theodore exited the locker room to see the referee erase Bob Bacon's name from the board. He had fought in the heavyweight sparring contest earlier in the day, and had won. Now the next contenders were being written on the board.

Harvard Intramural Semi-Finals

W. W. Coolidge, '79, 132 pounds

vs

T. Roosevelt, '80, 135 pounds

"Take the blooming Knickerbocker's head off!" yelled a bystander in the crowd, whose sympathies were evidently in favor of

William Williamson Coolidge. A senior classman and son of a state senator, Coolidge had a pretty stacked fan base, though maybe they were not aware that Theodore had handed Coolidge a tremendous thrashing in a prior match earlier in the season.

Theodore moved sturdily, calculated and cool, to jeers.

"One punch and he's down!" hollered another from the Coolidge crowd.

Theodore stared at his red-haired opponent already at the center of the ring, eyeing the gallery from where claps came. Alice was there; he could hear her voice through the crowd. He wished he could make her out, but his vision would only go so far. He imagined she was dressed finely, sitting on the bleachers on the second level. He had never known another woman to be in this arena. He was glad she would be the first. He could not wait to show her what he was capable of.

Wearing a sleeveless shirt, khaki trousers, and canvas shoes, Theodore broadened his high-arched chest and started his march to the ring. He drew closer and was struck by the expression on Coolidge's face: no fear, no hint of trepidation, only confidence. Theodore, with well-muscled arms and lean legs, stepped up to enter the ring, and his bulk of body felt strong as he dropped below the rope. He approached his opponent and gloved hands tapped one another. Theodore felt more than ready to take him down. The bell rang.

Round one: Right glove shot out, striking Coolidge's chin. The left followed in the same way and the man did not wince. With fighting blood in him roused, Theodore struck at the ribs and the scuffling commenced. The dance of the ring led the two of them into a whirl of blows. Coolidge stepped back and returned with attempts to strike Theodore's face, punches never landing. Theodore moved with such swiftness until Coolidge had his back against the ropes. He could not stop Theodore from pummeling his face, which turned as red as his hair.

Coolidge fell to his knees. Theodore gave him a moment, waiting for him to get back up. He beat him once, he would do it again. Coolidge rose unsteadily to his feet, and fists flew again, the blows so fierce that Coolidge was quickly down and out. Round one was not even over yet, and in two minutes' time, the match was over. Roosevelt took the bout.

The referee lifted Roosevelt's hand in the air, proclaiming him the winner. Roosevelt had always felt admiration for the fearless, the ones who could hold their own, no matter what. He started to feel among them.

The referee erased the chalked sign and scratched in the new match-up.

Harvard Intramural Championship

C. S. Hanks, '79, 133½ pounds

vs

T. Roosevelt, '80, 135 pounds

Theodore sat waiting for the announcers to call them out, fortunately giving him time to rest, though his spirit did not flag. It had taken years to get to this point, to the final round of a championship, and he thought back to that day long ago and that ride which spurred him to take up boxing.

ON A STAGECOACH headed to Moosehead Lake, his father had sent him off alone to get good air and clear his asthmatic lungs. That summer ride! And those other boys on it, they made his life miserable. They pushed him and kicked him, called him names and took swipes at him. Theodore could never forget how he tried desperately to fight back, though he could not do any damage whatsoever. And they handled him so easily. Theodore knew all along he did not have any natural gift to hold his own against boys like them. He made up his mind right there and then on that stagecoach that he would attain prowess through training, through boxing, to be ready.

"He's yours, Hanks!" a voice from the crowd shouted to welcome him into the gymnasium.

"Get him down, Hanks!" another yelled from the stands.

Theodore's focus was not on the naysayers, the critics on the floor, or in the bleachers. They did not count. Why not put yourself in the ring? he said to himself. You get no credit for sitting there, safe. The real credit goes to the person who is actually willing to go in, fail or not, win or lose, to be in the ring.

Into the ring went Theodore. "Roosevelt! Roosevelt!" He heard her from the bleachers.

Gloves tapped. The bell sounded.

Round one: Theodore made a rush for his opponent, landing a hard right. Hanks responded with a swinging left; Theodore did not even feel it. Side-stepping and ducking followed, each avoiding the other, until Hanks drove a left to Theodore's jaw, jarring Theodore to his heels. Swing after swing, Theodore missed the mark of Hank's head. He tried one more snap and heard Hanks's jaw crack.

"Time!" the timekeeper announced.

The shouts continued, some for Roosevelt, some for Hanks. The Hanks crowd infuriated him. Sure, they just wanted to point out when a man stumbles, or where the doer has done wrong. Why not do it yourself, just try, don't just hiss and holler.

Round two: Jab after jab at Hanks. Theodore wanted his speed to tire out his opponent, feinting, side-stepping, drawing his rush, moving at a quick clip. His own punches went wild of the intended mark, the mark in question being Hanks's head. Theodore swung and swung, coming up short again and then again.

Round three: Theodore felt dust and sweat on his face, and tasted blood. He kept fighting, willing to take the blows, willing to err, willing to fail, doing so with undiminished enthusiasm.

Round after round, Hanks's jabs found their mark, his longer reach allowing him to punish Theodore. A right-hand hit, ducking, avoiding a left-hand. Theodore pushed his opponent to the ropes. He swung and struck Hanks in the neck. A heavy hit to Theodore's head stunned him for a moment. Nine hard rounds, Theodore still stood, taking the blows.

Final round: Roosevelt refused to be pushed to the ropes and held his ground. If in the end he was unsuccessful, at least he could say he dared to achieve, at least he could say he was the man in the arena.

Here and there the name "Roosevelt" could be heard in cheers. A right strike to Theodore's head hit with the force of a logger splitting wood, leaving him staggering, leg muscles fluttering.

Time was called.

The fight was over.

Hanks was better all the way through, Theodore knew with certainty, the decision would go Hanks's way. Roosevelt dropped his gloves after a long, hard-fought battle. But before Theodore could shift, Hanks came in, striking a heavy blow to his nose. Blood shot to the floor.

"Unfair!" "Foul!" The hisses and shouts came loud from the gallery against Hanks and his ungentlemanlike action.

Alice yelled out, too. "Foul!"

Roosevelt didn't strike him back. He could not imagine that Hanks would do such a thing on purpose.

The hissing grew louder, taunts against Hanks, now.

Theodore flung his arm up to silence the crowd. "It's all right."

The hisses continued.

Theodore kept his arm up to command the crowd to calm down.

They did and went quiet. He gestured to the timekeeper, saying, "He didn't hear him." With a bleeding nose, he walked up to Hanks who apologized as they shook hands.

Theodore looked up to focus on Alice. She was standing up, and he could barely make her out, but he could hear her yell out, "All hail Roosevelt!"

Chapter Thirty-three

———◆•◆———

The Tintype Spree

CAMBRIDGE

Alice, seated on a low stool, leaned back against Rose who had taken the dark wood spindle chair. The background screen inside the Cambridge photography studio showed a large fireplace, and below Alice's feet spread a Persian rug of bold blue with burgundy accents.

"Positions, please," announced the photographer.

Theodore walked back and forth, talking to the two of them, so enthused by the day's event. They were there for the studio "tintype spree"—a series of photographs—to which he had invited them months ago.

Alice had pleaded with Rose to get their moms' approvals but need not have done so, because Rose had already accomplished it by telling them that the dancing master requested that the girls sit for photographs.

They wore button-to-the-top dresses. Rose's fabric was periwinkle blue with navy stripes, two vertical from shoulder to waist, and two horizontal across the skirt which had lovely pleats at the base. Alice wore light rose with a row of matching satin buttons all the way down with a lace tie at the neck which fell to her waist. Each wore their hair up with finger waves, and their hats, well, they were splendid. Rose's had bunches of ribbons falling gently. Alice's had a feather sitting against the fabric without any possibility of poking anyone's eye out.

"Here, at the lens, Miss Lee," the photographer said, pointing to the camera. Rose and Theodore were advised to look to their right.

Alice stared straight into the camera and gave the slightest of grins; she could not help it. She knew the style of the day was no smiling whatsoever, but in truth, she was happy, truly happy.

Standing behind Rose was her Theodore, in the most dapper of dress, wearing a brown three-piece suit with a three-button cutaway coat, his gold watch chain visible, a top hat in hand to match, and a gentleman's walking stick. His sideburns had even grown in completely by the day of the photograph.

"Three. Two. One." The camera clicked, and again, and a third time.

The photographer suggested a new pose, asking Rose and Theodore to switch places, seating Theodore next to Alice who adjusted her stool so as to sit upright; she would not dare be in a photograph leaning into Theodore. This left Rose standing, hands on the chair back. Again, the photographer asked only Alice to focus straight into the camera, and though she did, she noticed in her side vision Theodore gazing at her. When the camera went click, he looked away from her.

The camera clicked several times. "Fin" announced the photographer.

"When can we see them?" asked Rose.

"It will take several days before you may view them. The process is a complicated one. One cannot rush art. The photographic image will be created on a thin sheet of iron which will then be coated in a dark enamel and left to develop in my darkroom. It takes time. And Miss Lee, may I have a word?"

Alice was surprised by the request, but obliged him. Theodore eyed the man disapprovingly. She approached, and without hesitation he asked her, "Have you considered the profession of a mannequin?"

Theodore came closer. "A mannequin?" Theodore asked.

"Yes." The photographer, kept his eyes on her. "Couture fashion houses, Worth and Pingat, are seeking models of fashion, and you, my dear, would make a fine mannequin."

"With all due respect," Theodore said, motioning for the ladies to leave. They obliged for they had plans to meet Martha outside the studio following the photography session.

Rose was giddy as they left. "Imagine you a mannequin!" She laughed and laughed. Alice gave her a good long stare. She was sure Theodore must be giving that photographer a tongue lashing for just asking such a question.

Martha was prompt, waiting outside the studio door as they exited.

"Martha, wait until you hear this! The photographer wants Alice to be a model for French designer Emile Pingat or possibly Charles Worth."

Martha did not respond to Rose's comment, and instead queried, "May I ask, with whom were you being photographed?"

"Roosevelt," answered Rose.

"Your photograph included Mister Roosevelt?"

"Yes." Alice was confused.

"Are you sure you want to be in a tintype with him?"

"Whatever do you mean?" snapped Alice.

"Well, I've been investigating this fellow and what I found out, no one else knows. What I have since learned exclusively about this Roosevelt fellow will have you running so fast away from him, you'll not be able to look back. What he is, it's what he is, that you will not like."

"How dare you say such a thing!" Alice was fuming at this.

"Do you know he has stuffed birds in his room? Stuffed rodents? Did you know that?"

She did not.

"More than that he stuffs them himself!"

Alice felt sick to her stomach hearing this, hoping it be a lie.

"He is a taxidermist, Miss Lee, like that creepy fellow in town."

"Mister Bisbee?" Rose asked.

"Whatever his name is. And what about Mister Roosevelt's peculiar violent vehemence of speech and manner, and an overwhelming interest in everything? What would you want with a man such as this! Why, he's a campus freak!"

Part IV

---◆---

It sometimes seems as if I were having too happy a time to have it last.

—THEODORE ROOSEVELT

Chapter Thirty-four

———◄•►———

Here Roams Theodore

COWBOY LAND, NORTH DAKOTA

SPRING 1886

THE PRESENT

The storm has passed, one that turned the sky inky black. I leave Manitou and clamber out from our hiding place to discover an antelope, standing still, surrounded by fallen hail. "Our lives are a grim and an evil fate," I mutter to the poor animal. It reminds me of myself—dazed and stunned and helpless. Understandable, after what we have been through.

A towering mass of clouds unleashed wings of rain, enveloping anything attempting to escape its path. Pillars of wind followed, shrieking and slapping the air, forming a whirlwind. Seeing the center of it, I spurred hard with loose reins to get out of the open. The first gust caught me fairly across my back. A wipe from the tail almost seized me from the saddle. Galloping fast at the risk of our necks, I finally reached the edge of a deep washout and its offer of protection underneath a windward bank. I huddled and waited with my horse next to me. The center of the storm swept by, and suddenly, hail fell with the velocity of bullets. I tried to shield myself but to no avail. When it was over, I climbed out, beaten and bruised, everywhere there were hailstones as large as pigeon eggs that you could gather by the bushels.

Here we remain, Manitou, me, and the antelope which is beginning to find its legs. The air is now so very cold that my skin stings, but inside me hurts more; the sad thoughts, they pound against me like those hailstones, even after I have been here in cowboy land for sixteen months. I question why I even raced from the whirlwind. Why not be caught in it? It makes no difference what becomes of me. Suffering finds no escape—it burrows into your soul and there becomes firmly established.

Thick mist rolls in; a new storm forms in the distance but the booms are louder, drawing near. The reverberations carry through me. The rain sheds its tears. Nightfall comes fast, so I return with Manitou to our hiding spot, my boots squelching in the wet dirt, and I sit my soaked self against a hill to wait for the day. What shall I do? I know what not to do. I shall not think because every time I do, I think of Alice, and that pains me too much, true agony, physical and real. No, tonight, instead, I will take every memory of her and lock each away inside my heart. Where can I throw the key?

Through the hours, sounds emerge from the darkness, the long howling of a wolf echoes out of the deep canyons.

I remember what a friend out here, Bill Sewall, told me once: "Time heals them over, these troubles." Maybe the only thing for me to do is forget the past. Accept the event as finished and out of my life. To dwell on it, and above all to talk of it with anyone, is weak. Why I even spoke about any of it to Bill Sewall, I do not know.

As the night goes on, the hush sometimes breaks with the strange call of owls and the far-off, unearthly laughter of a loon.

Yes, from this time forth, to the world, I'll put on a brave and cheerful front no matter what I feel. And I pledge to myself that I will never speak one word of the matter with anyone. In the long future, when the memory is too dead to throb, maybe I shall speak of it once more. But if I can be wise, I will not speak of it now.

"When you get to feeling differently," Sewall told me, "you will want to get back where you can do more and be more benefit to the world than you can here, driving cattle." I answered, "I can serve no benefit at home. It is no use saying that I would like a chance at something I could do; at present, I see nothing whatever ahead." Then he added this: "If you cannot think of anything else to do, you can go home and start a reform. You always want to make things better instead of worse." I told him, "Every reform movement has a lunatic fringe," to which he responded, "You would make a good reformer."

The antelope bounds across my vision, then across a flowing storm-wash and out of sight. I know it will find its way. I should follow its lead.

———◄•►———

Chapter Thirty-five

The Débutante Ball

MILTON

NOVEMBER 1879

THE PAST

Alice stood last in line, her mind filled with angst. Violins played, their melody echoing up the red-carpeted staircase festooned with sparkling gold ribbons that reflected the light of the grand chandelier. From the ballroom floor rose the muffled voices of the crowd made up of mostly collegians. Upon the landing she waited with a dozen young women, hailing from Boston's most elite families, ready to be presented to high society. As she took the first step, Mamma raced over, adjusted the feathery aigrette in her hair, spritzed her with a flowery, overly sugary fragrance, and reminded her, "Hold your chin high and pushed forward, and drift, my darling, like a weeping willow."

Her intricate dress of pink taffeta with shirring and ruffling and laced rosettes was her mother's, which she had worn when she came out those years ago, and it itched. Alice fell behind to give her back one good final scratch and another at the front where she felt the heavy beat of her heart. For the first waltz she was promised to the son of the family that had granted approval for the ball to be held on this estate, and her mother felt obliged to grant the second as well with Alice. If not for the precision of her finishing school education which she had attended nearly every day for the past months, which taught her to smile delicately, answer questions kindly, step noise-lessly, and dance gracefully, she might not have completed her walk down the steps, onto the ballroom floor, and into the waiting arms of Hodges Chate.

"You are a vision, Miss Lee—a galaxy of beauty and poetry and sentiment." He spoke with his nasal voice, gazing at her.

She was silent, trying to hold her breath so as not to smell her pungent self. One step after another as the first waltz played, she kept her focus over Hodges's shoulder, studying instead the ball-room's long French windows and their striped curtains in ivory and bold red, which flowed from ceiling to floor, and there that counter with polished gentlemen serving champagne and pink sherbet.

"What a rapid and triumphant success this night is." His tight-set jaw reminded her that she despised this man. "Isn't my estate magnificent?"

Her eyes did not part from the sherbet. "Thank you for the kind reception," she blurted her prepared remarks with a rehearsed smile; outside of those words, she added nothing. She imagined the sherbet must be delectable being Fannie had created it, likely with cherries, yes, it must be cherries, she thought, due to its strong coloring.

Hundreds of invites to the finest bachelors had been sent for the débutante ball. From the looks of things, everyone accepted, many of them dancing with her fellow pearl-, feather-, and floret-accoutremented ladies.

How did you arrive at this place, Alice? Why are you here, danc-ing, candy-scented? This is not you. It makes no sense, she debated herself. Then, she remembered why.

The summer just passed, and it had been long and perhaps the most trying ever. Those weeks after the tintype spree may have been the worst and most extended spell she had ever experienced. In bed, waking only for broth and elixirs, the shakes and nervous fits refused to dissipate, her head refused to clear. Doctor Francis came and went, warning of a dire outcome, and Mamma paced in hysterics. She had to listen to her mother talking and talking about how her health must be revived for the ball, for the ball. Even when she moved from lying to sitting, her mother went on, next about boys and how Alice should not consider any relationship before the party, especially one with this New York boy. Mamma learned what Martha had revealed to her. *He has stuffed birds in his room . . . Stuffed rodents . . . Stuffs them himself. A taxidermist, like that creepy fellow in town. Why, he's a campus freak!* Alice discovered everything she said was true, and Mamma did, too. "Trophies? I thought he had trophies, not trophies!" Alice knew what her mother meant. More elixirs and baths followed. She appreciated how Papa tried to help, sitting by her side in the evenings, and even supporting her as she completed her application for Harvard. Mamma, after careful consideration and nudging by Papa, said she would speak to the Chates about it, being they knew Mrs. Agassiz. What made the time that followed all the more terrible was not hearing back from Harvard. A sickly girl lacking in education was all she was. She realized it was at that very moment that she stopped finding strength to argue with Mamma anymore, and so she did what was asked—attended finishing school full-time and followed the precise steps taught by the school's instructor.

"There is nothing more that can be done," Alice told herself now as she moved about the dance floor. "Give up and give in."

In the room, seated in gilded chairs with red velvet cushions, were the mothers who for as far back as Alice could remember had spoken of this day, the one that marked teenagers as eligible marriage prospects. The elders must have felt immense pride, she thought, for the young women danced finely, each with shoulders back, chins up and forward, satin-gloved hands softly settling on their partners' shoulders, and as she noticed the same closed smile planted firmly on each face, she knew how they felt: alone.

Alice glided over the polished floor. Her heeled gold satin shoe, one with the lowest heel possible because her mother did not want her taller than the gents, peeked out from the bottom of the ruffle of her dress. She felt numb, so she let her feet be guided by habit. One, two, three; one, two, three. They rhythmically carried her as they had been taught from an exorbitant amount of lessoning that included scrunching a cloth with only her toes, adding an elastic band, and spreading out her toes, and placing a tennis ball between the ankle bones as they relevéd and lowered in parallel.

She sighed a bit too loudly as Hodges released her to a new partner. And so the dances passed and monotony set in: she smiled when the men smiled; she replied to their questions of the trifling kind, none outside the realm of the ones she had been schooled on how to answer; she spun when they led her into a spin which followed in the exact rules of the specific waltz; and all the while she listened to the music, focusing on the harmonic connections, the notes carrying her through the mist of emptiness.

After the last of the ten bachelors her mother assigned, rogue ones circled her like moths to a flame requesting a dance. She declined and walked over next to her mother who gave her a piece of advice: "Never be afraid of blushing, my dear." Mamma examined her dance log, considering another partner. Fortunately, another fancy mother grabbed Mamma's attention to discuss how the sherbet matched the rosettes on Alice's dress splendidly.

The talk of pink coloring pushed her thoughts to Fannie's dessert, the imagined sweetness swirling about her tongue, the cold lingering inside her mouth. How exquisite it would be to taste it right now, but there were too many people to get through. Someone would ask for another dance. It was too much effort; instead, she decided to stand here and admire it.

She zeroed in on one of the gentlemen by the sherbet. She felt light, and she smiled, full and true; she had not seen him in many months. Mister Roosevelt walked toward her and, in each hand, he carried a bowl. How joyful she felt, how full of spirit and vigor, and she laughed.

His manner of walking had changed, now with a slight bent-over positioning which was the mode of the day. His hair was parted in the center adding a dignity to his appearance even though she usually was not fond of the middle part. It worked for him. Other than thick sideburns, he was clean shaved. He wore a black three-piece suit, a two-button dress coat open at the front, silk lapel facing, a U-shaped ivory waistcoat, his gold watch chain peeking out, and at the back, tails reaching to his knees. She noticed his trousers were tight and flared out slightly to cover his shiny black patent leather shoes.

He approached. "Would you care for some cherry sherbet?" When he spoke, his piercing blue eyes curved up at the ends, leaving her in doubt of any ability to carry through on her plan of what she was to say to him, the plan she had practiced many a time.

She accepted the bowl from him but placed it on the small high table near her. He did the same with his.

"If sherbet is not your pleasure, A.H.," he said, approaching her frightfully close, "then may I have this dance?"

He looked so handsome, more handsome than she remembered. She took in his smell, forest scented. Between them, there was a feeling that brought with it a degree of reciprocity, of respect, of reawakening. Her heart fluttered delightfully, encouraging her, telling her to "Gallop onto the floor with him"; but her inner voice directed her to say what she ought.

Chapter Thirty-six

————❖————

To and Fro

MILTON

Theodore drank in her smile. He waited for her to say "yes." She drew a breath; it hitched. He drew a breath. She smelled different, like sugared candy. The pause left him desperate to whisper in her ear, "I've missed you so. On October 18, 1878, I first saw your sweet face, and I fell in love with you. Love at first sight, Alice Hathaway Lee. You are my first love." He wanted to tell her how he had changed since their time apart. He withheld all those words. . . .

"May I have this dance?" he asked again, suddenly feeling less confident in her answer.

Alice's genuine smile disappeared, its departure making way for a forced grin with closed lips and a curve at the ends. The torture continues, he assumed. The past months had been spent agonizing over her, hardly having one good night's rest, some nights not even bothering with bed.

Another breath from her, and still no answer.

He wanted to tell her, "I have been pretty nearly crazy over you, my wayward, willful darling." Again, he said not one word of it.

After a pause that lasted longer than one should wait for an answer to a simple dance, she rushed the words: "Forgive me, sir." She grabbed a bowl of sherbet from the table and pivoted away from him, the whoosh lifting her dress just enough to show—were those trousers under her gown? Couldn't be.

Theodore watched her go, puzzled. "Sir." She had called him "sir"? Add to that her refusal of his invitation to dance when the beauty had danced with ten men already—twice with Hodges Chate!—and he felt so irked he wanted to tussle with that man right out there in the middle of the dance floor. But he kept his composure, knowing that would be no help, and he knew envy was as evil a thing as arrogance. Still, he sighed with a note of delight, because for a single instant, he had seen a sparkle in her when she first glanced his way; for him, that was an assurance of a new beginning.

"Women are fickle," Minot said to him with a strong pat on the back.

Theodore threw his hands up in the air. "Oh the changeableness of the female mind." His flippant answer did not reflect the truth, he knew this, for his mind and the whole of his inner world were absorbed in her. Placing a hand in his trouser pocket, he walked with Minot to the champagne counter. A crowd of ladies approached them. One débutante shouted, "Theodore Roosevelt, you are certainly a gay deceiver! You promised us a dance and here you are getting champagne without us." Another called him a flirt. And still, another told him that the gals had compared notes and determined that indeed he had promised each a dance and offered none an invitation to the floor.

He carried on, complying with their requests, laughing and joking, and dancing, then dancing some more. His status had been on a steady rise at the end of junior year, albeit that one stint in the woods that Richard seemed to have kept on the quiet. In the terrible summer just past, when Alice had shunned him every time he had requested a visit, he used that time—after he calmed himself—to make a plan. He would change, and he did, deciding his hobby of taxidermy was done, finished. A career in natural science would not fit in her world, and it was in that world he most wanted to be. Today, he took account in his head of his accomplishments, hoping they would be considered enough for her: being librarian of the Porcellian, secretary of the Hasty Pudding Club, treasurer of the O.K., president of the Alpha Delta Phi, committee member for Class Day, and a quasi-editor of the *Harvard Advocate,* being that he had written a number of articles. His feelings for her were indeed true and not a passing fancy; he fell in love with Alice Hathaway Lee a year ago, and everything was subordinate to winning her. Being a true society man might help. It certainly couldn't hurt.

He knew that being a senior classman now added to his stature, and he made sure to crowd the gap of her absence by making his days altogether too full, even packing his time with enjoyments like having a most delightful call on Miss Carow, whom he had known from childhood. She acted the same lovely little flirt as ever.

But now, as he whirled with different gals about the floor, he focused only on Alice and watched as she finished her bowl of sherbet.

In all of the spinning and additional partners on the ballroom floor, he saw Alice return to the table to retrieve his bowl of sherbet and begin to eat that one, too. This made him chuckle. He wondered why she was not enjoying her own party until her cousin Rose became his dancing partner and they had a little symposium while moving, which gave him the news that explained everything.

Chapter Thirty-seven

---◈---

The Power of Sherbet

"Whatever do you mean you told him the truth?" The next morning Alice, seated on her bed, could not believe her ears.

"I had to, Al," stated Rose, who was standing and holding something behind her back.

"You told him what Martha told me, about him being a campus freak!"

"He already knew *that* because I had told Richard who told him. And you know what happened? Which I feel terrible about and may have been my doing? A few weeks after our picture-taking, days before summer when Richard told Theodore about the 'campus freak' remarks, Thee ran off into the woods because he was so upset."

"The woods?"

"Yes, he was in the woods for days."

"And you didn't tell me this!"

"I couldn't. You were so upset already. He told Richard when he was sitting up against a tree that he did not think he could win your heart and that he was nearly crazy at the mere thought of losing you."

"No."

"Yes. Roosevelt seemed constantly afraid that someone would run off with you, and he threatened to duel any man who tried. He actually sent abroad for a set of French dueling pistols and even got them through the customhouse, with great difficulty of course. And I would have told you all of this but you were confined to your room with fever, and Auntie Caroline told me not to upset you further because you had finishing school to focus on after you finally finished being bedridden, and she made me promise and promise again not to say anything until after your ball, so how could I say any of this to you, especially after the whole Harvard thing?"

"You told Thee about Harvard?"

"Indeed, I told him. It had to be done, Al, what does it matter? So you didn't hear from Harvard. Focus instead on everything you have. Every bachelor wants to marry you. The débutante was a splendid success. And you have so much to offer without one of those silly paper scrolls."

"A diploma?"

"Whatever you call it."

"It's the only thing I ever really wanted, Ro. It would have been the only thing that was truly mine, my dream, my goal, my future. They clearly didn't want me."

"Well, there is this." She brought around her hand which held a thick ivory-colored envelope, the size of notebook paper. "Before I let you open it, Minot Weld bade me tell you that Theodore is done with collecting."

"Collecting?"

". . . Specimens. He does not approve of too much slaughter any longer."

"Too much slaughter? He should approve of NO slaughter!"

"Very well, I'll have Richard pass that along. But he for certain won't be becoming another Mister Bisbee or anything, and he's abandoned all thought of being a scientist, but maybe instead a political scientist."

"A politician?"

"Oh, I don't know, but not the scientist that likes to cut things under a microscope, for sure not that, nor that observing kind of scientist who walks around looking at outdoor things and such. He's done with that. I think you changed his mind . . . by not approving, so to speak."

"I never said such a thing, that I didn't approve of natural science." Alice started to open the envelope.

Rose shrugged. "So, in this envelope, Thee told me, are papers . . . that you inspired him to write, and he's making a submission to Harvard to deliver this speech at the upcoming commencement ceremonies. Apparently, this kind of thing has to be approved by a hundred men or some such. Anyways, he told me that he pledges to convince them to allow him to present the essay at the graduation ceremony. Can you believe it? You are the inspiration for it! But I was asked to tell you to read it all through and then make a judgment as to whether it would be worth your time to see Theodore again. I'm going to leave you alone so I can have a try of that cornbread in the oven—I can smell it from here—and I expect the right answer when I come back."

Alice began to remove the papers from the envelope.

"And one more thing. Do you know what he asked me?"

"What?"

"He wanted to know if you wore trousers."

"He did?" Oh, she thought, they must have shown when she pivoted away from him.

"Isn't that silly?" Rose's eyes rolled. "We know he's a unique character. Did you see Martha dance with Thee at the end of the night?"

Alice nodded.

"I don't believe everything she says, but guess what he told her?"

"What?"

"Thee pointed to you and said, 'See that girl?' You were across the room. 'I am going to marry her. She won't have me, but I am going to have HER!' Then, Martha told him, 'She does not want to marry you.'"

Alice had difficulty processing all of the information Rose disclosed to her, and she was stunned her cousin had kept it secret for all this time.

"Oh, and one more thing: Martha danced with Bob Bacon and walked outside alone with him, and you know what that means—that means I am out of luck. So please be happy that at least you have a crowd to choose from, unlike me, although I did enjoy dancing with Minot." She started to walk out. "And one more thing," Rose added, turning back at the doorway. "Martha says that you and Hodgie looked darling dancing together, and the Chate family thinks the match is a certainty. Blab. Blab. Blab."

"He would be the last man I would choose. And Ro?"

"Yes."

"Bring me some of that cornbread."

She closed the door behind her.

From the envelope, Alice pulled out eight loose papers that had been torn out of a notebook, the threading still partially attached at the edge. She brought them to the window bench, leaned the pages toward the sunlight, and began reading his neat penmanship, those letters spaced evenly, placed on the blue lines in perfect formation. She decided to read it through entirely before making any judgment.

Practicability of Giving Men & Women Equal Rights.

In advocating any measure we must consider not only it's justice but it's practicability. Viewed purely in the abstract,

I think there can be no question that women should have equal rights with men; that is, in an ideally perfect state of society strict justice would at once place both sexes on an equality. The qualities needed in the world as it now is being so different from those required in the world as it should be, I shall, in discussing the present question, merely consider the possibility of equalizing men and women before the law, society being still in it's semibarbarous state.

Only paying attention to the practical side of the question, there certainly seem to be very great, if not insuperable, obstacles in the way. The chief of these arises from the fact that women are as a rule physically inferior to men. All these objections would apply just as well if one caste of males were weaker than another caste. And of course we are merely taking each sex as a whole; individually many women are superior to the general run of men. The artificial rules of society, moreover, make many of these distinctions; if we could once thoroughly get rid of the feeling that an old maid is more to be looked down upon than an old bachelor, or that woman's work, though equally good, should not be paid as well as man's, we should have taken a long stride in advance.

But, entirely apart from considerations of what might be done in a state of society radically different from ours, I contend that, even as the world now is, it is not only feasible but advisable to make women equal to men before the law, leaving out for the time being all question of the franchise. A cripple or a consumptive in the eye of the law is equal to the strongest athlete or the deepest thinker; and the same justice should be shown to a woman, whether she is, or is not, the equal of man.

As regards the laws relating to marraige there should be

the most absolute equality preserved between the two sexes. I do not think the woman should assume the man's name. The man should have no more right over the person or property of his wife than she has over the person or property of her husband. I would have the word "obey" used no more by the wife than by the husband. The woman, too, should have at least as much voice as the man in everything regarding the children; indeed, I should say, more.

Even taking things as they are, a woman, though placed by education and surroundings at a disadvantage compared with man, is yet able to derive full benefit from the law; she is in no wise inferior as regards quickness or acuteness to man, and certainly even now would be very often able to hold her own, so that I should unhesitantly approve giving her absolute equality with man before the law.

Alice went back to the beginning and read his essay through again, stopping here and there, noticing how he underlined each individual word in this one sentence: "I do not think the woman should assume the man's name." What a novel idea; she had never realized that was possible. His ideas were well expressed, clear. Alice could hardly believe the man dared to put his reputation on the line.

She read through his writing once more and felt the words this time. In deciphering the full meaning, clarity struck. Her opinions made an impression on him! Her opinions mattered to him. Such a sensation of pride ignited in her and instantly seized her with joyfulness. The old maid! She laughed. The old bachelor!

Even with his misspellings, bits of incorrect punctuation, and the need for further explanations, she realized as she looked over the passage yet again that this could be the dawning of a new day. "I think there can be no question that women should have equal rights with men," she read aloud. She recalled what Rose had said about him wanting to present this speech before a crowd at commencement. This is what was needed to move the cause, make society get rid of those artificial rules. Yes, this would be a step.

"So . . ."

Was that faint voice coming from outside, Theodore Roosevelt's?

"What do you think, A.H.?" she could hear him say. He was standing in the grass looking up at her window.

What she thought, as she jumped from her seat, and raced from her room, is that she did not have to pretend to be someone she was not around Theodore. His writings sparked a most exhilarating moment: Thee believed that her authentic self was worthy of love. She rushed downstairs and out the door. Honest, her truest self, he liked her for her. And not only that, she felt safe around him, not for protection, but for growth, intellectual growth. Had she met the person who completed her? Her legs moved swiftly nearer to him. Theodore Roosevelt trusted her, understood her, gave her strength, conquered every obstacle she put in his way, and even knew the precise time to bring her dessert. She leaped into his arms. He made her life come to life. He was her cherry sherbet!

Chapter Thirty-eight

—◈—

As Time Passes

The months that followed, when autumn folded into winter and winter into spring, became a dream come true for Theodore after Alice agreed to be his girl, again. He closed his eyes and sat back in bed against a pillow, remembering when she leaped into his arms, and when she waltzed with him that night at Memorial Hall. The violins played. The crowd filled the banquet room, but he only saw her. When the musical notes reached a crescendo, her hand squeezed his hand, and she leaned into him, saying softly, "Thee, how I missed you so." These words made him feel powerful as a ship charging through the ocean's waves, and when, in a private corner away from noise, their lips joined together, softly, longingly, heaven itself opened. His heart leaped and had not come down since.

No man, he believed wholeheartedly, could lead a more ideal life than him. He now spent several nights, usually five a week, at Chestnut Hill. He really was leading the very happiest life a mortal had ever led. He was doing well in his senior year studies, having a royally good time with the club, his horse, and above all one sweet, pretty girl at Chestnut Hill.

He left his bed for his desk, reveling in his good fortune while trying to forget the one cloud that hung over him. There was that news he decided to tell no one, not even Alice, although she did notice his puffy eyes and pale complexion. Either way, he was not going to listen to the advice from the doctor: "Your heart is weak," Theodore recalled the doctor's solemn tone a week prior, "and you must beware of too much exertion, must, in fact, avoid even running upstairs, otherwise, Mister Roosevelt, your life will be a short one." The doctor's advice would go unheeded, he decided, because if he had to follow the life the doctor suggested, he would rather die young. At least the doctor said his lungs worked better; asthma had not given him much trouble as of late.

He put those thoughts aside as he relished the days of capital fun. Revisiting his writings in his diary, he realized he had spent the past year and four months in such incessant action, an eager, restless, passionate pursuit of one all-absorbing object. He turned the pages of his diary, reading his notes about his days with Alice since her debut:

> I took a long ride in the cart with Alice; got caught in the rain and had to borrow an umbrella from a strange house. In the afternoon went out for a long walk with Alice and Rose, who were just as funny as they could be, making me buy candy etc.

> We played lawn tennis; and stayed to tea and spent the evening, dancing till I was nearly dead.

> In the afternoon I drove in a buggy to Chestnut Hill, and went out walking with the girls.

In the evening I went to town . . . I took Alice there and from it, sitting by her; and the whole thing was a great success.

I dined at the Lees, in the evening taking a walk with Alice.

I had the most glorious ride. I spent the afternoon walking with Alice; dined at the Lees; and spent the evening dancing, talking, etc., riding back at 10 o'clock.

It was Rose's birthday; I rode over to Chestnut Hill where I lunched and spent the day, bringing over two fans for Rose and Alice. En passant, those two young ladies have cost me over $150 so far. In the evening we went to the strawberry night of the O.K.

He sat back in his chair and gazed at the framed tintype from their spree last spring: Alice gazing beautifully into the camera, Rose in between them appearing uncomfortable, and Theodore remembering how he skipped an extra step that day realizing he would have a photo of his love for all time. He was not happy with the photographer trying to talk privately with Alice, but that is what life would be like with his girl—every man wanted to be near her.

He read on in his journal:

We started in a special car to see the "Great Harvard-Yale Race" which Harvard won easily. I have hardly ever enjoyed myself more. We did not get home till 2 am, and I have absolutely no voice left; thanks to the shouting. We sang during most of the return journey. I spent a large proportion of my time with Alice, who never looked prettier.

Gave a lunch party of 34 persons up in the Porcellian. It was the greatest success imaginable. Everything went off to perfection; the dinner was capital, the flowers very pretty, and we had great fun with the toasts and speeches. All the girls looked extremely pretty, the wine was good, and the fellows all gentlemen.

It seems hardly possible that I can kiss her and hold her in my arms; she is so pure and so innocent. I have never done anything to deserve such good fortune.

Spent the day with the family; drove to a great family dinner at the Lees. The drive home, in the bright, cold moonlight over the smooth, frozen roads was just perfect.

I have had so much happiness in my life so far that I feel, no matter what sorrows come, the joys will have overbalanced them.

He hardly knew what to do with his bottled-up enjoyment. His own beautiful queen was the same as ever and yet with a certain added charm he did not know how to describe. "I cannot take my eyes off you, Alice Hathaway Lee," he whispered, alone in his room. He dropped his head into his hands with his elbows leaned on the desk. "I cannot bear to have you a minute out of my arms."

And he went deep into thought, remembering that one day as they sat in the shade by the clear, calm Charles River with the blooms emitting an aromatic, heady smell, and the water reflecting the varied colors of the soft red sky. Everything came alive that day, including the sound from the trees with a whistling note of *lu lu lu lu*. The nightingale's song, an outpouring of melodic notes led her to ask, "Could there be anything more beautiful than birdsong?"

"Only you," he replied.

She moved closer to his side and he could feel her hip on his hip. His shoulder felt her head gracefully lean on it, and her eyes looked up with a new luster. She sighed and murmured his name, his full name. He turned his face to her and gently kissed her cheek, placing his hand below her chin. His lips found hers. Her mouth was delicate, soft, inviting. Every inch of him felt her energy, as she said the words he so longed to hear: "I love you, Theodore Roosevelt."

Chapter Thirty-nine

———◦◦◦———

The Special Day

CAMBRIDGE

She loved how he loved her. She put her arm through his and together they strolled Harvard Yard. Blue skies darkened. An almost imperceptible breeze carrying the scent of fresh-cut grass cooled the air.

Class Day 1880: A day of revelry to honor the upcoming graduates brought hundreds into the Quadrangle, which appeared like a carnival. Alice scanned the Japanese flamed lanterns up above their heads, strung with ribbons tree to tree, an awning of illumination stretched over the whole of the yard. Each looked distinct in varying colors and shapes, some displaying the college's coat of arms, others the societies of Harvard, and many with the "1880" painted on them.

"There must be thousands of them," she said as Theodore brought her into his strong arms and held her tight.

"Thirty-two hundred, altogether."

"A Class Day committee member, of course, would know such details."

Theodore pointed up to a lantern above her head, which displayed on one side, the flag of the United States, and on the other the flag of Japan. "This one was actually used at the reception of General Grant when he visited there."

She smiled just thinking of the story he told her about his sister: "The general named after your pony?"

"You remembered." He laughed.

"How could I forget." She watched the dance of shadows from the lanterns swaying on their ribbons as the day's light faded. "Today could not be more perfect."

"You could not be more perfect." He moved her through the crowd, holding her hand tightly. His smile the entire day was full and bright, and now he conversed in gentle fashion about the weeks of events leading to graduation that they would attend together, the teas, the dances, the president's reception. He halted and stared into her eyes, and told her with enthusiasm bubbling over like she had never seen from him before: "I am elated to have you with me tonight."

True happiness, she felt it too, as well as the essence of what laid at its core: freedom. "I am happy, too, Thee. And after putting in four years of hard work, there is a great reason for you to be overjoyed, especially during a celebration as this."

Theodore found them a spot against an elm.

"I think I recognize this very tree." She thought it appeared to be the same one as after their first visit to the Porcellian. She never did answer his question from that day about being his forever. She should have said yes back then, ten months ago. How she wasted so much time.

"The fireworks are about to begin."

"How thrilling! Teddy, you are too sweet to me in everything."

He reached over and kissed her cheek. "Teddy?"

"I can't use a name everyone else uses. Is Teddy acceptable to you?"

"Only for you."

"Teddy. Thee. Theodore. I love every one of your names, Mister Roosevelt."

"Come here close." He brought her back against his chest and encircled her waist with his arms. "And what may I call you?"

"Any name you please?"

"Darling Queen . . . Laughing Love . . . My Little Witch!"

She giggled about that last one.

"I don't think there was ever anyone like you in this world. You are the purest, gentlest, and noblest of women."

The first salvo sounded; a simple spark launched and burst into a mighty flame. The second sunburst of fireworks dazzled in the empty sky. She could hear his excitement in her ear and feel his warm breath at her neck. The magical atmosphere sparkled like diamonds, and brilliant shells sounded as rockets before they ignited up high in reds and greens and blues. A bouquet of shells mutated into a crimson circle and within it spelled out the college's cheer, "Rah!" Another leaped into the sky and again a "Rah!" as the onlookers yelled it out. A third burst of "Rah!" led to a shout followed by resounding applause. The spectacle brightened the sky in light. A succession of spinning wheels and different shapes led to the grand finale that ended with the year 1880 in blue light.

"Not even all the fireworks in the world could light up my world as you do," he spoke softly, and as if planned, the glee club began to sing and the night could not have been more glorious for her.

Her cheek fell upon his stubbled one. "I adore you."

Theodore angled her toward him. "When I hold you in my arms there is nothing on earth left to wish for."

She closed her eyes waiting for his lips to touch hers.

"If ever a man has been blessed by a merciful providence, I am he."

When she felt nothing, she opened her eyes to see him on one knee.

"Alice Hathaway Lee, will you be mine . . . forever? Will you marry me?"

The moment she had envisioned since childhood, wondering what would it be like—that moment was here. That moment was now. This moment was perfection. He lit up her life. She wanted him. She needed him.

"Yes, Theodore Roosevelt. A thousand yesses!"

He leaped to embrace her. "If loving you with my whole heart and soul can make you happy, then happy you shall be."

He gazed into her eyes, and she could see his eyes welling up. She traced the tears gently down his cheek. "Oh, Thee."

"Like a star of heaven, a pure flower, a pearl, how infinitely blessed is my lot."

She kissed the very spot the tears fell.

"My Alice, I can hardly realize my wonderful good fortune."

She allowed her heart to open to his love, unafraid and unfaltering, and there in Harvard Yard, she became his. "How I love you, Thee, and will for forever and a day."

Chapter Forty

———◈◈◈———

A Summer's Dream

Time moved swiftly with love in the air. Now in the bedroom he shared with his brother, Elliott, overlooking the grounds along the Long Island Sound, he took a moment to reflect. "Whom first we love we seldom wed," he thought aloud. "But we shall prove an exception to this rule." Everything was settled. She was the girl he was going to marry in three months, and he could not have been more contented that she and her cousins and brother had joined him for an extended weekend. He took the four of them on several adventures, wanting to give them a most entertaining weekend, days of great unique fun that each of them would always remember. Alone with Alice, he drove the lovely paths to Syosset and Laurelton.

He sat by his desk, staring out the window. As he waited for the gals to change into their bathing dresses, he pulled out his journal and wrote:

> How I love her! and I would trust her to the end
> of the world. Whatever troubles come upon me—

losses or griefs or sickness—I know she will only be more true and loving and tender than ever; she is so radiantly pure and good and beautiful that I almost feel like worshipping her. Not one thing is ever hidden between us. No matter how long I live I know my love for her will only grow deeper and tenderer day by day; and she shall always be mistress over all that I have.

He closed the journal, thinking how bewitchingly pretty she is. "I cannot help petting and caressing her all the time. And she is such a perfect little sunshine," he said to himself. He opened the rectangular red leather box, with a dove-shaped gold clasp, that contained their love letters. These papers were a treasure, kept since their engagement. He read a few, one after the next:

Darling Alice,

I have just written to my family that I am coming on next Saturday, as I have something important to tell them; of course, they will guess what it is.

My sweet, pretty queen, how I long to see you! I am so happy, that I hardly dare trust in my own happiness; last Sunday evening seems almost like a dream.

Goodbye, darling,
Your Loving
Thee

Dearest Teddy,

I have just received your letter. Teddy, I do miss you so much and long for the 16th so as to have you back again at Chestnut Hill. I love you with my whole heart, and you are always in my thoughts. I must stop this prim love letter, with a great deal of love ever

Your loving
Alice

Darling Alice,

Will you be at home next Wednesday? If you are, I shall come over in the morning. My ring has come, and I want to put it on your sweet little hand myself. I shall be heartily glad when a week from Monday comes; I am all the time thinking of you, and wishing to be with you. I wonder what makes me love you so! Darling, I care more for you than for everything else in the world.

Goodbye, sweetheart.
Your Loving
Thee

My dearest Thee,

I have just time to write you a few lines before it is time to go to bed. You cannot imagine how much I miss you. I shall be the happiest girl that you ever saw. Tomorrow I am going down to New Bedford to Grandpa's funeral. Mamma and Papa did not hear of his death which was sudden at the last. I hope you are feeling better than you did when you left Chestnut Hill, and do not get all tired out.

With many kisses and much
love . . . always
Your loving
Alice

Darling Little Sunshine,

You sweet, pretty darling, I perfectly long to be with you; I perfectly hate to think it will be a week before I shall see you. My own, sunny faced Queen, I don't think you are ever absent ten minutes from my thoughts; I know every one of your saucy, bewitching little ways, and every expression of your sweet, bright, pretty face. Darling, how <u>can</u> you be so perfectly bewitching? I can really almost see as I write your slender, graceful figure, the pretty poise of your head, and your pure, innocent little face. Sweetest, I love you with my whole heart.

> Your Loving
> Thee

"We are ready!" he heard Alice say. Theodore folded each letter neatly. He could read these over and over and never tire of them. He placed them back into the rectangular box. He had planned out a full day for them.

STANDING IN THE heat, breathing in the salty air, Theodore devoured the scene before his eyes. Alice looked like an angel, barefoot on the sand, wearing a belted long white linen bathing dress by the water's edge, her hair up in a tail. Could there be any picture so divine? And the day was idyllic with the cerulean-blue water dipping itself onto the gold-shaded sand, seagulls' calls of *huoh-huoh-huoh* in the near distance.

"Tranquility!" she shouted, arms stretched wide, eyes closed. "I love an amble by the shore. Don't you?" she asked George, Richard, and Rose, standing nearby.

"Tranquility?" Rose rubbed her right foot while balancing on the other.

"There is not a vestige of a breeze on the Sound," Alice said and released her hair. "Almost as calm as glass."

"For the last three days, Thee, this place you call tranquility has been nothing but Spartan." Rose set down her foot. "With the obstacle course, and the swimming, and the horseback riding, and the lawn tennis."

Theodore laughed; he so enjoyed Alice's family.

Rose tossed her hands to her hips. "Anything less tranquil could hardly be imagined."

"What do you say we return home, Thee?" Alice's smile brightened like morning rays when she turned to him.

He took her hand and started the walk back, every step feeling warm on his toes.

"Rosy cheeks on Rosie." George, ahead of them, pointed to her face.

"Because we rowed and rowed under the blazing sun." Rose wiped her brow as she went.

"After you gallantly trooped through Fleets Woods!" exclaimed Alice. "Those lilies we picked smelled like summer in our hands."

Rose stretched out her hands. "And did you forget the mosquitoes were the size of bats, swarming us in clouds."

"Ha! Yes, there was that. However, I thought it was delightful." Alice smiled wildly at Theodore. "Especially when we arrived at Friendship Spring and drank the waters to ensure lifelong friendship. And hearing the thrush in the treetops and seeing the bobolinks in the tall reeds. Just magical!"

Theodore appreciated how Alice was always ready for adventure.

"And Ro, we did win Thee's obstacle course on Cooper Bluff."

"Al, you made me race down that big sand bluff." Rose's brow furrowed. "What agony! As you are well aware, I don't run."

"I can run!" George sprinted. "At top speed!" he shouted over his shoulder.

"By thunder! You should have been number one, Georgie," Theodore said loudly.

"I shouldn't've tripped and fell," he said, returning to them. "Got me this on my knee." The spot was puffy and red.

"As they say, as falls on Mount Avernus a thunder-smitten oak," chuckled Richard.

Theodore reached the boy to give him a hug. "By Georgie, that was bully."

Alice came over to George.

Richard walked nearer to them. "At least, Rose, you enjoyed the games in the old barn. They were jolly good fun, especially watching Georgie burrow his way into the haystack for hide-and-seek."

"You seen me?" He appeared forlorn.

"I would rather, if you wouldn't mind, that we focus on the less anxiety-ridden activities." Rose stopped to catch her breath.

"Well, you did enjoy those word puzzles under the big trees at Yellowbanks," added Richard. "Crambo."

Rose scratched her head. "Is that the one where we pick a question from a hat and from another hat we pick a word and have to answer the question in verse which must include the word drawn?"

"That's the one!" Theodore affirmed.

"I did like that one," confirmed Rose.

"We shall begin a new round of competition tonight!" Theodore sat George down on a rock. "Georgie, take off your wet shoes. The sand on the beach will be warm on your bare feet."

He obliged and the group of them walked with Theodore and Alice trailing.

"How I wish it could last forever," Alice spoke into Theodore's ear, grasping his hand.

Theodore relished her big wide smile. "I can never express how

I love you. And if I should love you twice as much and as tenderly it would not be nearly as much as you deserve. I never can understand how I won you."

"It is I who has won the greatest of prizes."

THAT DAY'S SETTING sun provided an ideal background for a picnic under the canopy of a large oak by the summer house. Picnicking was his mother's favorite recreation at Oyster Bay, and Theodore felt a special joy to see her, gathered in a little knot with Alice and his sister Bamie, each in broad-rimmed straw hats, drinking lemonade and eating lobster rolls. Rose, Richard, and George were taking a much-needed nap inside.

Theodore stood behind another tree eavesdropping with his brother Elliott nearby. "I find the serene composure irritating," Elliott joked to him, "like a cow chewing its cud in the shade." Theodore pushed him out of the way, frustrated that Elliott had not taken much part in any activities since Alice arrived, and continued to listen.

"I must inform you, dear Alice, that Thee bites," Bamie revealed to his girl.

"Oh?" responded Alice, sounding mildly surprised.

"He bit me right on my arm. I still have his little teeth marks by my elbow." She rolled up her loose blouse. "You see, right here."

"You failed to mention I was age four," Theodore interrupted.

"A mischievous four," chimed in his mother, laughing.

"We wondered how long it would take for you to reveal yourself," added Bamie in a mocking tone.

"You have won a great prize, Alice." Mother flashed her usual charming grin, with a slight twist of cynicism.

"Oh, Motherling, here we go again," sighed Theodore impatiently as he slowly stepped back from their circle.

His mother grabbed hold of his pantleg, yanking him toward her. "You must know these things, darling Alice, in case your children inherit the gene." She spoke briskly, reaching into a basket of goodies. "Would you care for a sandwich?" He said no. "He was quite the bad boy, I must tell you." She handed him a lobster roll in one hand, and on the other, she landed a gentle slap. "Did you know, after the biting incident, he ran away into the kitchen, stole some dough from the cook, and crawled under the kitchen table?"

"Father stormed the house in search of him," Bamie added details, "and found him with the help of the cook."

"Our cook had a characteristic contempt for informers, but her casting an eye under the table was enough to find this one." Motherling mimicked the action.

"Father dropped on all fours and darted for me." He mimicked this, too. "I feebly heaved the dough at him, and having the advantage of being small enough, I could stand up under the table which allowed me a fair start for the stairs. Father quickly caught up."

"Never bit me again. My protector," Bamie said thoughtfully. "I only wish our father could have met you, Alice. Theodore is the one of us truly like Father and the one on whom we all greatly lean. We know with you, he will lead the life worthy of our father's name."

Motherling nodded kindly. "And my dear Alice, where is your darling little brother?"

"He was in need of a rest after playing bear with Teddy on the piazza."

"It seems my acting became too realistic, and Georgie began to have a horrible suspicion that perhaps I really *was* a bear."

His mother sounded a resounding laugh. "You must know, darling Alice, despite all of his misbehaving"—she turned a curious eye toward him—"how very dear Thee is to us and now how very dear you are to us. We are so very proud to welcome you into our family circle."

Theodore could not have been happier to hear such loving words from his mother.

"I assure you, my heart is full of gratitude." Alice's words were just as sincere. "How kind of you and what a pleasure it is for me to know all of his loved ones. How happy I am, I cannot begin to tell you."

"We received the wedding invitation and are overjoyed." His mother now poured lemonade evenly as Bamie held two glasses, then two more.

Theodore was relieved that his mother refrained from speaking of her annoyance over the Roosevelt name being left off, and Alice's name, too. How could he forget the wording:

> *Mr. and Mrs. George C. Lee*
> *request the pleasure of your company*
> *at the marriage of their daughter*
> *Wednesday, October Twenty-seventh*
> *at Twelve o'clock*
> *Unitarian Church*
> *Brookline*

"Such a joy it will be having you as a sister." Bamie clinked glasses with Theodore and Mother and Alice, who added, "I can only endeavor to make Theodore as happy as he has made me. And you both, dear Bamie and Mrs. Roosevelt, you have made everything so comfortable."

"Please feel free to call me Motherling."

Theodore chuckled about how she always did like his nickname for her.

"So gracious of you," replied Alice.

"Believe me, my darling little friend, we will be spending many wonderful days together now with Theodore beginning Columbia Law School. I am here for you always. And I failed to ask earlier how you enjoyed his speech before Harvard at commencement?" His mother smiled, taking a drink. "He revealed to me that you were the inspiration for it."

"And I was honored. Theodore, as I know you are aware, is naturally gifted with an ability to get other men to listen."

"Our Theodore never was a supporter of armchair criticism. An opinion is one thing, but he has strong convictions and the courage to follow through with them. My dearest husband always said politics should be in his future."

"And will you be keeping your name, Alice?" asked Bamie.

"Alice Hathaway Lee Roosevelt is what I've decided," she answered, turning to Theodore. He was comfortable with whatever name she wanted to be called. He let her make that choice.

"How lovely for the both of you." His mother smiled. "There was a time that I thought our Thee would be melancholic about his departure from Harvard, but he certainly has a bright future with you, my dear."

"I suppose under other circumstances, I might," added Theodore. "But who could feel blue with so fond a bride elect!"

Alice took hold of his hand.

"Now I told Thee to make sure you were comfortable with the brothers' trip before the wedding."

From the moment Theodore said yes to the six-week excursion with Elliott, he had second thoughts. "I quite regret now deciding to go."

"It seems after four years of hard work, he deserves this time away," added Alice.

"The air will do my boys some good, I suppose."

Alice set down her lemonade, a glow on her cheeks, and looked at the group of them. "I must tell you, Motherling, how very pleased you've made me here at Oyster Bay."

With Alice happy, Theodore's happiness was complete.

Chapter Forty-one

———◈———

The Confession

CHESTNUT HILL

Only a week to go; the wedding day neared. Alice kept hold of his love letters and hers. She had every one of them which gave her a thrill, and at the bottom she kept the ones which she despised reading. In those, he was truly a naughty boy writing that he did not deserve her, that it would have been better for her if they had never met. Those, of course, were written during his trip, which ended early in an unexpected way: Theodore was struck down by colic, soaked through in a rainstorm, nearly froze to death in a gale, bitten by a snake, and thrown headfirst out of a horse wagon! But now she would forever more take good care of him. He did surprise her with the announcement that they owned ranches now—the Elkhorn and the Chimney Butte. "They lie along the eastern border of the cattle country, where the Little Missouri flows through the heart of the Bad Lands," he had told her with utter enthusiasm. She'd never heard of the place, but if he wanted land, she would support him.

They promised not to see each other until the day of the nuptials. At least she had love in her hands—this pretty stack of letters. She sat by her window, admiring the sapphire engagement ring on her finger that her Mamma considered extravagant, and read through the sentimental words written to each other:

Darling Queenie,

I am going to church in a few minutes, but I can't resist writing you a line or two. Elliott comes this morning, and tomorrow he and I start on our travels—with what success remains to be seen; I hope we have good sport, or, at any rate, that I get into good health. I am feeling pretty well now, and the Doctor said the very best thing for me was to go. The last two days have been spent in getting my things packed, playing lawn tennis and walking. Mother talks of you all the time, and so lovingly; you have won all hearts, sweet mistress.

Little Sunshine, I have been missing you more than I can tell; I perfectly long to hold you in my arms and kiss your sweet, bright face; you are never absent from my thoughts.

I have just received your dear little letter, which Elliott has brought out of town (he has arrived a minute ago); it is the sweetest little note I have ever read, and makes me long to be with you even more than before, if possible. Sweet, blue-eyed queen, I prize your letters so! Do write me often. And remember the more good times you have—dancing, visiting or doing anything else you like—the happier I am.

Mother and Elliott have just come in from feeding the horses with sugar, and send their best love to my darling.

I do love you so, and I have such complete trust in your love for me; I know you love me so that you will <u>like</u> to get married to me—for you will always be your own mistress, and mine too. Give my love to all,

Your Lover
Thee

My Own dearest Teddy,

You must excuse my answering your nice letter in pencil, but Doctor Francis thought it would be better for me to stay in bed today, so as to get perfectly rested, although I told him I felt all right. I do miss you so very much Teddy, I do not know what I shall do when you go out West for six weeks. What a good time we did have at Oyster Bay, I loved so much our pleasant little evenings in the summer house and our lovely drives together. Teddy, I love you with my whole heart and am never happier than I am when I am with you and how glad I shall be to have you back again at Chestnut Hill with me. With a great deal of love to all, and much for your own dear self, I am

Your loving
Alice

Tell Bamie I shall write her tomorrow.

My Dearest Love,

You are too good to write me so often, when you have so much to do; I hope you are not all tired out with the work. But at any rate you will have complete rest, and then you shall do just as you please in every thing.

Oh my darling, I do so hope and pray I can make you happy. I shall try very hard to be as unselfish and sunny tempered as you are, and I shall save you from every care I can. My own true love, you have made my happiness almost too great; and I feel I can do so little for you in return. I worship you so that it seems almost desecration to touch you; and yet when I am with you I can hardly let you a moment out of my arms. My purest queen, no man was worthy of your love; but I shall try very hard to deserve it, at least in part.

Goodbye, my own heart's darling,

> Your Loving
> Thee

My dearest Teddy,

I have been so tired all day that I have again put off my writing till night. I was not tired from sitting up late but very early this morning. I did not sleep much after that. We have had a great change in the weather. Teddykins, I do so wish you were here, we could have gone for a nice walk this afternoon, to see the surf which I know you would have enjoyed. Teddy, I long so for some nice quiet little evenings with you alone; it makes me so homesick to think I shall not see you for so long, for I love to be with you so much. Don't you think I am pretty good to write you every day? I suppose you laugh and say, these funny letters, they sound just like Alice. Good night and sweet dreams.

> Your loving
> Alice

Do keep well and enjoy yourself.

Darling,

Yesterday evening I took the six o'clock train from Bismarck, and sat up till ten playing whist with a party of jolly young Englishmen. Then I tumbled into my bunk and at two o'clock tumbled out, at Little Missouri station. It was bitterly cold. At breakfast (before which we all washed in the same tin basin) I met a wide awake Yankee, who received me with the greatest cordiality, and got me to at once shift my things over to the company's ranch building, where I have a room to myself and am very comfortable. He also took me out for a ride over the surrounding country. It is a very desolate place, high, barren hills, scantily clad with coarse grass and here and there in sheltered places a few stunted cottonwood trees; "washouts," deepening at times into great canyons, and steep cliffs of most curious formation about everywhere, and it was a marvel to me to see how easily our mustangs scrambled over the frightful ground which we crossed, while trying to get up to the grassy plateaus, over which we could gallop.

If I do not have time to write I will telegraph, saying when I will be with you. I shall pray for you every night; good bye my doubly dear,

Ever Your Loving
Thee

My own dearest Teddy,

How I wish it was three weeks from today, our wedding day. I perfectly remember my promise not to have the faintest alarm Teddy, and I know that I shall not; as I just long to be with you all the time and never separate from you, even for three weeks. Teddykins, I know you can make me happy and you must never think it would have been better for me, if we had never met; I should die without you now, Teddy and there is not another man I ever could have loved in this world. You are a naughty boy to write me such a blue letter. You must not think that I think you the least exacting, Teddy,

I am going to try and be a good wife for you. I shall write you again tomorrow, with much love

> Your loving
> Alice

Darling,

Last night I reached here in safety and have been having a very pleasant time. I am of course a good deal laid up, but unless I become very much worse I shall try to stay out here, as I like the country air and think it good. Today—I feel as badly sitting still as walking—I took a long stroll, quite forgetting my own unhappiness. Give my best love to all the other dear ones.

Goodbye my own heart's blessing, you don't know how I miss you.

> Ever Your Fond
> Thee

My dearest Teddy,

I have a few moments before dinner to write you in. Teddy-kins I heard someone say, that they did not think you looked well, every time I think of you I get more and more blue, do take good care of yourself. I will take care of you, for I am going to try very hard to be a good wife to you. Teddy, I shall be so very happy, it seems too good to be true that we are going to be married. I just long for the time to come. I do love you so very much Teddy. You must excuse the looks of this letter paper and ink, it is all I can do to write. Give a great deal of love to all and much for yourself dear Teddy.

> Ever your loving
> Alice

Alice folded the letters, just thinking how her life was an unexpected adventure with her Theodore Roosevelt. And ranch owners! How exciting. She longed for the days she would be with him on those lands.

THE WEDDING DAY: October 27, 1880. An apple-crisp afternoon, the air fresh, sweet, aromatic with autumn's scents. Fluffy clouds dotted a blue sky. Alice peered out with wet eyes at an oak tree outside Unitarian Church, where through the rust-colored leaves the bright red head of her favorite bird couldn't distract her from the tension. With the carriage parked, she lifted her lace-gloved hand to wipe tears from her cheeks before they might stain her white silk gown with its slight puff sleeve. In the other hand, she held the locket with Nana's picture; Alice needed her guidance today after what she had learned. The timing of her mother's confession could not have been worse with just the two of them inside the carriage as Alice was about to marry the man of her dreams. Today of all days! The news left Alice numb.

"At least the weather is nice," her mother remarked, as if minutes before she had not brought ruin to Alice's wedding day.

Sniffles and quiet sobs came from Alice; she could not help but cry.

"Oh, Alice, stop with the theatrics."

Alice recognized that scowl disguised as a smirk. "Theatrics? This is my life you are talking about." Her hands began to tremble with anger.

Mamma's face reddened, then she shrugged. "I'd no other choice. It was Harvard or finishing school, and the finishing school needed a final answer and the answer was yes, of course. You could not go into your débutante without your certificate. You know that."

"I worked with Papa for a month on that application for collegiate studies."

"You agreed to attend finishing school."

"You had me so drunk on elixirs for weeks. How could I think correctly?"

"And don't you be running to your father—he knows nothing of this." Mamma's face contorted, her mouth crooked. "That's the last thing he needs after today. You, leaving New England to move to New York of all places. I hear there's a fever there, rampant. Typhoid, they call it."

"How? How did you do it?"

"Darling, what does it matter now?" Her aloofness disturbed Alice even more. "I decided to finally get this information off my chest to prevent you from sulking for the rest of your days about being denied."

Alice started to feel light-headed. "How did you do it?"

"I have my ways, dear." She lifted her chin high.

Alice glared at her.

"The Chates offered their assistance and had the application pulled before it reached committee. You should be thanking them . . . and me."

Alice stayed silent, calmed her tears, and focused her eyes out the window again to see the bird perched on a branch, and spoke: "I spent so many years studying, working to grow mentally, intellectually. You know this would have meant the world to me. How could you do such a thing to your only daughter, Mamma?"

"Excuse me?"

"A mother is supposed to help her daughter."

"Look at you, Alice, all wet with tears. This is no way to walk into a church." She knocked on the glass to the carriage driver. "We are headed home," she barked.

"What are you doing?"

The carriage began to rock with forward movement.

"How could you go through with the nuptials, being so emotional as you are."

Alice grasped the locket with her nana's picture in her hand, recalling her words: *A baby bird can spread its wings, but the mother helps her fly.* She leaned over her mother, knocked on the glass, and gestured to the driver to stop moving the carriage. "You should have been there for me," she whispered at her mother, biting off each word.

"Oh, please. You'd have become an old maid."

Furor welled up inside of her. "And if I wanted to be an old maid, then damn it, Mamma, you should have supported me in becoming an old maid. That's what mothers are for, to support their baby girls and teach them to fly."

Her eyebrows jutted up.

"When I have a daughter, I'll tell you what I will do. I'll let her wear trousers!"

Mamma gasped.

"Just like I did under my débutante gown!"

Choking breaths came from the woman.

"And I'll let my little girl mess up her bed pillows if she wants, and pile her clothes in the closet if she wants, and not clean the kitchen if she doesn't want to, and you know what else I will let her do, Mamma?"

Mamma pursed her lips.

"I'll let her speak for herself, and I will support her in becoming not who I want her to be, but exactly the woman she wants to be, in the life of her choosing. And do you know what I am going to do now?"

A harumph came from her mother.

"I am going to marry the man who I fell in love with, the man who believes in me, and loves me for who I am." Alice marched out of the carriage and saw the redheaded bird flapping its wings.

Chapter Forty-two

Passion's Embrace

MASSASOIT HOTEL, SPRINGFIELD

The nuptials became quite tumultuous with Alice and her mother, both in tears after the ceremony. This, thankfully, did not continue through the reception for there was a kind of reconciliation with the two of them huddled and finally finding some type of peace after Mister Lee stepped in to calm Mrs. Lee's nerves, and Theodore brought Alice onto the banquet floor and kept her close to him.

And now Theodore noticed the sounds, logs snapping in the hearth and his heart thumping. Wearing a satin robe, he poured champagne into long-stem flutes; a whoosh, fizzing, champagne bubbles bursting, chattering. Every detail, his mind made a note of. Would he wake up from this fantasy? He could hardly believe his luck, and yet, stars sparkled outside the window of the honeymoon suite. His dream had come true.

A new sound: her footsteps. With a brush over the floor, each step brought her closer to the fire's light. A log crackled. He felt his mouth drop. The nightgown revealed his Alice. Sheer to the ground, her bare body shown through, her breasts touching the fabric. Feelings stirred in him as his heart beat louder. Her hips moved side to side, rounded and more beautiful than he could have imagined. "I could never have envisioned a picture so pretty," released from his mouth.

Her breath hitched as she arrived into his arms, sweet-smelling Alice, and her face rested on his, trembling. Cheek to cheek, he said softly, "I am living in a dreamland." He laid a kiss on her forehead.

A snap from the fire as flames roared, their flickering reflected in her eyes. He offered her a glass. She received it without releasing him from her gaze.

He had prepared what he would say to her, the words he'd wanted to speak all that time ago on the night of her débutante:

"I first saw you October 18, 1878, and fell in love with you as soon as I saw your face."

She sighed, her voice barely above a whisper. "Teddy, you never told me."

He wanted her to know this. He wanted her to know everything. "Love at first sight, Alice Hathaway Lee Roosevelt. You are my first love."

"As you are mine."

A faint clink came from the glasses touching, bubbles easing. He leaned into her ear. "'Who ever loved, that loved not at first sight?'"

Her cheeks glowed. "You charm me with Shakespeare."

A first sip tasted cool, effervescent.

"And 'I would not wish any companion in the world but you,'" she quoted.

He placed his lips upon hers, hearing a gentle sucking. She tasted heavenly, of bubbly.

"'My bounty is as boundless as the sea,' Alice, 'my love as deep. The more I give to thee, the more I have . . .'"

"'For both are infinite,'" she finished delicately and took another sip, slow and long. Shadows and light danced from the hearth. She smiled a sort of smile he had not seen before. A tempting curve to her lips, a sensuality she now shared with him, her husband. Her husband!

His hand reached around and touched the pure skin of her back, the gown low-cut. He held there, listening to her breathe in and out, champagne bubbles sparkling and alive; the moment raised him to another plane. Her head fell upon his shoulder. They swayed to the beat of their hearts, glasses still in hand. The heat of her body on his, the intensity too much. "When I hold you in my arms there is nothing on earth left to wish for," he murmured between kisses.

Her body stilled. "Shakespeare?"

He paused, then cupped her face into his hand. "Roosevelt."

She beamed.

He placed the flutes on the table near the fire with a tap and returned to her. Her hands landed full against his chest and smoothly moved the satin, releasing him from his garment. His muscles, she explored, first on his shoulders, and his arms, and then reached for his back. She leaned down, kissed his neck, and a whimper released from his lips.

His hands reached behind her neck and unclasped her bound hair, the strands tickling as they fell across his shoulders. Her eyes closed as he caressed her about the nape of her neck, kissing her from left to right.

"I perfectly worship you." His mouth she allowed to do what it wished, and it nibbled on her ear so that she tittered. He placed his hands about her hips and drew her close to where their hips were joined and he could feel each curve. He held her there, for there was no other place he ever wanted to be more than this. "What, Mrs. Roosevelt, can I give you to make you the happiest wife who has ever lived?"

"You."

Lips explored each other, and every inhibition erased from his mind.

"I am yours and you are mine," she tenderly breathed into his ear.

I am yours and you are mine. Never had he felt so close to her. Tongues lingered. He slipped the gown off her shoulders, then stepped back, her breasts holding the fabric from falling until gravity granted him his wish. His yearning for her grew more intense with every touch. He took hold of her, lifting her from the ground, carrying her to the bed with its softness like a cloud. Their bodies gave in to each other with pure, honest love, a sensation not before known, an intense happiness so sacred, it felt as if his soul joined in harmony with hers, as passion's embrace carried into the morning.

ECSTASY SHOULD HAVE followed them onto their European honeymoon but there was one problem: she had not gotten out of bed since they boarded the cruise liner. "I'm sicker than the devil and getting worse," she cried. "Don't leave me; when you're here at least I don't have any bad dreams."

Theodore knelt by her side inside the cabin. "I must tell you, my darling, our passage has been very nearly as gay as a funeral."

She clocked him on the head with a flirtatious tap.

"If ever a person heartily enjoyed a sea trip, it is certainly you," he laughed at her.

Her stomach grumbled. "I'm so hungry. Can you get me something to nibble on?"

"May I suggest my ear, because the last blessed meal you ate greeted me about twenty minutes later, with a gallop. Maybe we should ask the kind ship's doctor to come in and check on you."

"He'll suggest another mustard plaster. I cannot handle another one of those. It stuck to my face and emitted a most egregious smell."

"Even so."

"I know what would help. You putting on the hideous mustard seed mask and seeing how it makes you feel."

"Very well, no doctor. Would you like to continue your starveling existence on crackers again today?"

"On second thought, maybe you should get him: I feel another stomachic earthquake coming on." She sat up and held her belly. "I'm going to die! Here before the honeymoon even gets started. I'm going to die!"

"No one is dying on this trip, it's just seasickness."

"I hope so, but what if?"

FEELING VERY LIMP when they disembarked in Cork, Ireland, Alice displayed her marvelous powers of forgetting past woe, and in two hours' time, after having eaten several spoonfuls of beef stew, her head cleared, the shakes dissipated, and her stomach hungered for something else. The honeymoon had them kissing their way through Ireland with a special embrace amid wildflowers by the crumbling, ivy-covered, and picturesque old ruin of Blarney Castle.

FROM LONDON TO Liverpool, England, he had great fun as did she in the curious jaunting cars, the light two-wheeled carriages with the passengers' seat in front of the driver. They took hotels by storm, and when music was playing she had him dance every kind of dance, even those to which they did not quite know the steps. Their intimacy lasted well after midnight.

THEY SAILED THEIR way through the lakes of Italy and rowed the canals every evening in Venice. Alice had supreme enjoyments with eating and eating some more, then teasing Theodore about his lack of ability in the Italian language, moments which became quite comedic. His English with a smattering of German and some French proved useless. One night when they were served black coffee, which is all they wanted, Theodore gestured with his hand and added the dialectal, "c'est genuch." He thought the waiter understood that to mean, "that's enough." It seemed to have the opposite reaction for they were served pastry, cheeses, and fruit, all brought by the waiter in the hopes of satisfying this untranslatable request. Alice did not mind a bit and ate her way through.

IN PARIS, THEY debated their way through the City of Light. "Rembrandt or Rubens?" she asked, her hand holding his as they strolled through the Louvre Museum.

"Rembrandt," argued Theodore; "I am very much attracted by his strongly contrasting coloring, and I could sit for hours examining his heads, the features are so lifelike and expressive. By all odds, my favorite. Perhaps, the pictures I really most enjoy are the landscapes, the homely little Dutch and Flemish interiors, the faithful representations of how the people of those times lived and made merry and died."

"They bring out the life of that period."

"In a way no written history could do."

"Like the Baroque painter David Teniers the Younger."

"Or Adriaen Van Ostade of the Dutch Golden Age."

"I agree, and your feelings, Teddy, on Rubens?"

"I am not at all fond of his works."

Alice halted. "And how could you have such a distaste for the esteemed artist?"

"No painter can make the same face serve for Venus, the Virgin, and a Flemish lady. Rubens's three wives are represented in about fifty different ways."

"And here I thought you would have appreciated his women with their fleshy, swirling, sensuous extravagance."

"That did create a powerful impression."

She kissed him hard right there inside the art exhibit.

SAYING AU REVOIR to Paris, they traveled to Switzerland for a mountaineering adventure. The scenery was so captivating, it was beyond description; densely wooded to the water's edge, steep mountains surrounding them. Some of the cliffs overhung the edge and provided beautiful echoes, especially when their guide played his bugle. The sweet music repeated with a melody that was very eerie yet pleasing.

As he relished the imposing view, he expressed his deep feelings which grew more intense by the day, "It is perfectly impossible to tell you how much I love you."

"Mere words cannot express my love for you, either."

A kiss sealed their delight.

"Can you imagine a lovelier holiday?" she asked.

"This summer traveling with you, my dearest, through Europe, I have enjoyed greatly; the more I see, though, the better satisfied I am to return home with you where we are American." He held up his head, proudly. "Free born and free bred, where we acknowledge no person as our superior." He brought her into his arms in a tight embrace. "After my climb up the Matterhorn, let's go home, Mrs. Roosevelt."

Chapter Forty-three

———◄•►———

Sweet Home

MANHATTAN

Home. New York City. The months that had passed since the honeymoon felt invigorating. She liked just saying to herself, "I live in New York City!" Settling down here brought her true happiness. When with Theodore, she just adored how they spent hours talking as he drove them in his dogcart, sometimes along Riverside Drive, and other times they floated in swan boats in Central Park. When he was away from her, although she missed him, she was glad of how her time was filled exploring the museums and libraries and helping with charities, like the Newsboy House, where she and Motherling would bring homemade dinners. Alice made hot cross buns and had become quite good in the kitchen, although they did have help from a cook at the Roosevelt residence. Thankful she was to have Bamie, who so kindly laid out the long list of necessities to those working at the household. Alice let out a laugh remembering how Teddy, upon reading his sister's guide, commented about the one duty, as Bamie wrote: "Every morning the cook should meet the ashman with a pail of boiling water." Teddy demanded, "What has the poor ashman done to deserve a daily scalding?"

Theodore was studying law at Columbia University, and after much personal reflection had decided to run for political office, and had won. He was elected to the New York State Assembly for the 23rd district. His platform was clear: reform labor laws, outlaw racial segregation, advance park and forestry programs, and take on corrupt politicians. His father would have been immensely proud. She was proud, too, that Theodore would help usher in change in government. Much needed to be done.

As Alice waited for the doctor to arrive this morning for a last-minute appointment, she sat down at her desk and opened the rectangular box that was nearly filled to the top with their love letters. She needed to pass the time. Theodore would be returning for the weekend from Albany that afternoon:

My purest and sweetest little wife,
Oh, my sweetest true-love pray for nothing but that I may be worthy of you; you are the light and sunshine of my life, and I can never cease thanking the Good God who gave you to me; I could not live without you, and I care for <u>nothing whatever</u> else but you. I wish for nothing but to have you to love and cherish all the days of my life, and you have been more to me than any other wife could be to any other husband. You are, all in all, my heart's darling, and I care for nothing else; and you have given me more than I can ever repay.

The canvas is getting on superbly; there seems to be a good chance of my election, but I don't care, anyway. I enclose a piece from the Evening Post; be sure and keep all the newspaper scraps for me. I am

Your Ever Loving
Thee

You darling Teddy,

At night I miss your dear strong arm to lay my poor tired head on. I love you so much. I do hope you had a good rest last night in the cars; please try and get to bed before twelve every night; you are looking tired and not as well as your wife would wish; she will take good care of you. We had some very good games of tennis this morning. I beat Rose in a single-handed game much to her disgust. We had such a good time and it is delightful to see her so happy. This week we are going to be quite gay.

>   With love dearest Thee

>>   Your devoted wife
>>   Alice

My Blessed Little Wifie,

I felt as if my heart would break when I left, and I have just longed for her here in this beastly Hotel. I cannot say how I feel when I think of the cozy little room, with its pretty furniture and well stocked book shelves, a bright fire of soft coal in the grate, and above all my mistress, with some soft, dainty dress on, to sit and play backgammon with.

>   Here I am managing my canvas with great zeal. The fight is a very hot one; my chances of winning seem about even, but the result is impossible to foresee.

>>   Ever Your Loving
>>   Thee

My dearest Thee,

I have just received your little card. I do wish you would write me a little longer letter. I should like to hear a little more what you are doing. You are never out of my thoughts for a moment. Teddy, although you do tease me a little, I should so like to have you here just to kiss me.

With love

Your loving wife
Alice

Darling Wifie,

I have drawn blood by my speech, and have come in for any amount both of praise and abuse from the newspapers. It is rather the hit of the season so far, and I think I have made a success of it. Letters and telegrams of congratulation come pouring in on me from all quarters. But the fight is severe still, and today I got a repulse in endeavouring to call up the debate from the table. How it will turn out in the end no one can now tell.

I hope that you are getting well by this time, my poor, pretty, patient darling. I wish I could be with you while you have your nervous fits, to cheer you up and soothe you; I just long to hold her in my arms, and kiss her, and pet her, and love her. I am dreadfully sorry I cannot be with you. With best love to all

Ever Your Devoted
Thee

She did love his letters, especially when he sent drawings, little sketches of birds and boats. She kept them all, along with every article related to the elections. On November eighth, she remembered it well as her Theodore was elected by a 1,500-vote majority as its youngest member, at age twenty-three. The champagne toasts, the cheers, friends and family filled their home all through the night.

The reaction was not so celebratory in Albany, and it still irked her. When she joined Theodore on one trip, she read terrible things. They called her Theodore names in the papers, all kinds of names, like "young squirt," "weakling," or in the case of the Speaker of the House who said he was "just a damn fool." But what may have frustrated her to the core was when that same man assessed the strength of the party in the House as sixty and a half members. A half a member!

She continued reading:

Darling Wifie,
All—whether on the floor of the house or in the newspapers—
are now howling at me; and the hardest thing to stand is the
complacent pity of the shallow demagogues who delight to see
a better man than themselves stumble, or seem to stumble. I
would not care a snap of my finger if they would attack me
where I could hit back. Not a man has dared to say anything
to my face that I have not repaid him for with interest; but it is
the attacks I cannot answer that I mind. Still, I am rapidly getting hardened, and shall soon cease to care anything about it.
    With many kisses for your sweet self, I am
                                        Ever Your Fond
                                        Thee

My dearest Teddykins,
Your little card came this morning, how I do love to hear
from you. I think you are the dearest boy to write me so
much. Yesterday Ro and I went to Salem for the day. They
all asked after you and were awfully disappointed not to see
you. This morning Poor Mamma has been having one of her
ill turns; she suffers so with it but I am happy to say it did not
last more than an hour. We have not had one warm day since

I have been here; the wind is something frightful. I have got to go in town this morning. You dear old Teddy, I shall have you here next Saturday night. I shall not let anyone look at you as I shall want you all to myself.

> With love to all the family
> ever
> Your <u>baby</u> wife,
> Alice H. Roosevelt

Darling, best beloved, little Wife,
I am just going to bed, and sit down at my desk to talk to you for a minute. How I have missed my little teasing, laughing, pretty witch! My little, sweet, pure queen, I have had no one to jog my arm and make me blot the paper while I was writing; it always made me feel rather bad-tempered, but I loved it all the same. I feel dreadfully lonely going to bed without you. Be sure not to catch cold.

> Your Devoted Husband and
> Lover,
> Thee

You dearest Teddy,
It was so good of you to write me this sweet little card. How I should like to be with you. Your card made me more homesick, as I thought of you making your little <u>boats</u>, up till all hours in the night with no one to call you to bed. I wish it would be day all the time, as I miss you so much more at night; although you do tease me. I love it and you dearly. Everyone thinks I am looking so well and you must keep so.

> Your devoted wife,
> Alice

Darling Little Wife,

I have missed you more than I can tell; I have no little, pretty, teasing witch to greet me when I come in, or to take out riding; and I have to read the bible all to myself, without having pretty Queenie standing beside me in front of the looking glass, combing out her hair. There is no pretty, sleepy, little rosebud face to kiss and love when I wake in the morning; nor any sweet, loving heart to whom I can confide all the little joys and pains of the day. How I shall rejoice to be with you again!

I have just come upstairs, and as soon as I have finished this little letter I am going to bed.

I am longing more than words can express to hold my own sweetest, purest queen in my arms again,

Ever Your Devoted

Husband and Lover

He had arrived back from Albany; she had much to tell him on this hot and muggy July day, especially after the doctor's house call to her. Theodore had not given her a moment to talk since they had begun their stroll from their home on West Forty-fifth Street. The late afternoon sky displayed soft purple colors. The breeze smelled fresh and flowery, fragrant with pink lilies. Walking awhile, hearing the clops of hoofs and the squeak of the horse-drawn carriages, Alice headed them toward Central Park West.

"Being the youngest there has its challenges," he continued.

She let him go on, wrapping her arm around his.

"Have I told you that according to a *New York Sun* reporter, I'm known for my 'elastic movements, voluminous laughter, and wealth of mouth'?"

"Well, I like your mouth just fine." Her lace-gloved hand touched his bottom lip, though it kept moving as he talked.

"The House contains a rare set of scoundrels. Brains," both of his hands clutched his head, "less than a guinea pig." He turned to her as he picked up his pace. "Do you know what the governor told us upon our proposal to have the state establish Niagara Falls as a park?"

"What?'

"'But, gentlemen,'" Theodore made his voice falsely lofty. "'Why should we spend the people's money when just as much water will run over the Falls without a park as with it?'"

"Outrageous."

"Sooner or later the people of New York will realize that it is not sufficient merely to have a head of government, but that they must have one who shall also be entirely free from political entanglement."

She really did need to tell him her news, she almost could not wait another second, but decided it best to first arrive at the spot she had imagined as best suited for the revelation. "It seems New York needs you now more than ever."

"This host of sinecurists have no regard for rendering the people service, but only care for protecting political factions."

"And your speech on the corruption bill?" She knew the answer to this, having read the reaction in the papers.

"I think I made a nice strike. I did not do as well as I have sometimes done, but it still was one of my best speeches—though I do not know that that is saying much. I did not forget a word, nor was I at all embarrassed."

"Whatever do you mean?"

"I doubt if it pays to learn a speech by heart, for I felt just like a schoolboy reciting his piece. Besides, I do not speak enough from the chest."

"You jest?"

"My voice is not as powerful as it ought to be."

"I respectfully disagree and it seems so did the journalists. *The Evening Post* said you stated the arguments in an admirable speech with clearness and force. *The New York Times* wrote that your argument . . . was conclusive and unanswerable. I kept the papers for you." She found a nice garden bench for them to take a seat.

"By the way, our friends in Albany are all very much taken with you, Mrs. Roosevelt."

She chose this place knowing it was close to Theodore's heart. The American Museum of Natural History, a treasure with its Victorian Gothic architecture, stood five stories high. And of course, with his father having been one of the founders, it was an ideal place to share with him the news.

Theodore inhaled deeply, closed his eyes, placed his hands on his knees, feet flat, seeming to decipher the sounds in nature. "I think I hear your bird."

"My bird?"

"Birds."

"The cherry-headed one?"

"Yes, listen for the shrill call, followed by a sound like *charr, charr*. Must be a nest of them."

She mirrored his form, her hands on her knees. "I don't hear it."

"Concentrate, you'll hear." He leaned over and placed his hands right above hers. They were big and warm.

She disentangled from the noise around her—the sound of carriage wheels on gravel, steps on the stone path—and breathed. The welcome notes came through. She held herself for a moment in their calls, in the bliss. This is the time, she told herself. Speak, now. "Mister Roosevelt?" She opened her eyes to see his head tilt. "I believe we may be starting a nest of our own."

"A nest?"

"You're going to be a father." She studied him, concentrating, not shifting her eyes away from him.

He leaped from his seated position, and she tried to read all that was happening on his face. A flush in his cheek, something like a smile, his mouth shaping words but no speech coming. He waved his hands as if to signal his emotions, then bent over and slapped palms to knees. "This is true?"

"The doctor visited me today and he says I have every symptom of having a child!"

"A nest of our own? What capital news! A nest of our own!"

"I had him come and now I am so delighted as it has, at last, made me think I was truly to have a baby. Before it seemed too good to be true."

"Before?"

"I thought maybe, however, we know now for certain."

Falling to his knees, he brought her hand to his lips and kissed it. "When, my blessed heart's darling?"

"The doctor thought I ought to engage my nurse from the fifth of February as it is very likely to come between that time and the thirteenth or twentieth."

He placed his hands around her waist and dropped his head in her lap. "The world has given me more than I could ever wish."

She stroked his hair. "Do you think it might be a boy, or maybe a precious little girl?"

"Well now, if it's a girl, I will have fifty kisses for her." He reached up and kissed Alice on the forehead, and the nose, from one cheek to the other, and one that stayed for many heartbeats on her lips. "I shall love and prize the little thing. She will be very, very dear to my heart."

"And if it's a boy?"

"If it's a boy, a wee, wee, bunny baby boy—well," he stood up tall, head high, "I think he would grow up to be a great strapping Roosevelt!"

AS MONTHS PASSED, Bamie prepared the nursery, choosing the decor, and wanting it to be a grand surprise for Alice who was so grateful being that she had not been feeling all that well.

Today, Bamie escorted her, walking slowly to reveal what was behind the door. Alice felt excited and nervous at the same time, although she had complete trust in her decorator.

The handle turned. The door opened. And Alice immediately began to cry. Yellow and green wallpaper, decorated with hopping bunnies, and gold silk curtains held in place with bows of ribbons at the top along the rod; a wicker bassinet trimmed with muslin and lace with a canopy to match, and a most darling rocking chair with brass mounts.

"Bamie, it is perfect!"

"Believe me, my darling little friend, I am here for you always, and your children."

"Children?" Alice hugged her belly. "I would love a pile of them!"

A sound at the door. Motherling teared up upon entering.

Alice rushed to her and gave her the biggest of hugs. "Can you believe how beautiful it is?"

Motherling cried full, and Bamie joined in the embrace.

"Your Theodore will be most pleased," Motherling said, smiling a grand smile.

Together they walked from furniture piece to curtains, and even to a dresser with itsy-bitsy clothing inside.

What a thrill she felt, and what a blessing to have these two at her side, caring for her, and her baby.

"And my darling Alice, this letter just arrived for you."

They gave her privacy as she opened the envelope. It was from Theodore.

Darling Wife,

My own tender true love, I never cease to think fondly of you; and oh how doubly tenderly I feel towards you now. You have been the truest and tenderest of wives, and you will be the sweetest and happiest of all little mothers.

Goodbye, sweetheart,

Your Ever Loving
Thee

She headed to her bedchamber and sat at her desk to write him back:

My dearest Thee

Poor baby has been a "little under the weather" and has had to keep on her back for the last few days, or she would have written before. Ted, I do love you so much and just long for Tuesday to be with you again; please don't work this hard. I know you will get tired out. I have so much more to tell you, but it will have to wait. With love and many kisses ever,

Your loving wifie,

Alice H. Roosevelt

The days that followed were so busy with preparations for the baby, Alice hardly had a moment to sit down, except when her darling's letter arrived:

Darling Wifie,

I have just received your dear little note; I look forward so much to seeing you tomorrow. I wish I could be with you to rub you when you get "crampy."

Today I do not anticipate that there will be much fun in the legislature.

Ever Your Loving

Thee

Love between them grew stronger as the date neared. Alice highly anticipated his return, and then they would depart for Chestnut Hill. One last visit to her parents' home before the baby arrived.

LEAVE IT TO Mamma to quash a thoroughly enthusiastic day that included them arriving in Chestnut Hill by teatime to receive the news that Minot had asked for Rose's hand, that Bob Bacon had betrothed Martha Cowdin in a secret ceremony, and that Fannie Farmer had sent over cherry sherbet.

Alice and Theodore sat in the Lee parlor with Papa in his armchair. George and Rose sat next to Alice, who was excited to pass around the tintypes of Theodore's time out West before the wedding. Alice held up a funny picture of him in a frilled shirt. They laughed. Mamma sat with them, too, straight backed and not even pretending to mind the tintypes. Instead, she knit baby booties.

Mamma interrupted. "I don't mean to alarm you." Her eyes lifted from the knitting. She cocked her head and looked at Theodore. "I nearly died in childbirth with Alice."

A hush fell over the room. Theodore's posture straightened, his hand over his chest. He appeared stunned.

Mamma placed the needles down to pull an embroidered cloth from her sleeve and wipe her forehead. "I suffered hideous agony."

Alice tried to get up but tottered and fell back into the chair. "Please, Mamma. I cannot deal with exaggerations today." Once again, Mamma was being strange and rude, dousing Alice's happiness.

"This is complete truth. Tell her."

"That was a long time ago, Caroline," replied Papa.

"But the truth!" Her mother shot her father a look.

Papa rose from his chair and walked to Alice. "Yes, 'tis the truth. Your Mamma went in and out in a sort of delirium, speaking of this and that, of light, of dark. But after that, you were born, healthy," he said reassuringly. "And all was fine."

"Why did you think Georgie is so distant in years from you?" Mamma asked her. "I had nervous fits just the same as you. Still do. You have seen it yourself."

"All these years, you said nothing to me about childbirth."

Rose rushed to Alice's side, knelt down, and held her hand. "Oh, dear."

"Ladies do not speak on such subjects as childbirth." Mamma waved a dismissive hand at Alice. "But I felt it important you be forewarned. And Theodore, I am terribly sorry your mother could not accept the invitation for a visit."

Theodore was mum. Alice, too. She tried to reconcile in her mind this revelation and whether she should be worried deeply about the birth.

"Your mother?" Mamma queried. "I hear she's not well."

"She really seems much better," Alice answered, being that she had spent the morning with Motherling. "Her chest is still very uncomfortable, but she was well enough to be up and dressed and very busy with everyone in the house."

"I hear typhoid is rampant in Manhattan," snapped Mamma. "But we will be there nonetheless for the special day. And I hear your sister will be assisting Alice with the baby."

"Bamie is a dream come true, Mamma," Alice again answered. "She's been so beyond anything I could ask for." Thank goodness for Bamie and Motherling; she did not know what she would do without them and now was more eager than ever to get back to them.

"What of this swelling?" Mamma pointed to Alice's ankles. "Add to that, your face, your hands, and your feet are swollen, too."

"The doctor in New York prescribed rest. My indisposition is a symptom of being with child. That is all."

Theodore rushed over a footrest and helped lift Alice's feet as she mouthed "I'm sorry" to him. It was never easy being around Mamma, no matter how hard Alice tried to continue their relationship. There always seemed to be friction when they were together.

"All's well that ends well," said Papa, seeming to try to settle the matter.

Alice felt anything but well.

"Show me the horse!" George, whose attention had not left those pictures, requested of Theodore.

"What kind of place is this that you've bought yourself in the West?" Papa asked inquisitively, settling himself back into his armchair.

"Ranches," Theodore replied, shuffling through the pictures, but all the while Alice could feel his discomfort. He pulled out one of the landscape and walked over to hand it to her father. "Part of the great belt of grazing land that stretches from the rich wheat farms of Central Dakota to the Rocky Mountains, and southward to the Black Hills and the Big Horn chain." He showed him, then looked to Alice, then back at Papa. "Almost the only industry is stock-raising. The heart of broken country, some might say, dreary and foreboding."

"I like the triangle patch of white in his hair." George skipped over to Theodore with another picture.

"On the horse or me, Georgie?" Theodore leaned down to him and tapped his nose.

"Thee, show Georgie the one with your cowbay hat and boots?" Alice tried to lighten the mood, mostly her own.

"The fashion of the West," he said to George.

"What would you want with broken country, anyhows?" Mamma kept up her testy tone.

"Auntie Caroline, I hear its rugged beauty is striking," interjected Rose.

"And where do you clean yourself?" Mamma asked, curtly. "When you're in that godforsaken place."

Alice shook her head in disgust. "Mamma!"

Theodore took it in stride. "Not sure you are going to approve, but the truth is I was dirty—in fact, I had not taken off my clothes for two weeks."

Mamma's brows jutted up.

"Not even at night, except for one bath in the river—but I slept, ate, and worked as I never could do in ten years' time in the city. The Bad Lands make a good cattle country, plenty of nourishing grass," explained Theodore. "The cattle keep close to them in cold months, and in summer they wander on the broad prairies stretching back from them or come down on the river bottoms."

"Well, there can be no more disappearing now, to wherever that place is, especially with Alice in this condition," snipped Mamma.

Alice got herself up and stood by her husband. She held his hand and told him she loved him.

Chapter Forty-four

———◆◇◆———

The Departure

They left Chestnut Hill by the 5:48 p.m. train and reached Grand Central late that night. Theodore unpacked one bag and packed another, a larger case with clothes for a week in Albany. He left the next morning, slipping out of bed so as not to disturb Alice. As soon as he arrived in his chambers, a telegram was waiting for him, noting his mother had fallen sick. Theodore made quick plans to head right back home, until word came from Elliott that her fever had somewhat subsided.

The next day, Alice's letter arrived:

My dearest Teddy,
I suppose you have received my telegram telling you how sick your motherling has been. It was a bad attack of indigestion, which began from after we left New York and lasted late up into the afternoon, she suffered frightfully but is now very much better.

You dear boy, you don't know how I miss you. I have loved you so much; you must not dirty your new clothes or bile your handkerchiefs, unless you want me to fuss—I will write you how Mother is on Saturday. I hate so to have her sick and you must not show this note to anyone.

Your loving wife,
Alice H. Roosevelt

Good night you dear Thee, your little wife only wishes she might be with you tonight, she loves you so much.

Another letter arrived for him from Alice two days later. Angst filled him as soon as Theodore removed it from the envelope; the words were scrawled in pencil, the paper itself had been torn with jagged edges on the side:

Darling Thee,

I don't think you need feel worried about my being sick as the Dr told me this afternoon that I would not need my nurse before Thursday. I am feeling well tonight but am very much worried over the baby and your little Mother, her fever is still very high and the Dr is rather afraid of typhoid, it is not in the least catching. I will write again tomorrow and let you know just how she is—don't say anything about it till then. I do love my dear Thee _so_ much. I wish I could have my little new baby to look after.

Your loving wifie
Alice

Theodore had never needed the evening train to move faster; instead, it crawled. A hundred-forty-five-mile journey and the minutes were thick as the fog outside his window with wetness that left a person's coat moist.

"Mark it down. February thirteenth. It is suicidal weather." The ticket checker, as if he were the weather bureau, spoke aloud to no one as he walked up the aisle, pausing near Theodore to say, "Life does not seem worth living on a day such as today."

Theodore had seen him on every ride, and on every ride he did this sort of thing: waxing melancholy. Today was not the day to hear such things.

"Air that suggests death and decay in the dampness that fills the world, clings to the house door, drips from the fences, coats the streets with liquid nastiness, moistens one's garments, and paints the sky lead-color," the uniformed man said as he walked back, trying to get anyone's attention. "But, with blind faith, we cling to the old adage, 'The darkest day, live till to-morrow, will have pass'd away.'"

His words dredged up Theodore's concerns, returning his mind to the telegram he had received when on the Assembly chambers floor. A fellow member rushed over to him asking why he looked so troubled. He had no time to respond. He raced out within seconds, headed for the station.

He removed it from the satchel and read it again:

February 13, 1884
You have a little daughter. The mother only fairly well.

He recalled the words of her Mamma: "I almost died in child-birth."

He turned to the ticket checker. "What is the arrival time to Grand Central?"

"Forty minutes or so," answered the man.

Grey mist covered the glass of the window, the air chilly and raw. To distract himself, Theodore opened *The New York Times,* the pages in his lap:

Weather

The sun has risen, but we have not seen it. Daylight has come, but only in that uncertain, vague, and murky fashion peculiar to a meteorological condition from which the planets have been eliminated. Somewhere, the moon has been at her full. We have caught but one ravishing glimpse of her beauty. The stars are blotted out. The sky is veiled in a sombre fray that conceals the clouds, drops wetly down over towers, spires, and masts, and partially veils even the fierce white light of the electric lamps that blaze along the thoroughfares. The day is short, for it is curtailed at both ends by the phenomenal gloom that darkens the weeping sky.

Happy is he who can draw his curtains, light his lamp, and forget the dripping darkness that fills the world, outside. But the all-pervading moisture filters into every crevice and cranny of one's retreat. The atmosphere is laden with a chill.

A hiss told Theodore that the train was on approach to the station, the wheels oscillating before coming to a standstill. Porters bustled. Passengers neared the exit doors: an impatient merchant carrying his wares, a forlorn businessman wearing a black suit carrying a case, and a simple man kindly smiling, wrapping his belongings with a cloth.

The guard exited and blew his whistle. Theodore gathered his things to get out quickly, which he did, pardoning himself to be first off the train. The large clock on the platform read ten thirty, and Theodore rushed out of the station, following the lights of the lampposts until he arrived, No. 6 West Fifty-seventh Street, his motherling's address, the place his father breathed his last breaths six years prior, the place where his Alice was staying and blessing him now with a child. A glare of gaslight came from the window on the third floor; the baby must have been there with her.

He anxiously pounded at the door, with a heavy knock.

His brother Elliott answered, his face white as a ghost: "There is a curse on this house!"

Theodore raced in.

Elliott spoke, an ominous quiver about his lips. "Mother is dying, and Alice, too. If you want to see Motherling, you must do so at this moment. She has little time."

Chapter Forty-five

The Clock Strikes

MANHATTAN

Too many people in the room, Alice heard a rush of footsteps tapping the floor, a doctor, a nurse, Mamma, the doctor again. The sound became muffled as she drifted away.

what is happening to me where am i warm vapor fills this place that looks like a moor desolate i trudge through the thick murkiness i must find my way back back to where i hear a whistle no no not a whistle a cry

A dazzling heat forced her eyes to open. Alice shook her head hard. Before her was magic. As blue as the crystal blue ocean were her treasure's eyes.

"You ought to have been a little boy," Mamma's words came through clear.

The precious one could not have been more beautiful. "I love a little girl." Alice's words came breathy and broken, as if shaken out of her throat. Mamma helped Alice hold the baby, and she slowly lifted Alice's head to plant a kiss on her soft, full cheeks.

the grey haze interrupts foggy dismal am i going please no no there in the distance an emerging star that way i don't want to go i want to stay here here my feet plant themselves into the moist ash

"Wake up, Alice!" Her Papa's hands brought her back. He gently touched her cheeks, then her forehead.

curtains of gloom close from both sides of the room until they meet in the middle unbearable depressing my feet leave the ash and walk on the hot coals

"She's hot, too hot, get the doctor!" Papa hollered. "Stay with me, Alice."

what have you done between the clicks i held her nana i held my baby in my arms her cheeks are full eight and three-fourths pounds i kissed her i need to go back to her back to my baby

She heard the tapping of Mamma's heels on the floor until she was by her bedside, putting coldness on her forehead and laying a cool towel behind her neck. "The baby is beautiful, just like you, Alice. Her hair is light brown, with whisps of golden sunshine, like yours. She is a perfect little girl."

Why are you weeping, Mamma? she wanted to say, but her voice was silent. So thirsty; Papa helped her drink water from a glass like those days and nights bedridden, and Mamma now prayed: "O Lord God, I come to You for help and guidance. Give me grace to bear my child's sickness with strength and patience. Bless me, O Father, and restore my Alice to health. Help me do what is needed to protect her. Do not forsake us, but give us an assurance of Your loving Kingdom."

She has your eyes, Papa, like a crystal sky. What a beautiful toast you made on the day of the nuptials. How fitting it is now: The bright days are made brighter, and when the shadows come, they are made less dark by the fact that you have a true and loving heart to turn to for sympathy. We are ready to take you into our hearts and give to you a share of that love. Why are you crying, Papa?

The baby's cries in the distance hurt Alice's heart. Bring her back so I can see into her eyes, Mamma. There she was in Bamie's arms. Bamie, you're here, thank goodness, you are here, keep the baby close, Bamie. Tell her, Bamie, to be the girl she wants to be. A tiny sneeze came from the child. "Please, please, don't let my baby catch cold," Alice whispered, her voice returning.

"I hear you, Alice, I hear you."

The baby sneezed again.

"Bamie . . ."

"I promise you, Alice, I will. I will keep her safe."

tears fall from a weeping sky my nightdress drips wet on my skin a clearing in the old growth the haze is lifting the darkness changing to brightness with a fierce golden blaze

A shot of unexpected sweetness touched her lips. Love.

"I am here, my blessed heart's darling. I am here."

Peace rushed through her, the pain disappearing. Did you feel it, Teddy, in your heart? Our baby found a place in mine to snuggle. Kisses on Alice's cheeks. It's as if I came out of my own body and embraced her until my soul was too full! She wanted to say these words but words refused to release from her lips. Kisses on Alice's head. Tell her, Teddy, to be the girl she wants to be. Run wild. Make trouble. Wear trousers, little one. Wear lace. Wear whatever you want, and worry not about the bed pillows lined in formation, for those things will take care of themselves. His head on her chest. Isn't she more than anything we could have ever dreamed? We did it, Teddy. We made a perfect little girl. The world is yours now, Teddy. Make the world a better place for our little girl. Please, Teddy. Please. He was kneeling. He rose and climbed into bed with her. He laid next to her and wrapped his arms around her.

open the curtain says motherling see the sunrise the clock's hand strikes brilliance enters every pore glorious dawns birth beautiful adventures light lifts her floating aren't they beautiful the wings

fly Alice i will help you.

Forty-six

———◆◆◆———

Here Roams Theodore

COWBOY LAND, NORTH DAKOTA

SUMMER 1886

THE PRESENT

I miss her today. I missed her yesterday and all the days since that day more than two years ago when she was in my arms, and I did not want her to go, and I begged her to breathe. *Breathe, Alice. Breathe.*

I travel now with no light but that of the stars as the westering moon sinks out of sight. My horse treads his own way down to the creek bottom, which is sometimes filled with quicksand or mud holes. This one looks to be simply a grass meadow.

My mind sits on those prior years of happiness such as rarely come to man and woman. On that February day, our baby girl was born. In the hours afterward my wife became insensible, and died in my arms at two o'clock on Thursday afternoon, February 14, Saint Valentine's Day. When my heart's dearest died, the light left me, and I believed wholeheartedly that for joy, for sorrow, my life had been lived out. I remember that large X that I drew in my journal that day.

A half mile to go ahead of me. From the sides of the meadow abruptly rise steep, high buttes with jagged crests.

I watch the sky turn crimson with the glow of the unrisen sun. Chains upon chains of steep hills fill the landscape, broken country that extends for miles, except for that deep valley. Toward there, I ride.

Such a strange and terrible fate when death came to her. I begin to hum the hymn from that grim day of her funeral, as I move:

While I draw this fleeting breath,
When mine eyelids close in death,
When I rise to worlds unknown,
And behold Thee on Thy throne,
Rock of Ages, cleft for me,
Let me hide myself in Thee.

She was truly beautiful in face and form, and lovelier still in spirit; as a flower, she grew, and as a fair young flower she died. Her life had been always in the sunshine, tender and happy as a young wife; and when she had just become a mother, when her life seemed to be but just begun, when the future seemed so bright ahead of her—she was stolen from me, robbed of her years.

The eastern heavens grow brighter, and a dark form suddenly appears against the skyline in that direction, on the crest of a bluff directly ahead of me. A good look tells me that it is an antelope, which stands motionless, like so many silhouettes, its outstretched horns vividly outlined against the light, as if to welcome me.

The pastor that day at the funeral, with those words so truthful: "There is something very peculiar and unusual in the conditions in which we are gathered together. That two members of the same church, two members of the same family, dwelling together in the same house, should on the same day be taken out of this mortal life, and on the same day, with the same services, to their last resting-place—this is surely something very peculiar, very solemnizing, deeply affecting."

Oh, how could Bright's disease, undiagnosed for years, take your life? And how could typhoid fever take Motherling's? "Motherling, how I miss you," I say aloud, eyeing the heavens. "I'm sure Father had missed you more."

"Death means more than taking us out of this life," is what the pastor preached. "The death of a believer means the taking of him into the life above—the heavenly and glorious life, the highest being, the loftiest society." The words I will keep close.

Near a brushy ravine, I guide Manitou to a place where he will neither stumble nor strike his hooves against rocks. Then I dismount a little up the side of the hill. I remove the simple tools from my leather satchel and near a stream, beside sagebrush, and I begin to dig. The quick and bold odor of sage fills the air; dirt from my spade flies to and fro.

The tops of the hills grow rosy as I pause to focus again. The antelope is still there. I return to the satchel and retrieve the framed picture. I have kept this one treasure with me, today holding it to my chest, reminding me of the day my life was complete. She was so beautiful in her white lace gown.

"Our baby girl has your eyes," I tell her, although she knows, for I have told her a thousand times, and she saw our precious herself, she did. Those dazzling blue eyes and a pile of hair. Bamie gave our little girl a locket of your hair to have something of you with her forever. How Bamie loved you. And she has loved our girl as her own. She's written down so many loving memories of you and has told our little one how you loved her so dearly.

I don't bother to wipe my tears as into the dirt hole I place our wedding picture. If I'm to carry on somehow, I cannot take you with me. I cannot even say your name. I cannot go on that way. This is the only way. Here in this very spot, the sun will always rise upon you.

I set myself down onto the dirt, eyes upwards, and wait and listen.

Why did I leave home in the first place? I could never answer that question when people asked me, except to think the loneliness and freedom, and the half-adventurous nature of existence out here, allowed me to breathe.

Suddenly, sunrise bursts into striking shades. Sweet pink folds into a fiery red. Icy blue melts into deep cobalt. Warm yellow blends into a bar of bright gold. Slopes of color softly ascend and descend. The sounds of birds awakening to a new day sing nearby, quick, tinkling, tender notes. I lean over the picture and cover it with dirt.

I wasn't sure what to do until last night when I had those cherries, the only fruit I have had since I left New York. And I finally realized what you've been showing me all along. I asked myself, who will bring our precious girl cherry sherbet? And who will kiss our little one a hundred times? And who will offer her a shoulder to rest upon? Knowing what's right doesn't mean much unless you do what's right, I know this. All the resources I need are in the mind. I should teach her to listen to nature and to cherish these lands. I should give her the opportunity to dare mighty things. I should empower our girl to be exactly who she cares to be. How is it that I hadn't realized you are still with me in her? I cannot live another moment without seeing our child, without seeing us through her. And I asked myself, who will love her as much as I love you?

If I have learned anything from being here, it is that courage is not having the strength to go on; it is going on when you don't have the strength.

Today, I shall go home.

After Alice

How have we come to an end without the ending I would have wanted to write? If only Alice had lived. If only these newlyweds had enjoyed life together. I wanted a different ending, but I could not change history. The love letters, diary entries, photographs, and ephemera found to create this story were real. What went missing after over a century was the rest. I used the research of the world surrounding them, often making Alice a symbol of her generation and the times. What happened upon his return from the Badlands was this: Theodore Roosevelt asked that the name Alice never be used in his presence. Theodore called his daughter Baby Lee even though she was named after her mother. Roosevelt served as New York City Police Commissioner, then governor, and ultimately the twenty-sixth president of the United States of America. Roosevelt remarried in December of 1886 and had five children with Edith Carow. Baby Lee grew up to become a memorable first daughter, known for wearing trousers and demanding access to meetings traditionally only attended by men. Theodore rarely spoke of his first marriage but often said, "I would not have been President had it not been for my experience in North Dakota."

Acknowledgments

Words cannot express my gratitude for the keepers of history. Because of the archivists at libraries and historical societies around the country who preserved the century-old documents, this story was fully discovered. Special thanks to Harvard University's Houghton Library for the comprehensive collection of letters, manuscripts, and books in the Alice R. Longworth Collection, the Library of Congress, Sagamore Hill National Historic Site, Theodore Roosevelt Birthplace National Historic Site, Theodore Roosevelt Association, American Museum of National History, Harvard Radcliffe Institute, Theodore Roosevelt National Park, Theodore Roosevelt Institute at Long Island University, Theodore Roosevelt Sanctuary and Audubon Center, the Costume Institute at the Metropolitan Museum of Art, and New York Public Library.

Special thanks to the Roosevelt family, most especially Tweed, who kept me laughing for days over our conversation about a young Teddy, and the Saltonstall family for providing me with insight and inspiration as the story began to unfold.

A million thank-yous to my beyond brilliant editor, Elizabeth Beier, for your superb insight and support; if not for you, this book may never have been written. To the whole team at St. Martin's

Press—Brigitte Dale, Donna Noetzel, Michael Storrings, Lizz Blaise, Lisa Davis, Paul Hochman, Michelle Cashman, Katie Bassel, Gail Friedman, and Jennifer Rohrbach—my gratitude.

Boundless thank-yous to my dear friend and longtime agent, Sandy Montag.

And thanks most of all to my family. To my husband, Michael, for your love and support, and to our children, Michael, Alexandra, and Christopher, for giving me the encouragement to keep writing. To our big crowd of relatives, who supported me and helped me, I can't thank you enough.

And for my friend Andrea Smyth for pushing me forward, and the many others, including Michael Downs, Danielle Parker, and Dana Tyler, I am beyond grateful for your assistance.

Thank you from the bottom of my heart to the readers, who give the reason for authors to keep searching for new stories to tell.

Resources

Agassiz, Elizabeth Cabot Cary. *Seaside Studies in Natural History*. Boston: Ticknor and Fields, 1865.

Joseph H. Choate's Speech before the Harvard Club of New York, *The Harvard Register,* King, Moses, 1853–1909. Harvard University.

Laughlin, J. Laurence. "Roosevelt at Harvard." *The American Review of Reviews*, July-December 1924.

Leach, Abigail. Association of Collegiate Alumnae (U.S.). *Publications of the Association of Collegiate Alumnae. Some Present Needs in Education* Richmond Hill, N.Y.: The Association v.3, no 1–8, 1898–1903.

Morison, Elting E. "The letters of Theodore Roosevelt." *Harvard Library Bulletin* v (1), 1951.

Parsons, Frances Theodora. *Perchance Some Day*. Privately printed, 1951.

Paton, Lucy Allen. *Elizabeth Cary Agassiz: A Biography*. Boston: Houghton Mifflin, 1919.

Pringle, Henry H. *Theodore Roosevelt: A Biography*. New York: Harcourt, Brace and Company, 1931.

Putnam, Carleton. *Theodore Roosevelt: The Formative Years*, Vol. (1). New York: Charles Scribner's Sons, 1958.

Radcliffe College Archives subject files, 1869–2007. Admissions— Brochure, 1879–1880; application, 1968; data re: classes, 1960s-2000 RG XXIV, Series 5, folder 1.6. Schlesinger Library, Radcliffe Institute, Harvard University, Cambridge, Mass.

Riis, Jacob. *Theodore Roosevelt: The Citizen*. New York: The Macmillan Company, 1912.

Roosevelt, Alice Hathaway (Lee), 1861–1884. 16 letters to Theodore Roosevelt. Alice Roosevelt Longworth family papers, MS Am 1541.9. Houghton Library.

Roosevelt, Alice Hathaway (Lee), 1861–1884. 3 letters to Martha (Bulloch) Roosevelt. Alice Roosevelt Longworth family papers, MS Am 1541.9. Houghton Library.

Roosevelt, Alice Hathaway (Lee), 1861–1884. 4 letters to Anna (Roosevelt) Cowles. Alice Roosevelt Longworth family papers, MS Am 1541.9. Houghton Library.

Roosevelt Robinson, Corinne. *My Brother Theodore Roosevelt*. New York: Charles Scribner's Sons, 1928.

Roosevelt, Theodore. 1858–1919. "Practicability of giving men and women equal rights." Harvard College Class of 1879 and Harvard College Class of 1880 class day and commencement documents, 1879–1880. HUC 6879. Harvard University Archives, Harvard University, Cambridge, Mass.

Roosevelt, Theodore. *In Memory of my darling wife Alice Hathaway Roosevelt and of my beloved mother Martha Bulloch Roosevelt,* New York: G. P. Putnam's Sons, 1884.

Roosevelt, Theodore, Green, F.V., *The Works of Theodore Roosevelt*, Volume 6, New York: P. F. Collier & Son, 1882–1908.

Roosevelt, Theodore, 1858–1919. 23 letters to Alice Hathaway (Lee) Roosevelt. Alice Roosevelt Longworth family papers, MS Am 1541.9. Houghton Library.

Roosevelt, Theodore. Theodore Roosevelt Papers: Series 8: Personal Diaries, 1878–1884; Vol. 1, Jan. 1-Dec. 31. 1878. Manuscript/Mixed Material. mss38299, reel 429. Library of Congress.

Roosevelt, Theodore. *Theodore Roosevelt: An Autobiography*. New York: The Macmillan Company, 1916.

Roosevelt, Theodore. *Theodore Roosevelt's Diaries of Boyhood and Youth*. New York and London: Charles Scribner's Sons, 1928.

Roosevelt, Theodore. *Hunting Trips of a Ranchman*. Philadelphia: Gebbie and Company, 1902.

Roosevelt, Theodore. *Theodore Roosevelt's Letters to his Children*. New York: Charles Scribner's Sons, 1919.

Roosevelt, Theodore, 1858–1919; Minot, H. D., 1859–1890, *The summer birds of the Adirondacks in Franklin County, N.Y.* 1877.

Sedgwick, John. "Brotherhood of the Pig." *GQ: Gentlemen's Quarterly* 58, November 1988.

Ware, C. (1880). Illuminations and Fireworks. *The Harvard Register*, Volumes (1–2), p. 142.

The Weather. (1884, February 13). *The New York Times*, p. 4.

Wister, Owen. *Roosevelt. The Story of a Friendship*. New York: The Macmillan Company, 1930.

Further Reading

Charles Dickens. *American Notes for General Circulation.* London: Chapman & Hall, Ltd, 1913.

Cutright, Paul Russell. *Theodore Roosevelt The Naturalist.* New York: Harper & Brothers, 1956.

Farmer, Fannie Merritt. *The Boston cooking-school cook book.* Boston: Little, Brown, and Company, 1918.

Hagedorn, Hermann, *The Boys' Life of Theodore Roosevelt.* New York and London: Harper & Brothers, 1918.

Iglehart, Ferdinand Cowle, *Theodore Roosevelt: The Man as I knew Him.* New York: The Christian Herald, 1919.

Longworth, Alice Roosevelt. *Crowded Hours.* New York: Scribner's, 1934.

Monk, William Everett. *Theodore and Alice: A Love Story.* New York: Empire State Books, 1994.

Morris, Edmund. *The Rise of Theodore Roosevelt.* New York: Coward, McCann & Geoghegan, 1979.

Morris, Edmund. *Theodore Rex.* New York: Random House, 2001.

Roosevelt, Theodore III. *All in the Family.* New York and London: G. P. Putnam's Sons, 1929.

Sewall, William Wingate. *Bill Sewall's Story of T. R.* New York and London: Harper & Brothers, 1919.

Vail, R. W. G. "Your Loving." *Collier's: The National Weekly*, December 20, 1924.

Wilhelm, Donald George. *Theodore Roosevelt as an Undergraduate.* Boston: John W. Luce and Company, 1910.

Wood, Fred. *Roosevelt As We Knew Him.* Philadelphia and Chicago: The John C. Winston Company, 1927.

Wood, F. S. *Roosevelt As We Knew Him: The Personal Recollections of One Hundred and Fifty of His Friends and Associates.* Philadelphia: The John C. Winston Company, 1927.